THE MAN OF DANGEROUS

SECRETS

Maxwell March is the pseudonym of Margery Allingham. She was born in Ealing, London in 1904 to a family immersed in literature. Her first novel, *Blackkerchief Dick*, was published in 1923 when she was just 19. In 1928 she published her first work of detective fiction, *The White Cottage Mystery*, after it was serialized in the *Daily Express*, but her breakthrough came in 1929 with the publication of *The Crime at Black Dudley* and the introduction of Albert Campion.

Whilst her Albert Campion mystery series was taking off, she turned her attention to what she termed her 'thrillers'; serialized stories for magazines featuring larger than life characters and page turning plots. For this venture she adopted the name Maxwell March and the resulting three novels were later published under the same pseudonym.

Campion continued to flourish. He proved so successful that Allingham made him the centerpiece of a further 17 novels and over 20 short stories, continuing into the 1960s.

Allingham's writing marked the arrival of a new breed of more sophisticated detective fiction defined by sharply drawn characters, wry observations and a flash of eccentricity. Allingham has been called the 'Dickens of detective writing' and sits alongside Agatha Christie as one of the Four Queens of Crime.

Margery Allingham died in 1966.

The Man of Dangerous Secrets

Maxwell March

ipso books

This edition published in 2017 by Ipso Books

First published in Great Britain as *Other Man's Danger* by Collins 1933

Ipso Books is a division of Peters Fraser + Dunlop Ltd

Drury House, 34-43 Russell Street, London WC2B 5HA

CHAPTER ONE
ACCIDENT OR MURDER?

There are few places more romantic, more exciting, more subtly sinister than the arrival platform of a great London station just after midnight, when the ordinary work of the day is done and the terminus sleeps fitfully under half-lights, waiting, one eye open, for the night boat train from the Continent.

The young man in the raincoat standing in the shadow of a closed bookstall thought so at any rate, and his mild brown eyes twinkled as he glanced down the concrete way where sleepy porters and a handful of anxious relatives or faithful friends awaited passengers from the train.

Robin Grey waited in the capacity neither of relative nor friend. His was a peculiar mission, but then he was a peculiar person. There were a good many people in London who would have given a great deal to learn the exact standing of that sturdy thickset figure with the fair hair, cherubic face, and mild, friendly expression. The most his friends knew of him was that he was a bachelor, the owner of a smart flat in the Adelphi, that he possessed a reasonable income and had been known on occasions to become involved in adventures which would have whitened the hair of any ordinary private detective.

But there were others, prominent people, people in the know, who recognized Robin Grey for what he was, one of the most valuable men in the complicated machinery of civil administration which controls the underworld of Europe.

A brilliant Home Secretary had realized that there arise sometimes matters requiring delicacy, secrecy, and integrity, which do not come under the jurisdiction of Scotland Yard, the C. I. D., or the Home Office, but which fall somewhere between the three, and it was for precisely these affairs that the curious unofficial post held by Mr. Grey was created. His friend, Inspector Whybrow of the Yard, called him "the man of dangerous secrets," and the inspector was not a person notorious for overstatement.

Robin was not bound by any officialdom. His net was thrown far and wide, and sometimes it was from private clients that his most valuable secrets came, secrets which smashed dope rings and broke gangs of international thieves.

He was still young, barely thirty-two, and on the whole he looked younger, for there was something boyish in his smile, something misleadingly innocent and bland in his expression of polite inquiry.

This habit of meeting the boat train at Waterloo was growing on him, he reflected. In his experience so many strange stories began from just this point. For nearly a month now he had been waiting every night to meet someone in whom the Foreign Office were peculiarly interested. So far this doubtful visitor had not come.

He had been waiting on the station for perhaps fifteen minutes when he first noticed the man in the interpreter's cap. The stooping, somewhat seedy figure passed him at a leisurely stride and went on into the misty yellow gloom at the other end of the platform.

Robin studied the back of this individual with interest. One of Mr. Grey's most useful gifts, and one which his friend the inspector privately considered was an advanced form of second sight, was the instinctive ability to detect a disguise, however simple or elaborate, at sight. Most of the people on the platform wore oldish clothes, but they presented nothing out of the ordinary to the young man who looked on at humanity through such a microscope of special knowledge.

But the man in the uniform of an interpreter was different. Robin knew at a glance that the frayed blue serge trousers were not bagged by the knees which they now covered; the disconsolate ruck on the shoulders was not quite in the right place; the cap, greasy on the band, was some inches away from the collar which should have caused the shininess.

He was interested at once. It was details like these which always roused his attention, and he sauntered down the platform after the man.

He passed him and came back so that he could see the face beneath the peak.

To the ordinary observer the man was typical; clean-shaven, slightly pale, a little bored-looking, a bulky sheaf of papers in his unmanicured hand and a weary shuffle in his walk. But as soon as Robin caught sight of him the customary urbanity which was almost second nature with the young man was almost visibly disrupted. One of Robin's other gifts, which was almost part of the first, had been called into use. The young man's memory for faces was proverbial among those men who made such a memory part of their business. He saw people as a camera sees them, searchingly, relentlessly. Twins who confused their own relations were completely different in his eyes; a facial trick or mannerism was never lost upon him.

Nevertheless he walked down to the full length of the station and back again to catch one more glimpse of the strange interpreter before he was satisfied. Then he returned to his position in the shadow of the bookstall and blinked.

It was incredible, but it was true. He was certain of it.

At that first glance he had been inclined to believe his powers were deserting him or that he was suffering from unsuspected nervous hallucinations. The second time had convinced him that what he saw was a reality.

The man masquerading as an interpreter was Ferdinand Shawle, the chairman of the United Metropolitan Bank & Trust Company, one of the wealthiest and most important men in the city of London.

There was no doubt at all about the fact in his mind after that second glance, but the explanation eluded him. At first he was inclined to suspect a wager of some sort, but after some reflection he decided that Sir Ferdinand Shawle was the last person on earth to undertake any such undignified escapade. He was a man notoriously without humour, a man whose type is mercifully becoming extinct in the realms of high finance. His career had been one long story of a forceful personality unhampered by scruples or by any weakness which kind-heartedness or charity might have dictated, smashing its way through to the top with complete disregard of all obstacles. His courage was a byword, but although there were business men who professed to admire him and many who were frankly afraid of him, there was none who could profess to like him for himself or for any disinterested action.

In view of all this, his appearance in this ingenious disguise was bewildering in the extreme. Robin was puzzled, and as usual on these occasions, his interest, at once his chief asset and his chief charm, was roused to fever pitch. He edged towards the man as the train came thundering into the station.

Instantly the great station came to life, the sleepy porters forgot their weariness, the strip of platform which had been as stark and desolate as a suburban pavement on early-closing day became miraculously crowded. Time-hardened travellers set about disembarking themselves and their luggage with methodical ease. Sleepy, irritable tourists, home after an unusual holiday, became hysterical, lost themselves, their children, and their baggage a dozen times in five minutes.

Robin kept his eyes fixed upon the man in the interpreter's cap. His own quarry was temporarily forgotten. The man hovered uncertainly. Once or twice he forgot the role he was playing, and when an excited elderly lady seized him by the arm in mistake for a porter he brushed her aside abruptly.

Robin, watching him, saw him stiffen suddenly, however, and advance down the platform. The young man followed, and presently he saw his objective.

A young man had descended from one of the first-class carriages and now stood talking to someone within. He was an attractive type, very fair, tall, and good-looking, with that profusion of graces which nature sometimes bestows upon the older aristocracy.

"Wait here, all of you, and I'll find the luggage and a porter."

The voice was pleasant and controlled. The man in the interpreter's cap quickened his step, and, as the boy came out into the crowd, moved back a little, making an oasis to which the youngster naturally gravitated.

The next thing that happened took place with such incredible swiftness and seemed so utterly illogical and unlikely in the circumstances that Robin, who had seen many strange sights, could scarcely credit his own eyes.

The man in the peaked cap went up to the boy and thrust the bundle of papers he carried into his face. Robin, who was behind, caught the youngster's startled expression changing to one of annoyance, and then without warning to one of blank surprise as he put up his hand to his face and staggered back a little.

Even while Robin looked, the colour drained from his cheeks and he reeled. The interpreter caught him by the arm with a husky, "Now then, sir, look out! What's up?" which somehow had not quite the right intonation, and led him out of the way of a porter with a barrow, who had been held up by the momentary delay.

The young man staggered. He stretched out his hands blindly. One or two people turned to glance at him, but the crowd swept them on, and the man in the peaked cap thrust an arm round the boy's waist and hustled him across the platform.

Robin followed. He could hear the badly simulated whine continuing: "You're all right, sir, you're all right. Come along now. Easy there."

And then in a flash it happened.

The platform was very narrow at this point. It was also overcrowded, and on the opposite side to the boat train was an unoccupied suburban electric line.

As the two men reached the edge of the concrete way, the man in the cap stumbled, and as he was then supporting the full weight of the younger man they both slipped to the ground. The man in the interpreter's cap dropped to his knees on the concrete, but his protégé was pitched forward onto the suburban line, where he lay floundering.

Robin felt a thrill of horror run down his spine. The boy's hand was a few inches from the live pick-up rail. Should he touch it, death must be instantaneous. With the swiftness which always seemed extraordinary for a man of his bulk, Robin dropped onto the line and drew the younger man back to safety.

It was a ticklish job. The youngster was heavy, the perilous line very near, but Robin was sufficiently used to situations where prompt and sure action was essential to keep his head. Moreover, something had aroused him. When he had first bent over the boy he had noticed something which had at once confirmed his suspicions and added to his mystification: the sweet, sickly, unmistakable smell of chloroform.

Meanwhile, the incident had aroused attention. There was a deep crowd on the platform. Excited railway officials had appeared as if by magic.

"For heaven's sake be careful, sir!" The red face of a terrified porter was thrust into Robin's own as he forced his unconscious burden onto the platform. Willing hands drew the boy onto the concrete way, and with care Robin followed him.

The confusion was tremendous, and the excited jabber which surrounds any accident had broken out, shrill and incessant.

Robin was explaining as best he could to an excited group that neither he nor the stranger was drunk or suicidal, when the crowd parted and a girl flung herself on her knees beside the prostrate boy, who now showed signs of recovering consciousness.

"Oh, Tony, Tony, what's happened?"

Her voice had a ring of real terror in it, and Robin turned to look at her.

At that moment she raised her eyes and met his own, and for the first time in his life Robin Grey felt an inexplicable thrill at the sight of a woman's face. It was not that she was merely lovely. He had seen great grey eyes and regular features in an oval face before, but here was something different. The face that looked into his own had the calm, tranquil loveliness of a great masterpiece. He could not tell what colour her hair was, whether her lips were painted, whether she was short or tall, but he knew that he had seen true beauty suddenly manifest before him in the chill dinginess of Waterloo Station.

For a moment he forgot everything else and stood looking at her, but the boy on the ground had begun to stir, and in an instant she had bent over him again. Robin pulled himself together as his mind clicked back to the business in hand.

Far down the platform he caught a glimpse of a peaked cap hastening away towards the exit, and, brushing aside the bewildered officials who were trying to question him, keep back the crowd, and revive the boy at the same time, he plunged off through the press after the retreating figure.

As he ran, his mind worked furiously. The papers had concealed a chloroform spray, then. The stumble had been clumsily simulated. It would not have deceived a child. But why in the name of everything extraordinary should the whole incredible incident have taken place at all?

He was held up by a porter just inside the barrier and had the chagrin of seeing the peaked cap disappear down the subway. He vaulted a pile of trunks, to the astonishment of their charge, and rushed after his quarry.

In the long underground way to the road he saw the peaked cap again. It was moving swiftly now.

Once again fate hindered him. The suitcase of a man in front of him suddenly burst open, and he stepped aside

involuntarily to avoid the shower of linen and toilet acces-
sories which were poured at his feet. When he looked up
again, the peaked cap had disappeared.

He came out of the station into the dank, ill-lit Waterloo
Road just in time to see the back of a sleek, noiseless limousine gliding swiftly out into the stream of traffic over the
bridge.

Robin Grey walked back to his flat through the cold
bright night. It was useless to return to the station platform now. If the Foreign Office's visitor had arrived, he had
come in unseen, and as for the victim of the extraordinary
attack he had just witnessed, Robin had no desire to receive
profuse thanks. The explanation of the story, he felt, was
not there; the boy had been too surprised, too completely
unprepared for the attack.

He walked slowly, pondering the problem thrust so
unceremoniously under his nose. In cold blood the facts
were incredible, but experience had taught him that the
incredible does sometimes occur.

Once he paused and swore at himself softly, for through
the mesh of clearly balanced thought which he should have
applied to this problem, as he did to every other, he was
haunted by the face of a girl, a girl lovely beyond all imagining, with stark terror in her wide grey eyes.

CHAPTER TWO
STRANGE BETROTHAL

At four o'clock on the following afternoon Robin sat at his desk in his small study in the Adelphi flat and looked at a paragraph in the folded newspaper in front of him. He had noticed it first early that morning, and all through the day his eyes had returned to it. As he read it through again, a frown spread over his forehead, and a puzzled expression crept again into his mild brown eyes.

"TRAGIC HEIRESS AGAIN." The headline topped a news paragraph. *"An unpleasant incident marred the return of Miss Jennifer Fern to London last night after her holiday on the Riviera with a party of young people, when one of their number, Mr. Tony Bellew, became giddy upon the arrival platform at Waterloo and accidentally fell onto an electrified suburban line. Had it not been for the timely assistance of a fellow traveller, as yet unidentified, Mr. Bellew must have floundered onto the live rail and become electrocuted.*

"Miss Fern has been called 'the tragic heiress.' Her engagement to Mr. Richard Grey in 1929 was ended by the latter's death later on in the same year, when his fishing boat was accidentally capsized by a steam yacht three days before his wedding should have taken place. In 1931 it was announced that a marriage would take place between Miss Fern and Mr. Philip Crawford, but by a tragic

coincidence this romance was also ended by death. Mr. Crawford lost his life motoring in the Alpes Maritimes in the autumn of the same year, when his body was discovered by the side of his car in a ravine not far from the famous Col de Breuil.

"When our correspondent called on Miss Fern at her hotel this morning she denied that there was ever any likelihood of an engagement between herself and Mr. Bellew."

It was an extraordinary story. The more he thought of it the more extraordinary it became.

He was still pondering over it when the miracle happened. Mrs. Phipps, his housekeeper, came trotting into the room in a palpable flutter, her prim coiffure disarranged and two bright spots of colour in her faded cheeks.

"A lady to see you, Mr. Robin."

Had Mrs. Phipps announced that a boa constrictor awaited him she could not have sounded more concerned, and somehow or other he knew whom to expect, so that he was standing by his desk conscious of an odd breathlessness which no other visitor had ever aroused in him when she came in.

It was the girl of Waterloo Station. He knew her at once, although she was now revealed as a tall, slender beauty with honey-coloured hair showing under a little French hat that covered only one side of her head. A sleek fur coat hugged her figure and displayed a touch of coloured silk at her throat.

She met his eyes again, and he read in their depths the same haunting fear which he had observed on the night before, the same glance of terrified appeal which had touched him so poignantly.

Her first questioning glance gave place to one of surprise.

"You!" she said. "Why, you were there last night... I didn't know. I got your name from a friend, and——"

Robin stepped forward. "Look here," he said, "won't you sit down? We can sort out everything then, can't we?"

She granted him a faint, shy smile and sank down gratefully into the armchair he wheeled up for her.

"Now," he said as he seated himself at his desk, "my name is Robin Grey. Can I do anything to help you?"

"But you have," she said involuntarily. "You have already. You saved Tony's life last night. This is wonderful. But I suppose I'd better begin at the beginning. I was sent here by Lady Dorothy Fenton. You—you helped her and her husband some time last year, didn't you? When little Jack was kidnapped?"

Robin nodded. He disliked being reminded of his past exploits as a rule, but this extraordinary creature had the odd effect upon him of making him forget himself entirely in his wonder and delight in her.

"Well," she said, "I am in trouble—in curious, terrifying trouble—and I don't know what to do. So——"

She broke off awkwardly.

"You've come to me," he said helpfully. "Well, that's fine."

She shot him a grateful glance under her long lashes and began to speak slowly in her clear, soft voice.

"My name is Jennifer Fern," she began.

Acting on a sudden impulse, he picked up the paper and handed it to her.

"You've come to see me about this, haven't you?" he said.

She glanced from it to him in frank astonishment.

"Do you know everything?" she said. "Dorothy Fenton told me you were wonderful, but this is a miracle."

"It is, rather," he said involuntarily and added hastily, to cover his confusion, "It's very simple really. You see, naturally after witnessing the incident on the platform last night I connected it with this story which I read in this morning's paper. Then, when you walked into the room I recognized you, and there you are."

She looked relieved. "Oh, I see. Of course. I was a little frightened for a moment. There has been too much of the—well—uncanny, lately, in my life. You scared me."

There had been a curious inflection in her tone, and he found himself longing to comfort her, to tell her that, whatever the matter, everything would eventually be well.

"Suppose you tell me all about it?" he said.

Her eyelids fluttered for a moment, and then she regarded him gravely.

"Well," she said, "everything in this paragraph is true, except for one thing. I know you won't believe me, I know you'll probably think I'm quite mad even to suggest such a thing, but I tell you I know that someone tried to murder Tony last night."

Robin sat looking at her, and there was no expression at all upon his round face.

"Of course you don't believe me," the girl went on passionately. "I know it sounds ridiculous. But if you're going to help me you've got to believe it, and you've got to believe as I do that Richard and poor Philip were both murdered. They were murdered because of me." She rose to her feet and took a few uncertain steps towards him. There was no colour at all in her beautiful face, and her eyes were appealing and afraid.

"It's always happened," she said, "just before I was to be married. I've thought it was coincidence, one of those dreadful tragic coincidences that happen sometimes. But after last night I'm sure it can't be that. There's something else, something terrible, something sinister. I was going to marry Tony this afternoon. Now I've told him I'll never even speak to him again. We were going to be married secretly. I didn't think anyone knew except our closest friends, and yet you see *it* got to know."

"It?" he inquired gently.

She nodded. "The thing that's haunting me. The thing that's walking behind me. The thing that brings death to any man who wants to marry me."

Robin looked at the girl sharply. He saw signs of nervous exhaustion in her face, saw her hands twitching.

"Sit down," he said sharply. "Sit down. Pull yourself together. I'll do all I can to help you."

She sank down again, and he went over to the door and shouted to Mrs. Phipps to bring tea. He steadfastly refused to speak seriously again until the girl was sitting up sipping the strong fragrant stuff and he noticed the colour returning to her cheeks.

"Now," he said, "I believe you. Get that well into your head. I believe you implicitly. What do you want me to do?"

She put down her cup and saucer on the table by her side and leant forward, her slim brown hands folded tightly in front of her.

"There's one thing I haven't told you, Mr. Grey," she said. "A thing that explains why I've come here, really. I like Tony very, very much."

"I see," he said. "You want me to protect Mr. Bellew."

"Well, yes, of course. But not only that. I want you to find out what is the meaning of this terrible scourge which follows me. It's like a curse, the sort of thing that happened hundreds of years ago. I've never done anyone any harm. Why should anyone want to ruin my happiness?—anyone or any *thing*?"

Robin nodded, and the frown returned to his forehead. "It's a difficult problem," he said slowly. "You see, Mr. Philip Crawford and Mr. Richard Grey died some time ago. It will be hard to collect sufficient detail concerning their deaths to form any real comparison between the two and the attack on Mr. Bellew last night. That seems the most obvious approach to the problem, doesn't it?"

The girl nodded absently. A sombre expression had come into her eyes, and for some moments she was silent. Then she spoke without looking at him.

"There is one other way," she said. "But I don't think I could ask you to take that. And yet it would make it so much more simple and——" She broke off and looked up to find his brown eyes looking solemnly into hers.

"I had thought of that," he said. "But naturally I didn't like to suggest it. If your engagement to me was publicly announced it would be rather challenging the enemy, wouldn't it?"

The dusky colour rose slowly up her throat and suffused her face.

"I couldn't ask you to do that," she said.

"My dear young lady, you could ask me to do anything," he said involuntarily and added hastily, "This is a most extraordinary problem you bring me. I'm tremendously anxious to get to the bottom of it. Yes, if our engagement is announced in every London paper tomorrow morning, with the prospect of a speedy marriage clearly indicated, we should at least force your malignant fate to show its hand. After all, you know," he added with an attempt at light-ness, "there may be nothing in it after all. It may be just coincidence."

"Oh, but it isn't," she said earnestly. "You mustn't dream of doing this if you don't believe in it. And somehow I don't think you ought to do it anyhow. Don't you see what it means? Think of the danger."

Robin smiled. "That," he said truthfully, "is the one thing I never permit myself the luxury of thinking about. Very well then, that's agreed, is it? A notice of our engagement shall appear in every important London paper tomorrow morning."

She hesitated. "It's awfully kind of you, but I mean to say, won't you—well, won't there be personal complications for you?"

He smiled. "I'm not married, if that's what you mean, and I haven't a fiancée." He too hesitated. This was delicate ground. "How about Mr. Bellew?" he inquired awkwardly.

She smiled. "That's all right. No need to worry about Tony. There's one person you'll have to pretend with, however, and that's my father. I'm afraid he'll have to think that we're—well, properly engaged."

He looked at her curiously. Sir Henry Fern was a well-known shipping owner, and in spite of his retiring disposition, which made him avoid interviews and photographs, he was often to be seen in the better-known London restaurants. Robin knew him quite well by sight.

She went on timidly. "I've thought it all out," she said. "I suppose it was an awfully impudent thing to do, but this did seem the obvious way if it could be arranged. I thought we might go along and see my father. Although sometimes I feel he doesn't want me to get married, ever, he won't object. It'll only mean you'll have to go to dinner with him, probably. And yet—oh, this is a ridiculous situation! I can't ask you to go through with it."

"Why not?" he said gently. "Don't worry. I've had many commissions, some of them quite as extraordinary as this. Look here, since we're engaged, let's go out and have a cocktail somewhere to celebrate, shall we?"

She looked at him timidly. There was more colour in her cheeks, but the terrified expression still lurked in her eyes.

"I should like to," she said. "Besides, we shall probably find my father in the little cocktail bar at the Savoy. But

16

there's one matter we haven't touched on, and it's very awkward, so I'd like to get it over. I'm an heiress, you know, in
my own right. My mother left me all her money. So whatever—er—your fees are, Mr. Grey, well, you won't find me
parsimonious."

The words were blurted out awkwardly, and he realized
that she was embarrassed.

He bent forward. "Suppose we leave that until I succeed?" he said. "Meanwhile, I have a whole hour to spare.
Shall we go down to the Savoy and interview your father?"

As Robin Grey walked into the Savoy and turned to the
left towards the small cocktail bar overlooking the embank-
ment, he glanced at the girl at his side and marvelled at
the extraordinary situation which had developed in the
last twenty-four hours. At one o'clock in the morning he
had set eyes upon the first woman who had ever struck him
as being flawlessly beautiful, in peculiar circumstances, to
say the least, and at four o'clock in the afternoon of the
same day he found himself engaged to her, to shield from
unquestionable danger the man she had practically admitted loving. And here he was, sober and in his right mind,
going to interview her father.

It was an experience in itself, he found, to escort Jennifer
Fern. Her air of quiet elegance, her carriage, and her flawlessly lovely face commanded attention wherever she went,
and as they paused for a moment in the entrance of the
little green-and-gold bar everyone in the room turned to
look at her.

"There he is," she said, and Robin, looking round,
became aware of the ship owner coming towards them.

He was a big clumsy man whom no amount of tailor-
ing could render smart. His grey hair was short and finely
cropped. He had a square, good-natured face, very blue

eyes, and a sleepy, lazy smile which bespoke at once his shyness and his friendliness.

Jennifer effected the introduction with an ease which Robin appreciated. The old man shook the boy's hand vigorously.

"How d'you do!" he said. "Come over to my table. I've been having a business talk with an old friend, but that's over now."

"Wait a minute, Daddy." Jennifer laid a restraining hand on her father's arm. "I've got something to break to you. I'm afraid you're going to get a surprise, and I can't very well tell you in front of strangers. You see, it's like this. Er—Robin and I are very old friends, though you haven't met him before. This afternoon he asked me to marry him, and I've accepted. In fact, congratulate us; we're engaged."

"Engaged?" Robin found the blue eyes fixed on his face again, and although there was nothing in the man's expression to indicate it in any way, he received the unshakable impression that the news had been received not so much unfavourably as with absolute panic. In an instant, however, the lazy good nature had reasserted itself, and Robin felt his hand seized again.

"Congratulations, my boy! Congratulations! I can't say I'm surprised at your choice, but the news is a bit staggering, you know. Really, Jennifer, you shouldn't spring things like this on your old father before dinner. Well, well, we must talk this over. Come along, both of you. We must have a drink and a chat."

Robin followed the father and daughter across the room to a small table in an alcove where a third man was seated. He heard the ship owner's booming friendly voice: "F. S., I want you to meet Jennifer, my daughter. The young monkey's just given me the shock of my life. She turns up here as cool as a cucumber and announces she's engaged to be married. And here's the lucky youngster too. Grey, my boy, let me present you. A very old friend of mine."

Robin bent forward and came face to face with a man whom he recognized instantly, and, moreover, a man who, he saw, had recognized him.

Old Sir Henry's voice went on cheerfully behind them: "Shawle, this is Robin Grey. Grey, my boy, Sir Ferdinand Shawle. Look, F. S., he wants to marry my daughter."

"How do you do, my boy! Congratulations!"

A lean cold hand took Robin's own for an instant. He eyed the man curiously, but after that first swift telltale glance of recognition Sir Ferdinand Shawle gave no other indication of the thoughts which must have been passing through his mind.

Instead, he seemed to go out of his way to make himself as affable as possible, and Robin, playing his part carefully, decided to take his cue from the other.

Of the quartette at the small table, these two, the lean elderly man with the cruel mouth and the blank expressionless eyes, and the boy, young, ingenuous-looking, and friendly, were perhaps most at ease.

Jennifer was pale and uncommunicative, while there was frank consternation in Sir Henry's eyes in spite of his frantic efforts to hide it.

"When's the ceremony to take place?"

Sir Ferdinand spoke casually enough, but he glanced sharply at the boy and waited for an answer.

Robin turned to Jennifer.

"That entirely rests with you, my dear," he said.

He did not meet her eyes and did not see the colour which came into her face. She laughed nervously.

"I haven't thought about it yet," she said. "After all, we only got engaged this afternoon."

"I hope you won't do anything precipitate." Sir Henry's voice and manner betrayed more anxiety than ordinary parental concern would dictate. "Marriage is a serious business," he added lamely. "You don't want to jump at it."

He stopped abruptly, and Robin, looking up, intercepted a glance which passed between Sir Ferdinand and his friend. It was swift, warning, and apparently effective, for Sir Henry dropped his eyes, and an uncomfortable pause might have ensued had the banker not taken charge of the conversation by introducing a new subject.

"Since the engagement is so recent," he said, "perhaps you would do me the honour of celebrating it at my house? It isn't such an extraordinary request as you might think," he went on, turning to Robin. "After all, Henry and I are very old friends, and I've taken an avuncular interest in Jennifer ever since she was a baby. I'm an old bachelor with more money than is good for me, a great lonely house in Grosvenor Square, and no children for whom to entertain."

He paused and, turning to the elder man, continued with an enthusiasm not wholly simulated.

"I've set my heart on it, Henry. Let me give a dinner party tomorrow night for these young people. Madame Julie will be delighted to make all the necessary arrangements. Perhaps you would ring her up about the names of the guests? I won't hear any denial."

Robin glanced at Sir Henry. Apart from the fact that the invitation was rather an extraordinary breach of etiquette, unless Sir Ferdinand was an even greater friend of the family than he appeared to be, the man really did seem motivated by kindness. Sir Henry's red face betrayed nothing but embarrassment, and his bright blue eyes were troubled. He spoke affably enough, however.

"That's very nice of you, F. S. Of course we shall be pleased to accept. I'll ring up Madame Julie this evening. It's rather short notice, but I expect we shall get those people who really matter to come."

They sat for perhaps another five minutes, chatting with apparent idleness, although always there was the hint of something beneath the lightness of the conversation, something secret, something sinister.

Then Sir Ferdinand Shawle took his leave somewhat abruptly and went off, leaving the memory of a quiet, ruthless personality in their minds and an impression of a cool limp hand in their own.

As soon as he was out of earshot, Jennifer turned to her father.

"What an extraordinary man, Daddy! How can he have had an avuncular interest in me all my life? I've never seen him before. It was very nice of him to want to give us a dinner party at his house, but it was a little odd, wasn't it?"

Sir Henry shrugged his heavy shoulders and looked thoughtfully out across the cocktail bar with unseeing eyes.

"F. S. is a very odd man," he said slowly. "But a very influential man. Naturally I don't want to offend him. However, putting all that aside, I've known him for many years, and I expect having heard so much about you from me he does regard you as a kind of niece. Be a good girl and accept this invitation for my sake."

Jennifer laughed and patted his hand. "What's the matter with you?" she said. "After all, what's a dinner party? Of course we'll go, won't we, Robin?"

Robin smiled at her. "Of course—Jennifer," he said.

"Who is Madame Julie?" The girl had turned to her father again.

Sir Henry frowned. "She's a social secretary, my dear," he said. "A woman of quite good family, I believe, who attends to all Shawle's entertaining for him. It's very difficult for a man to do these things alone, you know. She's a very ordinary woman, but quite nice. She's been with him for two or three years, I should say. Anything else you want to know, Miss Inquisitive?"

"No, nothing. I'm perfectly satisfied." The girl's tone was conciliatory. Then she turned to Robin. "I'm going to send you home now," she said. "I'm not going to be one of those fiancées who keep you away from your work. You'll ring me in the morning, won't you?"

"Of course I will." Taken off his guard, Robin could not keep the enthusiasm out of his voice, and Sir Henry laughed, an explosion that was suddenly carefree and which chased the worry out of his eyes and the deep furrows from his forehead.

"That's the note I like to hear in a man's voice when he talks to his girl," he said. "Enthusiasm: there's not enough of it these days. I suppose the bar's too crowded, or are you going to kiss her here?"

"Daddy, don't be ridiculous!" Jennifer's face was scarlet to the eyebrows. "Of course he isn't. Run along, Robin. I shall be waiting for your call in the morning."

As Robin Grey walked out of Savoy Court into the Strand he whistled softly to himself. In the past twenty-four hours he had stumbled into the very midst of something which baffled him completely. In that brief interval he had caught glimpses of a web of intrigue and danger so closely knit that it seemed doubtful, if, once within it, one could ever escape.

But, because of the girl, he did not hesitate. It was one of Robin's peculiarities that he never deceived himself, and he knew now that, whatever Jennifer Fern's reaction towards himself might be, he had fallen completely and helplessly in love with her.

CHAPTER THREE
THE DEALER

"Well, Bourbon, I hope you're satisfied that the room is sound-proof. When you've finished prowling around the walls perhaps you'll sit down and show us some of that control we hear so much about."

The pathetic but rather terrible little figure in the wheeled chair spoke sharply, and his voice, never lovely, was almost unbearable with the sneer in its timbre.

The man who had been wandering round the panelled room with the aimless movement of one who finds the situation intolerable swung round now and came back to his seat at the head of the table.

Rex Bourbon, one of the best known of the younger brokers, was not prepossessing at the best of times, but now, with the colour drained out of his heavy face and his thick hands fidgeting together, damp and cold in the warm room, he was definitely unattractive.

He poured himself out a stiff whisky from the decanter in front of him and drank it down without answering the vitriolic figure who sat opposite him across the expanse of shining mahogany.

Irritated by his silence, the other man spoke again.

"You're drinking too much. I heard that some weeks ago. Be careful. It isn't only your own career you hold, remember."

Bourbon looked at the cripple with something like entreaty in his greasy eyes.

"For heaven's sake shut up, Fisher. Can't you see I'm all on edge? This is the second time in a fortnight we've been summoned. It's getting on my nerves, I tell you."

Caithby Fisher, chairman of Armaments Limited, stirred in his wheeled chair and laughed unpleasantly.

"You should have thought of that in the beginning," he said. "Fifteen years ago, when the temptation was offered, you fell like the rest of us. Now you've got to take the consequences, as we all have. Do I have to remind you that if one of us loses his nerve there is quite a variety of fates awaiting the rest of us? What would it be for you, Bourbon? The end of a promising career, certainly; but a prison sentence—fifteen years' hard labour, I should say. Or no—let me see—that clerk of yours died, didn't he? All the same, I doubt whether they could hang you."

"Shut up!" The younger man's voice rose to a scream. "I can't stand it."

The third man in the room, who until now had taken no part in the conversation, raised his head. Sir Ferdinand Shawle did not believe in interfering unless circumstances demanded it, but now his quiet, chilling voice echoed softly through the room.

"Do I have to remind you, Fisher, that this is my house? If you must bicker, save it for your own office. As for you, Rex, in the adjoining room my guests are gathering to celebrate the engagement of Jennifer Fern to the young man who is of such interest to us all. This panelling is sound-proof for all ordinary purposes, but I can't guarantee it to keep your hysteria a secret."

Bourbon threw out his hands. "I'm sorry, F. S.," he said. "Are we still waiting for Sir Henry? It's the waiting that gets on one's nerves."

He got no further. The door opened, and two men came in. Sir Henry Fern, pale and unhappy, was followed by his partner, Nelson Ash.

This individual was in many ways the most extraordinary man in the room.

He was above normal height, loose-limbed and gracelessly built, and his scanty hair was of that peculiarly unattractive type of colourless blond which does not seem to alter with age. He was now nearly fifty, but his hair and scant brows were both of this unattractive colour. For the rest, he had a thick white skin which puckered into folds over his small pale eyes, and his voice when he spoke was high and reedy.

The five men nodded to one another in silent greeting and took their places round the table. Sir Ferdinand appeared to have adopted the position of chairman by unanimous consent, for it was he who spoke briskly, jerking the troubled minds of the others to attention.

"Well," he said, "who has the message?"

No one spoke, and a frown of irritation passed over the banker's lean face.

"Come," he said. "We have no time to lose. We can't put off the evil day by fencing. Who has the message?"

Sir Henry Fern pulled himself together with an obvious effort.

"I'm sorry, F. S.," he said. "My mind was on other things. It came to me this time. Here it is."

From the breast pocket of his tail coat he drew out a wallet which he opened carefully on the table. A single slip of grey-blue paper fell out upon the wood, and, picking it up, he passed it to Bourbon, who sat next to him, who in turn handed it to Sir Ferdinand.

The banker read the paper, and the others, watching his face anxiously, saw no sign of the emotion which the message might have produced.

"The girl again," he said softly.

"Read it—read it!" Rex Bourbon's tone betrayed his agitation.

"All in good time. Your nerves are in a bad state, Bourbon. If our situation were less precarious," he said, with a sardonic smile, "I should suggest a visit to a psycho-analyst. But in the circumstances, despite professional etiquette, perhaps not. However, just to set your mind at rest, I will as usual read the message aloud."

He cleared his throat and began, his dry impersonal voice lending an added chill to the words.

" *Fern's daughter has become officially engaged to a man who is a professional detective, standing high with both Scotland Yard and the Secret Service. Since it seems highly probable that the engagement is an artifice entered into by the girl in an attempt to discover the truth of her position, it is obviously necessary that her association with this young man should cease instantly. In view of the disastrous and futile attempt upon Tony Bellew, I do not immediately advocate Grey's violent removal. Find some other method if possible. But should you be unsuccessful within one week from this date, then the more usual and direct method must be adopted.* THE DEALER.' "

There was silence after the cold voice had finished speaking. It was Bourbon who finally took the lead.

"I know you're all looking at me," he said. "I know you're all thinking that it was I who bungled the Bellew business. But it wasn't, I tell you. It wasn't. I knew at the secret ballot that you all thought I had drawn the name. But I hadn't. It was one of you others. I swear it."

A slow, unpleasant smile spread over Sir Ferdinand's mask-like face.

" 'Methinks the lady doth protest too much,' " he quoted softly, and went on in the briskly practical tone he assumed for business dealings: "Don't excite yourself, Bourbon. If the Dealer intends to punish he will doubtless do it in his own way. And now, as a matter of form, Henry, how did you receive this message?"

The old man rose to his feet. He looked much older. His shoulders drooped, and his very blue eyes were dull.

"In the usual way," he said. "When I came down to breakfast it lay on the top of my letters. The postmark was simply 'London.' Both the address and the summons which told me we should all meet here at seven o'clock tonight were typewritten. There was no clue," he went on, fighting to keep his voice steady, "no clue to tell me of the identity of this blackmailing fiend who has bled us white for all these years, the monster who has turned us into the slaves we are."

Bourbon poured himself out another drink. His hand was trembling so that the heavy cut decanter rattled against the glass disconcertingly.

"I can't stand it," he said thickly. "I can't stand it any longer. One of you," he went on, glaring round the room, "one of you is the Dealer. One of you sits and laughs at the agony of the others. Sometimes I feel I'd rather have the disgrace, I'd rather have the imprisonment, than this incessant mental torture, this uncertainty, this knowledge that any day one may be forced to pay new demands, or, worse still, to commit some crime for which the penalty may mean anything, even death."

"Very prettily said," snarled Caithby Fisher from his wheeled chair. "But if we're going to start one of those interminable arguments about the identity of the Dealer, then I am leaving. After all, as I see these things, I am not shocked by the wickedness of our—master." His voice sank. "I am impressed by the cleverness, the colossal power of the man. Think of it," he went on softly. "Here we are, five wealthy men. Fifteen years ago we were trapped, all of us, in different and ingenious ways. It was pointed out to me, so subtly that I hardly realized that the suggestion came from an outside agency, that the manufacture of a certain document bearing my signature and some others, exhibited only once in the right quarters, might be worth a quarter of a million to me. It was not until I had achieved my end that I awoke to discover the incriminating document spirited out of my safe and myself completely in the power of a man only known to me by his pseudonym—the Dealer."

He paused and looked round at the strained faces of the men seated at the table.

"You all have some such story," he said, his sharp, rather cruel little eyes gleaming as his glance travelled from face to face. "All except you, Sir Henry, whose case is, I think, even more unfortunate than my own. However, I tell you I have a respect for the Dealer, and if, as I believe, he is one of us seated round this table tonight, I offer him my sincere congratulations. Had I been as clever as he, I should sit where he is sitting now."

Bourbon opened his mouth to burst out impetuously, but the sinister significance of the last part of the cripple's remarks was not lost upon him and he checked himself in time.

Sir Ferdinand tapped on the table with his signet ring.

"If you are ready, gentlemen," he said, "as it is growing late I suggest that we follow our usual procedure when the Dealer sets us a specific task and take a secret ballot to decide which among us is to be responsible for the young man in question. As usual I will prepare slips of paper. Bourbon will mix them and we will draw in turn."

"Gentlemen, this must stop."

The words were so strangled that it was some moments before his audience realized that it was Sir Henry who had spoken. He tottered to his feet now and stood facing them, a pathetic and a desperate man.

"I must speak," he said. "You, Fisher, have pointed out the helplessness of our position very clearly. I am not a fool. I have given my money, I have seen myself beggared, and I have countenanced crimes from which as an honest man I shrink. But this merciless persecution of my child must stop."

He turned round and faced the men who stared at him, impressed in spite of themselves at the passionate earnestness of his appeal.

"My daughter is young," he went on. "She is beautiful. She has her life before her. Fortunately her mother left her well provided for. In a rational world nothing should come to her but happiness. Why must she be victimized? I am thought by some to be a timid man. Sometimes I see myself as a criminal weakling. But this cannot go on. Do what you like with me, but let the child have her life and her happiness. If the Dealer is here, if one of you under the guise of a companion in adversity conceals the mind which has brought us all to this infamous slavery, then I appeal to him to stop this thing."

There was silence as his voice died away. Even Sir Ferdinand, normally so calm and so cynical, drummed an embarrassed tattoo upon the table with his slender, bony fingers.

It was left to Nelson Ash, with his reedy voice and conciliatory manner, to answer the trembling old man who was his partner.

"We appreciate your point, Sir Henry," he said, blinking, his thick white eyelids almost covering his narrow eyes, "we appreciate your point. Of course we do. But consider the circumstances. After all, we're all in the same boat, you know. I'm sorry for you," he went on, the merest hint of unctuous hypocrisy in his thin voice. "I realize that from your point of view I myself am very much to blame. After all, you were away ill when the—er—regrettable incident occurred in our own case, which made the firm criminally responsible for the series of tragic happenings which led to the disgrace and suicide of our innocent accountant. But need I remind you that when you returned and the facts were made known to you, rather than risk the crash and disgrace which would have involved not only yourself but your innocent wife and daughter, you remained silent, and therefore rendered yourself liable to the machinations of our friend the Dealer."

Sir Henry Fern passed a trembling hand through his short grey hair as he sank down again at the table and sat bowed and helpless before the unanswerable logic of the man at his side.

Ash went on. He had not risen, but leant sprawled across the table, one white hand emphasizing the important words in his discourse with an insistent and irritating gesture.

"It is quite as painful to me as it must be to everyone else to bring up this next subject," he said. "But since you seem to have forgotten it I feel I must remind you. This persecution of your daughter, as you call it, has been forced upon the Dealer, if not by you, at least by a member of your family. In removing the chances of your daughter's marriage the Dealer is protecting himself and us. In Morton Blount's deed box lie all our fates."

The old man stirred. But as though he were enjoying the agony of his stricken partner, Nelson Ash went on.

"This is an old story," he said, "but I'm sure all our friends will forgive us if I repeat it to you. Sometimes I feel, Sir Henry, that you can never have understood it properly. Your brother-in-law, Morton Blount, was an extraordinary man. I need not go into his reputation as a criminologist, but when after many years spent in delving into our secrets, in tracing down one crime after another to our very doors, he suddenly gave up, to retire an apparently defeated man, there were many of us who wondered. It was not until his death, when we each received a copy of that dramatic little note, that we saw the truth and realized the terrible pitfall he had laid for us."

He leant further across the table towards the shrinking man. There was something sinister, something repulsive in his movement, and the hardened quartette who watched him were silent, fascinated by something almost subhuman in the intensity of his attack.

"I think I could repeat that note to you, Sir Henry, almost verbatim. Perhaps you did not pay sufficient attention to your copy. Let me remind you. The final paragraph was very illuminating. After revealing that he had proofs which would imprison us all, if the gallows did not claim at least two of our number, he finished, if I remember rightly, something like this: '*You may wonder why I have chosen to keep silent about these discoveries. Let me tell you. I realized from the beginning that there was one amongst you more culpable than the others. One whose pseudonym—the Dealer—hid the mind which held the rest of you in helpless bondage. I was determined that he should not escape his full toll of punishment. On continuing my investigations it came home to me one day that my own brother-in-law, the husband of the only woman I ever admired, the father of the child whom I loved as deeply as if she had been my own, was enmeshed so inextricably in this sordid web that I could not expose him without ruining my sister's life and her child's.*'"

Nelson Ash's voice had sunk, but its reedy tenor was still very clear in the quiet room.

"Shall I go on? The note was very clear, if you remember. *'Therefore,'* he wrote, *'I have placed my evidence and the proofs which I have collected against you, and which I have enumerated in the earlier part of this letter, in a deed box with a firm of solicitors which I shall naturally not name. Should my niece, Jennifer Fern, die, that box will be taken to the Public Prosecutor. In the event of her living, on the day she marries and acquires a husband who can take care of her, the solicitors are instructed to observe the same procedure.'*"

The thin voice ceased. Sir Henry had hidden his face in his hands and now sat silent, his grey head bowed over the table.

As though to end a situation which had become unbearable to them all, Sir Ferdinand Shawle rose to his feet.

"It is growing late," he said. "We should take the draw, I think. In view of what Ash has said tonight, I need hardly remind you how important the Dealer's instructions are for all our safety."

The ceremony took place in absolute silence. It had become a ritual with the five men by this time, a ritual which had grown more terrifying by repetition as on one occasion after another each man drew the marked slip which meant that he was responsible for the particular task the Dealer had set.

Ash prepared the slips, each one identical in shape and folding. Bourbon mixed them in his trembling hands and threw them down upon the polished surface of the table.

Sir Ferdinand Shawle chose first, Sir Henry's nerveless fingers took the second slip, Caithby Fisher, his eyes glinting curiously, snatched the third, Bourbon picked up the pellet nearest to him, and the folder took the last.

Each man examined his choice furtively, hiding its message from the others. Then, as was their custom, they rose. Each face was blank, and no one eyeing them, however carefully, could have told who out of the five had received the command to attend to Robin Grey.

Sir Ferdinand sighed, helped himself to a drink from the tantalus, and, after draining it, readjusted the set of his faultlessly fitting tail coat.

"Now, gentlemen," he said, "my guests await us."

Sir Henry shook his head. His face bore traces of the violent emotions to which he had been subjected.

"If you'll excuse me, F. S.," he said, "I won't join you immediately. I'm not well."

Sir Ferdinand shrugged his shoulders. "I shall see you at dinner, then," he said.

The old man stumbled out of the door, while his host moved over towards the panelling, which reached from floor to ceiling on the south side of the room. He touched a bolt and swept the great doors aside. They rolled back on well-oiled runners, so that the room in which they stood became part of the larger salon beyond.

Instantly the tense atmosphere was swept away. The sound of laughter and music burst in upon them, and the air became heavy with perfume and tobacco smoke. The salon was crowded with chattering young people, and in the center of the heavy Chinese carpet Jennifer stood beside Robin. Her cheeks were flushed with excitement, which even the sinister circumstances that had led to her present position could not subdue; her eyes were dancing, and the long slender folds of her white dress enhanced the slim beauty of her figure.

Robin, sleek, immaculate, and very much at ease, stood by her side. They made a striking couple. It seemed incredible that any shadow could hang over two such attractive, happy young people.

Sir Ferdinand was just about to step forward when a wiry hand clutched at his coat tail. He turned to find Caithby Fisher looking up at him from the depths of his wheeled chair.

"Is that the boy?" said the cripple, his dry voice crackling with interest. "Introduce me to him, won't you? I think I'd like to have a word with him."

The thin, unpleasant voice of Nelson Ash cut across the other's request.

"I should like to meet him too," he said. "After all, it's easier if you know them socially, don't you think?"

CHAPTER FOUR
STRANGE MEETINGS

"**Y**ou must put up with my questions, my boy. Consider them an old man's prerogative."

The harsh, unbeautiful voice of the cripple was softened into a semblance of friendliness as Caithby Fisher leant forward to speak to Robin.

The dinner party was almost over. The ladies had retired, and the men sat smoking and sipping their brandy until it should please their host to give them the signal to move.

On the whole the meal had not been such an ordeal for Jennifer as Robin had feared. Sir Henry Fern had not put in an appearance, and the young people were spared the discomfort of listening to speeches concerning their engagement.

Caithby Fisher had introduced himself in the salon before dinner, and now that Jennifer, on whose left he had sat, had retired, he had moved his wheeled chair forward dexterously so that he might speak confidentially to the young man.

Robin, who had been on his guard from the beginning, had not been attracted by the hunchback's personality, but he found it impossible to shake off the man. Presuming upon the advantages which his age and infirmity lent him, he had fired questions at him with the rapidity and searching quality of a prosecuting counsel.

"I expect you think my behaviour a little curious," he continued. "But you must forgive me. I'm a very old friend of Jennifer's father. Our business association has been close. In fact," he went on with a sly smile which the boy found oddly disturbing, "I think we may safely say that we share most of each other's secrets. Therefore it is only natural that I should be tremendously interested in meeting the man whom Jennifer is going to marry. I've already told you you're an extremely lucky man, haven't I?"

"I assure you, sir, I realize my own unworthiness," said Robin, realizing that the remark was stilted but feeling that nothing less was expected of him.

"Not at all, not at all." The narrow eyes of the little cripple ran over the boy's broad frame approvingly, almost enviously. "I don't doubt for a moment that in yourself you are everything that any girl could desire. The only question that ran through my mind—if you'll forgive me—touched upon a purely monetary matter. You are not, I take it, Mr. Grey, as wealthy as you would like to be?"

"I'm not rich," said Robin cautiously, wondering where this conversation was going to lead. "But Sir Henry quite understands my position."

"I know, I know." The cracked voice was soothing. "I appreciate your difficulties, my boy, and that's why I wondered if you would allow me as an old man who has taken a great interest in your future wife's career to make you an offer, shall I say to put something in your way? Here's my card."

He pressed a slip of pasteboard into the astonished young man's hand.

"Come and see me at Armaments House tomorrow. Let me see, make it three o'clock. I think I can offer you something that will interest you. No, no, no, don't thank me," he went on, waving away the startled words that had risen to the boy's lips. "We can't talk business here. It would hardly be polite to our host's brandy."

He turned away to join in the conversation upon his right, and Robin was prevented from speaking or even thinking any further upon the subject by the sudden appearance at his elbow of one of the footmen who had waited upon him at table.

"Excuse me, sir, but are you Mr. Robin Grey by any chance?"

Something that he could only regard as a premonition of evil sent a chill of alarm down Robin's spine at the simple question.

"Yes, what is it?"

"You're wanted on the phone, sir. Would you come this way?"

With a muttered word of apology to his host, Robin followed the servant out of the dining room and down a thickly carpeted corridor to a little telephone booth, which had been erected in a secluded corner of the hall. Shutting himself in securely, he picked up the receiver.

"Hullo."

"Hullo, Mr. Grey. Is that you? This is Danvers speaking. Can you hear me?"

"Yes; be quick." Robin recognized the voice and the name. Johnny Danvers was one of his most valued assistants, who even now was following up certain matters which had arisen in connection with the present case.

"I'm speaking from a Kensington call box," the voice continued. "I followed Bellew, as you instructed. I've had my eye on him all day. He went back to his flat about two hours ago. But I thought I'd better ring you. His man's just given the alarm. I haven't been able to get many details, but he's dead all right. Poison, they think. So long. I'll ring you at your place if anything else transpires."

The receiver almost dropped from Robin's fingers, and when he spoke he did not recognize his own voice.

"Here—Johnny!" he ejaculated. "Johnny, what did you say?"

But the only reply was a click as the man at the other end of the wire hung up.

For some moments Robin did not move. Johnny never spoke until he was sure. He knew as surely as if he stood looking down at the body that Tony Bellew, the last man openly to attach himself to Jennifer Fern, was dead, and although Johnny Danvers had not said it, the ugly word stuck in his mind—murdered.

"The gentlemen have joined the ladies, sir. Can I direct you to the drawing room?"

The polite manservant who accosted Robin on the threshold of the dining room looked at the young man curiously. It was evident that he had received bad news.

"Oh, have they? No, that's all right. I can find my way, thank you."

Robin crossed the hall and entered the big salon where they had foregathered before dinner. The one thought uppermost in his mind was that he must get Jennifer home before the tragic news could be broken to her in some casual and shocking manner.

At first he could not see her. He stood inside the door looking round anxiously, and had just made up his mind that she was not there when he caught a glimpse of her white dress half hidden by the heavy grey curtains which flanked an alcove in the far corner of the room. He hurried over to find her talking to a tall, dark-haired woman dressed smartly but severely in black, whom he recognized instantly as Madame Julie.

Sir Ferdinand Shawle's social secretary was tall and still slender, although the lines round her eyes proclaimed her age to be well over forty. She was still beautiful, however, in spite of the pallor of her skin and a certain intensity in her dark eyes fringed by long, drooping lashes.

As Robin came up he got the impression that Jennifer was embarrassed by something her hostess was saying. There were bright spots of colour in the girl's cheeks and a bewildered expression in her big grey eyes. She looked relieved to see him and turned towards him eagerly.

"Robin, you know Madame Julie, don't you? I've been telling her I think we ought to leave early. I'm so worried about Daddy. I can't understand why he didn't come to dinner. I know he meant to."

She laid her hand on Robin's arm as she spoke, and the intimate gesture thrilled him unreasonably.

"Of course," he said quickly. "I'll take you back at once, if Madame Julie will excuse us." He glanced inquiringly at the woman and was startled to see the curious intensity of expression in her face as she regarded them. Some of his surprise was apparent, and the woman's heavy lids fluttered down over her eyes, and an embarrassed little laugh escaped her.

"You must forgive me," she said. "I am old enough to be Jennifer's mother, and the sight of you two young people so very much in love reminded me of something very long ago. I am afraid it showed in my face. Of course you shall go if you want to. I can sympathize with you. These formal functions are very dull when one has so much that is more interesting to think about."

Robin dared not look at Jennifer. His own ears were burning. The situation was embarrassing. He mumbled some excuse and was about to draw the girl away when Madame Julie spoke again. She had a deep musical voice which long experience in the realms of tact had made soft and versed in every subtle modulation.

Robin, glancing at her, decided that only her eyes were sincere, and he was surprised by the expression that was almost passionate entreaty in their depths.

"All ceremonial is irksome at this time, isn't it?" she went on softly. "That's why I've been telling Jennifer that you two must regard me as your friend. I have a certain amount of influence. If you want to get married without any fuss or bother, I could arrange it for you within the next twenty-four hours. Please don't think my offer extraordinary," she went on, and Robin noticed to his astonishment that one of her slender white hands which held her jewelled vanity case was trembling. "I'm genuinely interested in you both. Perhaps I should explain. My own life was ruined many years ago by a delayed engagement. If I had married the man I loved immediately after he had proposed to me, my life would have been very different. Please see me as a sentimental old woman who wants to help."

The hurried story told so briefly in the deep musical voice was frankly not convincing, but even had it not been for the evidence of the trembling hand it was impossible to doubt the anxiety of the woman to persuade them to get married immediately.

Robin felt Jennifer trembling at his side, and with the nightmare project of breaking the news of Bellew's death to her he felt that this last extraordinary development was more than he could tackle. He pulled himself together.

"Thank you very much, Madame Julie," he said with a hint of stiffness in his manner. "Should Jennifer and I decide upon a hurried marriage we shall certainly come to you. As it is, she is tired and naturally a little worried about Sir Henry. If you would excuse us, I think we will go now."

"Of course. I quite understand." The woman's calm dignity had returned. The heavy lids had once again descended over the dark eyes, but the boy had the impression that there was frustration hidden in their depths, frustration and a shadow of disappointment.

She escorted Jennifer upstairs to get her cloak and handed the girl over to her escort some minutes later.

Jennifer's cheeks were very pink, and Robin noticed that she did not meet his eyes. It was not until they were sitting together in the back of Sir Henry's chauffeur-driven limousine that she spoke directly to him.

"It's—it's all rather awkward, isn't it?" she said. "I hope you weren't made too uncomfortable."

"Of course not," he said hastily, anxious to put her at her ease. "It can't have been very pleasant for you either. But after all, it was obvious from the moment when we came to our rather unconventional agreement that some sort of situation like this was bound to occur. We must learn to be unselfconscious, mustn't we?"

She shot him a shy, grateful glance from under her eyelashes.

"You're extraordinarily kind," she said, and repeated almost wonderingly, "extraordinarily kind."

Robin caught his breath. There were moments when his position as a disinterested investigator became very difficult.

The girl went on before he could speak again.

"That woman's behaviour was very strange, wasn't it?" she said. "The whole thing has been strange. First of all Sir Ferdinand's invitation, when he didn't really know us at all. And then Madame Julie's insistence that we should get married at once. Before you came up she had been talking to me about it. I suppose in the ordinary way I should have been offended, but somehow I got the impression that she really was trying to help. She was so anxious to get me alone too; so anxious to talk to me without Sir Ferdinand seeing her. I don't understand it. What possible effect could my marriage have on her?"

Much the same problem had been occupying Robin's mind, crowding out that other matter which he dreaded to mention.

"It's just one of the inexplicable things that we've got to sift out," he said. "And now, Jennifer, I want you to be very brave."

The light of a passing street lamp lit up the inside of the dark car for a moment, and in that fleeting instant he caught a glimpse of her face, white and terror-stricken.

"What is it? Not—not Daddy?"

"No," he said hastily. "No, not your father. But after dinner this evening I received a phone call from an assistant who has been shadowing Mr. Bellew. I am afraid there's bad news for you."

She caught her breath, and he felt, rather than heard, the tiny sound in her throat as she checked an exclamation.

"Not dead?" she whispered.

He laid a hand over hers. "I'm afraid so," he said. "I can't give you any details yet; I don't know them myself. But as soon as I've left you at your father's house I shall go on to see Inspector Whybrow of the Yard. And then I promise you you shall hear everything."

After his voice died away there was complete silence in the car. He could feel her trembling, and suddenly something splashed down upon his hand and he realized she was crying. A wave of helplessness passed over him, coupled with a sick feeling of loneliness and emotion which he dared not analyze.

"You were in love with him?" In spite of himself the words came dully.

"No," she said violently, her voice choked with sobs. "No. I never loved Tony. But I was fond of him. He was always so happy, so cheerful. Quite one of the dearest boys I ever met. No, it's not that. I'm shocked—horrified—terrified—I can't tell you what I feel."

She withdrew her hand from his, and he guessed she was dabbing her eyes with her tiny scented handkerchief.

"Oh, it's terrible!" she broke out suddenly. "I can't believe it. Don't you see, it's all through me? Tony was in love with me, and because he was so sweet about it I didn't send him away. If only I had, perhaps this wouldn't have happened. I've prayed that this fate which seems to hang over me was a series of coincidences, but you see it isn't. It's a living terror. It's as if I were poisonous!"

She began to sob, and Robin, unable to restrain himself any longer, put an arm round her comfortingly. She drew back from him as though he had hurt her.

"You must go away," she said, her voice muffled with tears. "I'll write and cancel our engagement tonight. Don't you see? You're in serious danger. I must go away. I must shut myself up somewhere, as though I were a—a leper."

"Hush, hush, my dear." The endearment escaped Robin in spite of himself. "Please don't," he went on. "I'm all right. Nothing in the world will make me give this thing up now. I'm satisfied that there is some logical if startling explanation for all this, and I'm going to set you free from it if it's the last thing I do."

The final phrase slipped out unconsciously, and she seized upon it.

"That's it," she said. "That's what I'm so afraid of. They might—might kill you."

Conquering an absurd impulse to take her in his arms and to tell her that the matter was immaterial to him so long as she was happy, Robin continued to reason with her gently.

"My dear, I'm a detective, if you like to look at it that way. A risk like this is part of my job. My life has been in danger from one source or another for the past ten years. I shall be all right. This persecution of you has got to stop. I'm sorry about young Bellew—desperately sorry. I ought to have realized that he was still in danger. As it was, I thought that my announcements would shift their fire. But I see we're up against a shrewd intelligence."

Jennifer was still crying. "I can't let you go on," she said. "I feel like a murderess already. Oh, Robin, what shall I do? What shall I do?" She spoke with the weary helplessness of a tired child, and he felt her sway towards him.

For the rest of the drive she sat with her face hidden against the rough sleeve of his coat, and he sat very still, hardly daring to breathe.

When they arrived at the big Regent's Park house he climbed out and half led and half carried the stricken girl into the brilliantly lighted hall.

The butler, a white-haired man who had been in the service of the family for many years, bustled forward with fatherly concern. At the sight of his anxious old face Jennifer pulled herself together.

"I'm all right, Williamson," she said. "Is Daddy in?"

"In the library, miss. He came in half an hour ago. If you'll excuse me saying so, I should compose yourself a little before you go in to him. Sir Henry seemed very worried, very worried indeed."

Jennifer nodded. "You're right," she said. "I will." Then, turning to Robin, she held out both her hands. "I'm very grateful to you," she said, and her grey eyes still swimming with tears were raised to his own. "You've been most kind—more kind than anyone I've ever met. But I can't let you go through with it."

For some moments Robin was silent. Williamson had withdrawn discreetly, and they were alone. He held the slim white hands very firmly in his own.

"Miss Fern," he said, using the more ceremonious form of address deliberately, "you're going to find it very difficult to get rid of me. You've employed me on a matter which I am convinced is of the greatest importance. You can't dismiss me now."

Her lips quivered piteously. "God knows I don't want to," she said. "But oh, Robin, if any harm should come to you——"

"How can it?" he said. And then, with a gallantry of which he would certainly not have considered himself capable thirty-six hours before, he raised her hands to his lips and kissed them.

While she stood looking at him, a half-frightened, half-bewildered expression in her eyes, he turned abruptly and hurried out of the house, hailed a passing taxi, and gave the driver laconic instructions: "Scotland Yard, and drive like hell."

Chapter Five

Father and Daughter

"Daddy, may I come in?"

Jennifer paused at the doorway of the long, low, book-lined room and looked across the expanse of red and blue Turkey carpet at the man who sat huddled over the carved desk pulled out before the fire.

Sir Henry Fern raised his head, and for a moment a smile lit up his face. He looked very tired, and there were deep lines of worry engraved upon his heavy features.

"Why, Jennifer," he said, "you're back early. What's the matter? Did anything happen at the party to send you home so soon?"

The sharp question came as a surprise to the girl and she frowned.

"Why, no," she said. "What could have happened?"

"Nothing, of course," he agreed dully. "Come and sit down."

She crossed the room obediently and sat down on a low chair by the fire.

"I was a bit worried about you, as a matter of fact," she said when the silence had become difficult. "Why didn't you turn up?"

He did not answer for some moments, and she repeated her question.

"Eh, my dear?" he said, swinging round in his chair and facing her. "Oh, I had a headache. I felt I couldn't sit through one of F. S.'s long ceremonial meals. You were all right, weren't you? I thought as you had young Grey to look after you you wouldn't mind."

He paused, and as she did not reply he went on lamely: "If I go to one of these formal dinners I eat a lot of things that don't suit me. I came back here and Williamson found me some cold chicken and a very good glass of '98."

"But I thought you'd only just come in?"

He looked startled. "Well, yes," he admitted. "I had one or two things to do first. I called in at the club and put in an hour talking with Fenton."

"You don't look well," said the girl suddenly. "Is something worrying you?"

He turned away from her and thrust his hand through his short grey hair, a gesture of his that she recognized. Suddenly he rose to his feet and paced restlessly up and down the room.

Jennifer stared into the fire. The room seemed to have become suddenly very cold.

"Daddy," she said, "Tony Bellew is dead. Robin told me as we came home in the car."

"What?"

Sir Henry paused in his stride and stared at his daughter, while she, arrested by the horror in his voice, turned to look at him. Whatever effect she had expected her words to make upon the old man, his reaction bewildered her. His face had gone grey, his eyes were dilated, and his mouth had fallen open.

Jennifer forestalled his flow of questions.

"I don't know any details. Robin only told me that he was dead. Oh, Daddy, what does it mean?"

Sir Henry wiped his face with his handkerchief and came over to the hearthrug.

"I don't know, my dear," he mumbled. "I don't know."

The girl was holding herself with an iron control. She forced herself to rise and stand facing him.

"Daddy," she said, "we've never openly mentioned this subject, but I feel it's got to come up now or I shall go mad. What is the reason for this string of tragedies which haunts me?"

The old man turned away from her. "I don't know what you mean, my dear," he said wretchedly.

She went up to him and put her hands on his shoulders.

"But, Daddy, you do," she said. "You know what I'm saying. What is there about me that makes every man who admires me walk in danger of his life?"

Sir Henry laid his hand over the girl's lips.

"Jennifer, don't say such things," he said wretchedly. "You're hysterical. You're imagining things."

The girl drew back from him, repulsed, and a spasm of pain passed over the old man's face. He took a half-step towards her, but changed his mind and sat down at his desk.

"Look here, my dear," he said, and there was tenderness in his tone despite his efforts to hide it, "I want to talk to you about your engagement. As you know, I've never interfered with your life if I could possibly help it, but I do feel that you are young and that marriage is a very important step which should not be taken lightly. Are you in love with this man Grey?"

There was something that was almost pleading in the very blue eyes. Jennifer dropped her own before it.

"Robin is very kind to me."

"I know, I know. But do you love him?"

"I—I think so." The half-truth was wrung from the girl awkwardly. "Do you want me to give him up?"

"No, no, I'm not advocating anything so drastic as that." Sir Henry spoke wretchedly. There were beads of sweat on his forehead. "I only beg you not to hurry. Wait—take your time—take plenty of time. Be very sure before you do anything rash. I like young Grey, but I don't know anything about him. And above all, Jennifer, put this—this mad idea of yours about your fate, as you call it, out of your mind. Above all, don't try to find out. Don't *employ* anyone to find out."

The girl looked up with startled eyes to meet his own fixed upon her earnestly, but in spite of the sternness of his tone and the purposeful harshness of his expression, the emotion which leapt into view at the back of the very blue eyes was stark fear and pleading; fear both for himself and for what was to him much more important, his daughter.

CHAPTER SIX
SCOTLAND YARD

"Whenever I see you walk into my office with that damned bland friendly look on your face I know you've come prying."

Inspector Whybrow, standing on the hearthrug of his airy white-walled room at the Yard, spoke cheerfully as he grinned at Robin, who had just entered. The inspector was one of those plump, good-tempered men who look as though any mental exercise would floor them completely. But, as many criminals knew to their cost, that quiet exterior hid one of the most astute brains in the Criminal Investigation Department.

Robin was a particular favourite of Whybrow's, and the two had worked together on more than one occasion.

"I'm sorry I haven't got on my tail coat," the inspector went on, eyeing the boy's sleek shoulders with amusement. "You're getting very grand these days. Marrying into society, or something, aren't you?"

Robin did not smile, and the other man grimaced at the calendar which hung on the wall opposite him and winked as though exchanging a confidence with an old friend.

"Well, it's nice of you to come round and see an old policeman pal," he went on aloud. "What's up?"

Robin perched himself on the edge of the battered mahogany desk.

"I want the inside story of the Anthony Bellew case, Jack," he said.

Inspector Whybrow raised his eyebrows. "You're onto that pretty quick, aren't you?" he said. "It came in too late for the evening papers, and they haven't run out a special. What do you know about it?"

"Nothing at all," said Robin frankly. "But to tell you the truth, Johnny Danvers was keeping an eye on that fellow Bellew for me, and he phoned me when I was having dinner with my—er—fiancée that the youngster had been found dead. I took Miss Fern home and came straight on. What's the dope?"

"Wait a minute, wait a minute." Inspector Whybrow eyed his young friend suspiciously, his little bright eyes sharp beneath their bushy brows. "Let me get this thing straight. You say you've had Danvers following Bellew all day? What for?"

Robin sighed wearily. "It's a long story," he said. "Let me have the facts, Jack. Be a good fellow. How did this youngster die? Was it accident, suicide, or murder?"

The other man's bushy eyebrows rose to their fullest extent.

"It isn't exactly in my province," he said guardedly. "Mowbray is actually handling the job. He was in here just before you came, and I won't say we didn't have a chat about it. But fair's fair. We pool all information, you know. Is that a bargain?"

"Of course. But don't beat about the bush. I tell you I've got a very special reason for hearing the facts before I tell you what are, after all, only suspicions on my part."

"Well." The inspector spread out his podgy hands. "Mowbray doesn't know much yet, naturally. As far as I could gather, the facts which have come to light are these: this lad Bellew came in from a cocktail party about half-past six this evening. He was perfectly sober and seemed very cheerful, so his manservant says. He has a small flat in West Kensington and seems to have lived very comfortably. The manservant doesn't spend the whole day there, but comes in the morning to give his master his breakfast and to tidy up, and then wanders off to attend to his own business and returns about four to valet the youngster and prepare dinner. On this occasion he put out the whisky and soda and young Bellew's dress clothes and went out into the kitchen."

Robin, who knew it was useless to hurry the inspector when he was outlining a case, waited patiently.

"At half-past six Bellew came in," the elder man repeated. "He walked into the dining room, helped himself to a whisky and soda, went into his bedroom to change, collapsed, and was dead before the servant could get a doctor. Poisoned."

"The whisky?" said Robin.

The inspector nodded. "Mowbray thinks so. Anyway, he collared the decanter for analysis. The Doc's performing an autopsy tonight. He couldn't tell offhand what poison had been used. Something unusual, he thought. All that he would say was that it was some kind of swift narcotic. There you are. Now let me put a few questions. Don't worry," he added, as he caught the boy's expression. "I know you're not making an official statement any more than I am. This is just a little chat among friends. First of all, why in the world did you put Danvers onto Bellew?"

"In strict confidence, I had him watched because I thought he might be in danger."

"Really? Why?"

Robin hesitated, and decided, after a moment's consideration, that if the inspector was not to be trusted there was no one in the world who was.

"Well," he said at last, "it's an extraordinary yarn, but I witnessed the so-called accident he had on Waterloo Station the other night. In fact, I saved his life."

"The devil you did!" The inspector was startled into an admission of surprise. "Anything fishy about the circumstances?"

"Yes," said Robin quietly. "A man tried to murder him by throwing him onto the live rail."

"Did you see the man?" Inspector Whybrow was alert now, looking for all the world like a Scotch terrier with his ears pricked.

"Yes."

"Recognize him?"

"I—I think so."

"If you say you think so, that means as much to me as another man's oath. Who was it?"

"Sir Ferdinand Shawle."

"Get away!" Inspector Whybrow's favourite exclamation of astonishment broke from his startled lips.

"I only said I thought so."

The elder man went over to him and looked into his eyes. "Like to do the drunks test?" he inquired.

Robin permitted a faint worried smile to spread over his face.

"I feel rather like that myself," he said. "And remember, this is completely unofficial. I was at a dinner party at Sir Ferdinand's house when Danvers' message came through."

The inspector was silent for a moment or two. "I'll keep your name well out of it, of course," he said. "But thanks for the tip. Unless——" He turned on his heel to regard the young man shrewdly once again. "What are you playing at, Robin? I've known you a good many years, but I didn't know you knew any of the smart set intimately. What's the inside story of this engagement of yours?"

Robin regarded the man whom he had cause to think of as his best friend and spoke quietly.

"This is a dead secret, Jack," he said. "Miss Fern is a client."

A smile of understanding passed over the other man's face.

"I see," he said. He took out his cigarette case and passed it over.

After they had been smoking for some time in a silence which betokened complete understanding rather than any lack of sympathy, the inspector spoke again.

"You don't remember Morton Blount, do you?" he said. "He died just before your time. He was Jennifer Fern's uncle. They do say that she and her mother were the only people who ever aroused any spark of feeling in that old misogynist's heart. He was on the track of something pretty big until he suddenly threw everything up and retired to the country to die. There hasn't been a man in our line since who could touch him. I've often felt there was a story there, if only we could hit on it."

Robin did not comment. His mind was still working furiously on the story of Tony Bellew's death.

The inspector cut into his thoughts.

"Thanks for the hint," he said. "I shall look into it. And if anything transpires I'll let you know. Some day I may have to ask you for full details. But if I do, you can rely on me to be discreet."

He paused and went on again with the speed of one who has made up his mind to say something awkward.

"In many ways the history of Miss Jennifer Fern has been an extraordinary one," he said. "Every man who has so much as looked at her has come a cropper. I can't get Morton Blount and the thought of what he may have discovered out of my mind. Well, you see what I'm driving at, don't you? Be careful. We can't do without you just yet."

Robin laughed and held out his hand. "Don't worry about me," he said. "I'm one of the lucky sort. Well, good-night, old man, and thanks for the information. You'll be hearing from me in a day or so."

"Well, I damned well hope so," said the inspector to the calendar as the door closed behind the young man. He was very fond of Robin.

Mrs. Phipps was pacing up and down the hall of the Adelphi flat like an outraged white hen when Robin let himself in fifteen minutes later. As soon as she caught sight of him she came forward, on the verge of actually clucking.

"D'you know the time?" she demanded.

Robin looked at her in astonishment. "About half-past ten or a quarter to eleven," he said. "What's the idea, Phippy? Don't you like your Robin out late?"

"Oh, it's not that, Mr. Grey. You know I wouldn't be so impertinent." Mrs. Phipps positively blushed at the inference. "It's her I'm thinking of. Coming here at this time of night to call on an unmarried young gentleman who, even if he is mixed up with the police, is perfectly respectable, and as nice a young fellow—if you'll forgive me saying so—as ever I happened to meet. It isn't that there's anyone who'll talk, but it's the principle of the thing I object to. I mean, you're younger than I am and very trusting, and probably you don't know. But——"

"Here, Phippy, Phippy! Hold on a moment." Robin caught the old woman by the shoulder and shook her gently, so that she stopped talking and looked at him in mild surprise. "Who's been here?" he inquired.

"A woman," said Mrs. Phipps, adding reluctantly, "I suppose she's a lady, really."

"Who was she? What did she want? When did she go?"

"She hasn't gone," said Mrs. Phipps, her indignation boiling over again. "She's in your sitting room now, and nothing I could say would move her, the—the—the person!"

Robin swept the old lady aside good-naturedly and hurried into his study in some trepidation.

A tall figure in a soft flowing fur coat rose up from his deep easy chair. He stared at her in complete astonishment, for as the light fell upon her face he found himself looking into the dark, curiously appealing eyes of Madame Julie.

Robin stared at the woman who had appeared so astonishingly before him, and she came forward, her hand outstretched.

"I had to see you. I hope you don't mind."

Her voice was low and soft, but there was intensity in its tone, and he realized that she was labouring beneath some suppressed excitement.

"Not at all," he said wonderingly. "Not at all. Won't you sit down?"

She seemed not to have heard the conventional phrase, for she stretched out her hand and laid it on his arm.

"Mr. Grey," she said, "I want you to be frank with me. I want you to forget that I am comparatively a stranger, that I am a woman, and that I have come to see you at what I am afraid is a very unconventional hour. I have come for your sake as much as my own. Tell me, are you in love with Jennifer Fern? Do you really love her?"

Robin looked at her helplessly. Her nervous manner and her extraordinary interest in what, after all, must be his own private affair naturally suggested an advanced case of chronic hysteria.

She seemed to read the thought in his face.

"This must seem very odd to you," she went on in an attempt at calmness. "But I tell you you must forgive me. You must be patient. Tell me, do you really love this girl?"

Something in her voice and in the passionate sincerity in the dark eyes convinced Robin that she was in earnest, that she was sane, and that she had some deep reason for her apparently extraordinary behaviour.

"Yes," he said truthfully. "Yes, I love Jennifer."

It was the first time that he had uttered the words aloud, and in spite of the tenseness of the moment their truth came home to him with a little shock of something very like dismay.

The woman seemed relieved.

"I believe you," she said. "I saw it in your eyes when you were talking to her this evening. Now you must trust me a little further. You two young people are in serious danger."

She swept aside his incredulous exclamation with an impatient gesture.

"I have come here at great risk," she said simply. "It is not likely that I should do this unless I had some very good reason. I am not a fool. Nor am I," she went on, the ghost of a smile flickering across her pale, still beautiful face, "the hysteric you seem to think, young man. Now, I have a way out for you both."

She opened her jewelled vanity case and produced two official-looking green-backed booklets, which she laid upon the table between them.

"These," she went on, tapping them with a slender finger, "are two reservations on the Orient liner *Orestes* which leaves Tilbury for Sydney on the morning tide. You have just time. If that girl loves you as you love her, and as I believe she does, you will have no difficulty in persuading her to come away with you."

For once in his life Robin was bewildered. Here was a person who every instinct told him was a shrewd, capable being in full possession of her senses deliberately persuading him to take a ridiculous and incomprehensible course.

But the woman was still talking, the words breaking from her lips in a stream of passionate pleading.

"Many people have eloped before. It may even appeal to her; there is a spice of romance in it. As soon as you are out of port, the captain can marry you on the high seas. Not a soul will know until it is done. Not a soul will be able to stop you. You will have the long voyage to Sydney and back again if you wish. By that time the danger will be past. It is your last chance. Will you take it?"

Robin picked up the documents from the table. A glance told him that they were indeed reservations for the *Orestes* and represented a very considerable amount of money spent.

Meanwhile the woman was watching him with big, terror-stricken eyes.

Robin sat down, motioning his visitor to a chair opposite.

"Don't you think you'd better explain a little more fully, Madame?" he said.

She still ignored his offer of a chair, and instead bent forward across the table, her pale face suffused with eagerness.

"Take this warning seriously, please," she said pleadingly. "I can't tell you any more. I can only repeat that you are in danger. I can only implore you to take this way out while there is still time."

Robin's ingenuous boyish face became troubled.

"My dear lady," he said, "how can I? The whole thing's preposterous."

"Not if you love her," she insisted, "and she loves you. What does it matter when you get married—tomorrow or in a year's time? Or where?—in a society church or on an ocean-going liner?"

Robin lowered his eyes before the woman's penetrating stare. The question she raised brought home to him the hopelessness of his situation with regard to Jennifer.

He pulled himself together and rose stiffly, his embarrassment lending his manner more coldness than it might otherwise have possessed.

"You've come to me with an impossible story, Madame," he said, "and an equally impossible request. While I do not insult you by suggesting that you are forcing yourself into an affair which is hardly any concern of yours, I must point out that my marriage is my own business, and at the moment I do not want to discuss it."

He heard her catch her breath, and, turning, saw to his astonishment that her eyes were full of tears. She winked them back instantly, however, and drew herself up, a curiously imperious gesture which lent her height an impressiveness.

"You want proof?"

The words were uttered very softly, but there was something in the inflection of her voice which sent a little thrill down his spine.

"Very well. I tell you you are in danger—you particularly. Her turn has not come yet. Since you don't believe me, I should examine your rooms very carefully before you go to sleep tonight. Something tells me, Mr. Grey, that if you neglect this warning, nothing very much will matter to you by this time tomorrow."

She was still speaking softly, almost lightly, but he could feel the underlying sincerity, the underlying menace almost, in every word.

He looked at her inscrutable face for a moment and then glanced sharply round the room. His quick, well-trained eye and orderly memory told him that nothing was out of place. Mrs. Phipps had conservative ideas both in regard to furniture and tidiness, and he could tell at a glance, after some years of her ministrations, if anyone other than she had been tampering with his things.

Madame Julie stood watching him, her lips smiling, her eyes wide, and with that hint of fear and pleading in their depths.

He turned into his bedroom, which led out of the other room.

Here everything was as usual. The bed had been turned down, he recognized, by Mrs. Phipps's careful hand.

He went on to the bathroom, a tiny white-tiled affair of a pattern which his good landlady had caused to be installed in every suite.

Robin's detective-trained mind went to work methodically. In all cases where a trap has been laid for a victim it is usually found that the intelligent criminal anticipates the normal actions of his prey so that death may come swiftly and completely unexpectedly. Robin considered his own habits upon going to bed.

He would take off his things by the big wardrobe, hang up his suit, change into pyjamas, come into the bathroom to wash.

He examined the basin carefully. His soap and sponge were where Mrs. Phipps always left them. His shaving brush he was certain had not been touched, since he had cleaned it himself that morning.

He picked up his toothbrush, peered at it under the electric light, and finally sniffed it dubiously.

He turned back and replaced it in its stand. As he did so he caught sight of his tube of toothpaste lying on the glass shelf beneath the shaving mirror.

Instantly his heart leapt uncomfortably and he stood staring at it. It lay on the wrong end of the shelf. Mrs. Phipps had set out his belongings in exactly the same order night after night for years, and she invariably put the toothpaste next to the shaving cream on the right. He had often remarked that he could have dressed himself quite well in the dark, so exact were these tiny arrangements.

He picked up the tube and turned it over. It was the brand he usually used, but he had an impression in the back of his mind that this was considerably fuller than the tube of the morning.

Holding the thing well away from him, he unscrewed the cap and squeezed out a little of its contents into a soap dish. The familiar ribbon of pink cream greeted his eyes, and he was inclined to laugh at himself for over-caution, when something inconsistent about the compound caught his attention.

He picked up the tube and sniffed it. The next moment the colour drained out of his face and he dropped the thing into the washbasin involuntarily.

Even the strong peppermint flavour of the paste had been unable to disguise the pungent, sinister scent of bitter almonds which even in that brief moment had set his nostrils tingling and dried the back of his throat.

Cyanide.

Cyanide, that most swift, most horrible of all the poisons, a touch of which on the tongue means almost instantaneous death.

"Of course it is traceable." The thought ran through Robin's mind immediately. Whoever had placed this death trap for him was taking a big risk.

The diabolical ingenuity of the scheme shocked him. The infrequency with which cyanide is used as a poison, save with suicides, is due principally to its well-known symptoms which make it most obvious to trace, and secondarily to this characteristic and powerful odour which warns any intended victim if it is placed in food.

There are few things that the average person puts straight into his mouth without hesitation. One of these is toothpaste. The metal cap on the tube prevented the smell of bitter almonds suffusing the room, yet Robin shuddered when he realized how easily he might have squeezed some of the infamous mixture onto his brush and used it unthinkingly.

He picked up the tube gingerly, replaced the cap, and, setting it down upon the soap dish, carried them carefully into his bedroom and locked them in the little wall safe above his bed.

He returned to the bathroom and washed his hands before he hurried back to the sitting room to interview his strange guest, who had turned out so astonishingly to be a deliverer. There were many thoughts in his mind, many questions on his lips.

As he turned into the room, however, a sense of frustration seized him. It was empty, and the door to the staircase stood ajar.

He went out into the hall. The whole house was dark and silent. The other lodgers had early habits, and Mrs. Phipps herself had retired.

He went downstairs cautiously, but although he searched the house no trace remained of his mysterious visitor save the soft fragrance of the perfume she used.

He came slowly back to his room, his forehead knotted, his eyes dark and troubled.

Lying on the table were the two reservations. He turned them over idly.

A strange woman, with a strange, all-impelling motive, he reflected.

He could not understand her behaviour. Her talk of an elopement, marriage on the high seas—it was all strange and incomprehensible. And then her dramatic warning, which had proved to be only too justified...

He passed his hand through his fair hair.

Then he sighed, and a faint, rueful smile passed over his face as he threw the reservations down upon the table again. There was something about the romantic picture which Madame Julie had painted which had been very tantalizing.

"If she loves you..." she had said. Robin shook his head sadly. That was not to be hoped for, he decided.

Chapter Seven
Sinister Coincidence

"Oh, Mr. Robin, how you startled me—sitting up in bed like that! You don't look as though you've slept a wink."

Mrs. Phipps set the cup of tea she carried on the little table at the side of Robin's bed and bustled round the room, pulling back the curtains and throwing the windows wide.

Robin sat hunched up in bed, his knees drawn up to his chin and his arms clasping his ankles. He looked tired, certainly, and there were lines of anxiety round his eyes. He had spent a wakeful night pondering over the peculiarities of the astonishing situation in which he found himself.

As a rule he was able to keep one side of his mind for his cases; never before had anything touched him quite so nearly. The personal element kept intruding itself into his thoughts, and he found it very difficult to think of Jennifer in any detached or disinterested manner.

Mrs. Phipps planted herself at the end of the bed and surveyed him with shrewd, motherly eyes.

As he caught sight of her inquisitive little face peering at him like some quizzical sparrow, he jerked his mind out of its train of thought, which largely concerned the most beautiful girl in the world, and returned to the business in hand.

"Phippy," he said, "did anyone else come up here last night—before I came in?"

Mrs. Phipps looked surprised. "Anyone else besides that—that——"

"Lady," suggested Robin.

"Lady," agreed Mrs. Phipps grudgingly. "That lady who was waiting here when you came back? Anyone besides her? Well, what a funny thing you should ask that! As I was dressing this morning I said to myself, 'There! I never told him about that poor old body.' I was so taken aback by that— that lady's impudence in coming so late, that everything else went clean out of my head. It wasn't even as if she was a relation, yet she came up here as bold as brass. That's what we used to call 'fast' when I was a girl."

Robin knew Mrs. Phipps too well to attempt to stop her before she was forced to take breath. At the first opportunity, however, he cut in.

"Who are you talking about?" he inquired.

"Why, the lady," said Mrs. Phipps. "The second lady."

Robin started.

"Oh. So there were two ladies who came up here last night?"

"Well, yes, I'm telling you." Mrs. Phipps looked pink and irritated. "The first one, poor dear old body, said she'd come up all the way from Somerset to see her son who's in hospital, and she called in on you because she hadn't seen you since you were a little boy. She waited until she'd have missed her last train if she hadn't gone. She looked so tired, but I made her a cup of tea and let her sit up here and drink it. I'd have told you first thing, but that other person coming put it clean out of my mind. Oh, that—that other one did annoy me!"

Robin restrained an impulse to get out of bed and shake a little coherence into the garrulous housekeeper.

"Now, Phippy," he said slowly, his voice having just that quality of sternness which made her realize that he was very much in earnest, "how much can you remember about this first visitor of mine? Did she give her name?"

"Of course she did! Would I have let her in if she hadn't? She said you'd recognize her name at once. Why, Mr. Robin, it was your old nurse, Mrs. Hester Branch, from Somerset."

She was looking at him with interest to catch the gleam of recognition which she felt sure would come into his face.

Robin's eyes remained grave, however.

"Oh, yes," he said noncommittally. He knew that it would hardly add to the speed of Mrs. Phipps's revelations if he volunteered the information that he had never had a nurse in his life. "How old was she?"

"Oh, getting along," said Mrs. Phipps complacently. "Between sixty-five and seventy. But wonderfully upright and strong-looking. She said her ears were still good, but she suffers with bronchial trouble which makes her very hoarse. She looked so tired, poor thing, and so grateful for the cup of tea."

Robin laughed, a short bitter explosion which made the old lady look at him in amazement.

"Phippy, you really are a darling," he said.

Mrs. Phipps positively blushed.

"Oh, Mr. Robin, go along with you!"

"I suppose you left her in my sitting room while you made the tea?"

"Yes, I did. There was a nice fire there, and I thought if she couldn't see you she'd be happy resting in your place."

Robin leant forward.

"Phippy," he said, "you're perfectly sure it *was* a woman?"

"Well, Mr. Robin!" Mrs. Phipps's mouth fell open as for the first time a faint inkling of the truth presented itself to her mind. She turned pale and clutched the bedrail with nervous, bony fingers. "Oh, Mr. Robin!" she repeated. "You don't mean to say that you don't know anybody of that name? Oh dear, oh dear, and I left her alone amongst all your things! I never imagined anyone could be so deceitful! Tell me," she went on anxiously, "nothing's been taken, has it?"

Robin shook his head. "No," he said slowly. "No, Phippy, nothing's been taken."

"Thank Heaven for that," said Mrs. Phipps piously.

Robin regarded her with affectionate dismay.

"In future," he said, "never show anyone in here unless you know them. Understand?"

"Yes, sir." Mrs. Phipps was conscience-stricken. "Oh, the wicked old thing!" she went on with sudden indignation. "The wicked old thing! Sitting there sipping my tea. I expect that's what she came for—just to get warm. It's very sad in a way, but very wrong."

Robin's lips grew grim, but he did not think it necessary to enlighten Mrs. Phipps concerning his strange visitor's real reason for calling.

Her protestations of regret were mercifully interrupted by a tap on the bedroom door. She started violently.

"Mercy on us! Who can that be?" she inquired, and advanced to face the intruder as if she expected burglars at least.

Inspector Jack Whybrow's friendly, good-humoured face confronted her as she opened the door, however, and with an audible sigh of relief she threw the door open wide.

"I'm sure *you* can come in, sir," she said.

"And me too, I hope, Mrs. Phipps. Or do you want to see my warrant?" said a different voice from the background as Inspector Mowbray, Whybrow's colleague and officer in charge of the investigation of the murder of Tony Bellew, followed his friend into the room.

With a nod to Robin, Mrs. Phipps tactfully withdrew, and the two distinguished members of the C. I. D. stood looking at the young man in bed.

"Hullo, what's this? An arrest?" Robin grinned at Mowbray as he spoke.

The inspector was a heavily built, florid individual, whose fine black moustache was a relic of the fashion of former days.

"Not yet, my lad," he said, seating himself on the end of the coverlet without ceremony. "Whybrow here tells me of something you told him in confidence about an incident you witnessed on Waterloo Station."

Robin frowned. He had not wished to be implicated in the affair, but he also knew his duty as a Yard man too well to refuse information when deliberately asked for it.

"Yes," he said. "I'll repeat it if you like."

He went through the story clearly.

Mowbray nodded and smiled at Whybrow.

"Exactly," he said. "You're a fine reporter, Jack. Now look here, Robin, I know your reputation where faces are concerned, and I don't want to put ideas into your head. But are you perfectly sure that the man you saw make an attempt on young Bellew's life was Sir Ferdinand Shawle?"

Robin shook his head. "No. I told Jack here that it looked like him, that's all."

Mowbray shrugged his shoulders. "We all know what that means with you," he said. "But look here, this is what I'm trying to get at: do you think there is a chance that this man you saw on the station was not Sir Ferdinand but"—he paused, and added softly—"Sir Henry Fern?"

"Sir Henry Fern?" Robin gasped at him. Then he laughed. "No," he said. "No, I'm sure of that. The man I saw on Waterloo Station was not even faintly like Sir Henry."

He caught the expression in the inspector's eyes and laughed abruptly.

"You needn't worry, Bill," he said. "I'm not shielding anyone. But I think I deserve an explanation."

"Sure you do," said the inspector slowly. "You shall have it."

It was evident that he was disappointed, however, and, in the silence which followed, Robin climbed out of bed, slipped on a dressing gown, and went over to the safe.

"Look here," he said. "What do you make of this?"

He brought out the soap dish which still contained its deadly burden and set it down upon the dressing table.

Mowbray looked puzzled, but Whybrow, who recognized the earnestness in Robin's face, inspected the exhibit cautiously.

Robin unscrewed the metal cap of the tube and squeezed some of the contents out upon the porcelain dish.

Whybrow sniffed, and he and his colleague exchanged swift inquiring glances. Finally Whybrow whistled softly through his teeth.

"Well," he ejaculated, "well, what do you make of that?"

The question was rhetorical.

Inspector Mowbray picked up the soap dish and peered cautiously at the deadly tube.

"Eh!" he said disgustedly. "That's as dirty as anything I've ever seen in my career. Where did you get it?"

Robin related his experiences of the evening before, omitting only the name of the woman who had warned him.

The two inspectors listened to the recital gravely. They were both men of deep experience, but there had been something about the callousness and ingenuity of the death trap which had shocked them both.

"It might so easily have succeeded," said Mowbray, taking out a large pocket handkerchief and absent-mindedly wiping his forehead. "It makes you think."

Inspector Whybrow pulled out an old and battered notebook.

"Now look here, Robin my lad," he said briskly, "you're too valuable to run risks of this sort. This kind of thing must be stopped. You must come across with all the information, as if you were an ordinary private individual. Now then, out with it—the whole of it."

Robin shook his head.

"You'll have to trust me, Jack," he said. "I can't give you the name of the woman who warned me just yet. It's vitally important to me that she should not be put on her guard by police questioning or anything of the kind. I can tell you one thing, however, and that is that I had a mysterious visitor late last night who spent some time in this suite alone, while my landlady was making her a cup of tea. She gave her name as Hester Branch and represented herself as an old nurse of mine from Somerset. Needless to say, I've never heard of her before. Mrs. Phipps was telling me about her when you both came in. Whoever she was, she took in Mrs. Phipps. As far as I can gather she was between sixty-five and seventy, and——" He broke off abruptly. "What's the matter with you two fellows?" he demanded.

The inspectors were staring at one another, sheer bewilderment upon Mowbray's face and a species of incredulous amazement on Whybrow's.

"This is absurd," said Whybrow at last. "You say your landlady saw this woman?"

"She certainly did. She left her in my sitting room and trotted down to make her a cup of tea. Then, as far as I can gather, she stood and watched the old dear drink it up and showed her out of the house."

Whybrow turned to Mowbray.

"Can you beat that?" he said and, striding across the suite, put his head out on the landing. His stentorian voice boomed through the house. "Mrs. Phipps! Mrs. Phipps!"

The good lady appeared with an alacrity which suggested that she had been lingering near at hand, and some moments later she was seated in a chair by the bedroom window undergoing a steady cross-examination from the two excited inspectors.

"Yes," she said defiantly. "I let her in, and I've apologized to Mr. Robin for it. But seeing that nothing's been taken I don't see——"

"Nothing taken!" ejaculated Whybrow, and would have continued, had not a warning glance from Robin silenced him in time.

"Mrs. Phipps," cut in Mowbray, "can you describe this stranger?"

Mrs. Phipps tried and floundered.

"She was old," she said. "She had a browny-black cloak, an old-fashioned pork-pie hat, rather pretty fluffy white hair, and an old lined face with no teeth."

Inspector Mowbray was flapping over the pages of his notebook.

"Would you say," he ventured cautiously, "that she was about five foot ten? That's very tall, you know. About an inch taller than Mr. Robin here. And would you say that she seemed rather vague in manner, and that her glasses were very thick?"

Mrs. Phipps started violently.

"Oh, how did you know? She's not some well-known thief, I hope? Because, if so, now she knows the way she'll come back. We shall lose everything—perhaps be murdered in our beds——"

"Don't worry about that, Phippy," Robin counselled gently. "Answer Inspector Mowbray's questions."

"There aren't any questions," said Mrs. Phipps. "He's described her as if he'd seen her. She was very tall and held herself very straight. She had the thickest glasses I ever saw, although she said her sight was good. And I noticed she hadn't any teeth. I felt like telling her about it. You can get a set of dentures so cheap nowadays that it really doesn't seem worthwhile going without."

The inspector shut his notebook with a snap.

"That's all for the moment," he said. "We may have to call on you again, Mrs. Phipps. Thank you very much."

He showed her courteously out of the room and came back to find Robin staring at him inquiringly.

"What's the explanation of all this?" Robin demanded. "Who is this mysterious visitor?"

"That's what we all want to know," said Mowbray. "Here is our story as far as it goes: We've been up half the night investigating the Tony Bellew murder. We've taken dozens of statements, and the only one that is of any great use is the story from the furnace and odd-job man in the block of flats where the boy lived. This man has a box in the hall of the block, but as he has to mingle a certain amount of general work with his duties as porter he doesn't use it very often.

"Yesterday afternoon he had several odd jobs to do— cleaning the windows in one flat, for one thing, re-laying the main stair carpet for another—so that although he was about the building all day he could not swear that he'd seen everybody who'd come into the house.

"Now the curious thing is that in his statement he says that during the afternoon an old woman in a brown-black cloak and well over average height went up the staircase towards Mr. Bellew's flat. He didn't see her go in, because he was on the fourth floor and she went up to the fifth, but as Bellew's flat took up the whole of the fifth floor—which is also the top—it seems reasonable to suppose that she went there."

He paused and looked at Robin shrewdly beneath his thick eyebrows.

"This janitor was working about all the rest of the afternoon. He does not deny that he was in and out of the lower flats, but thinks that the chance of anyone getting up and down the staircase without him seeing him was remote. However, the fact remains that he did not see the old woman come down, and no one else, as far as we can see, did either. We've inquired in every likely quarter. That old woman seems to have vanished into thin air from the time when she was seen going up to Tony Bellew's flat to the time when Mrs. Phipps admitted her into your room some hours later."

Robin was still assimilating these remarkable facts when Whybrow broke in softly.

"There's something else I think you ought to hear, Robin," he said, "for it affects you, in a way."

While the boy stared at him, a sick feeling of apprehension clutching at his heart, the older man went on inexorably:

"Included in the janitor's statement was something else. Half an hour after the old woman was seen going up to the flat, a man was seen coming down from the fifth floor. The janitor was surprised because, not only had he been unaware that he had gone up to the flat, but also, he recognized him. Moreover, he was a very observant fellow, and he noticed that not only was the man about the same height as the old woman, but that he carried a bulky brown-paper parcel, which might easily have contained articles of wearing apparel."

Robin looked from one to the other of the two men. His mouth was dry, and there was a startled expression in his eyes.

"You say the janitor recognized this man?" he said, and even to himself his words sounded staccato and unnatural.

"Yes. By chance, in the war the janitor had served on the ship of which this man had command."

"Who was it?" Robin knew the answer before Whybrow spoke.

Mowbray read his thoughts. "Yes," he said. "You're right. Sir Henry Fern. Queer thing, isn't it?"

"Of course it's not evidence," said Inspector Whybrow quickly after the pause which had followed his colleague's sensational announcement. "It's not evidence. We all know that. The janitor believes he saw Sir Henry coming downstairs from Tony Bellew's flat late yesterday afternoon. But that doesn't prove anything."

"Of course it doesn't," said Mowbray, a little nettled. "But at any rate it's something to go on. Now look here, Robin, we're going down to Sir Henry's house now."

"I'll come with you. If you'll wait for me for half a moment I'll be there."

Robin began to dress rapidly. His thoughts were busy with the extraordinary story the two inspectors had brought, and his chief concern was for Jennifer. He foresaw a very difficult time ahead for her.

Some minutes later, as they sat in the taxicab speeding towards Regent's Park, old Whybrow broached the subject again.

"There's no question of an arrest, of course," he murmured, eyeing Robin dubiously.

"I should hope not!" said the young man, aghast. "Neither Bill nor you have gone mad, I take it."

Inspector Mowbray grunted. "If he wasn't the person he is, he'd be detained," he said.

Robin shrugged his shoulders. "It is the fact that he is who he is that makes the whole thing preposterous," he remarked, and silence fell again upon the little company.

Old Williamson, Sir Henry's butler, admitted them with some surprise. It was evident that he did not approve of such early hours for callers.

Robin touched Whybrow's arm.

"I think, if you don't mind," he said, "you'd better see Sir Henry alone. I'll stay down here and see if I can't get a word with Jennifer."

Something in the inflection of his voice as he spoke the name made the old inspector look at him sharply, an interested expression in his shrewd eyes beneath their shaggy brows.

A deeper colour came into Robin's face, and the old man nodded to himself confidentially.

"Oh," he said softly. "So that's the way the wind blows, is it? Be careful, my boy. You're on dangerous ground."

Robin affected not to have heard this warning, for at that moment Williamson returned with the remark that the two gentlemen from Scotland Yard would see Sir Henry in the library.

The little procession moved off at once, Williamson stalking majestically in front, while Robin remained in the hall.

He was staring idly at the magnificent oak staircase, thinking of Jennifer, when she appeared, standing at the top of the flight in a trim blue morning dress, a gaily coloured scarf thrown negligently round her slender shoulders.

She gave a little cry as she saw him and came hurrying down the staircase, her hands outstretched.

He noticed that her face was pale beneath her honey-coloured curls and that there were faint dark shadows beneath her eyes.

"Oh, I'm glad you've come," she said, and then, as though the words had contained more warmth than she had realized or intended, the colour came into her face and she dropped her eyes.

"Look here," she said, "won't you come into the morning room? I want to ask you about Tony."

Robin followed her into the sunny little room, gay with white paint and brilliant chintz. His heart was pounding uncomfortably, and he realized with a sense of dismay that he was soon going to find it impossible to maintain the grave impersonal attitude of a professional man when dealing with this particular client. She made him breathless. He could not trust his voice to keep steady.

"What have they found out about Tony?" She spoke eagerly. "How did it happen? I saw in the paper this morning that he was poisoned. Do they know who did it?"

Robin shook his head. "I'm afraid I can't tell you. I don't know. Inspector Whybrow and Inspector Mowbray, who are in charge of the case, are here now talking to your father."

She stared at him, every hint of colour slowly draining out of her face.

"Talking to *Daddy?* Why? Oh, Robin, he doesn't know anything about it. Oh, my dear, they don't think that——"

She broke off and stood looking at him, horror in her vivid eyes.

Robin conquered the impulse to take her in his arms.

"Oh, no, it's nothing," he said, turning away from her. "Nothing to be alarmed about at all. They simply want to ask him a few questions. You've got to keep very brave and very level-headed. We all have. Then you'll find everything will come perfectly all right."

He heard his own voice speaking pedantically and without much conviction. The main part of his mind was idiotically preoccupied with the colour of her hair, the tilt of her chin, and her tiny fluttering white hands.

She did not speak for some moments, and, as he was standing with his back to her, he felt rather than saw her sit down wearily in the big leather armchair by the fireside.

Suddenly she spoke, and her voice was very small and childlike.

"Robin," she said, "this must stop. Daddy was talking to me last night. I think he must have guessed—about—about us, I mean."

Robin spun round. "What do you mean?" he demanded.

"Well, he questioned me about our engagement. Wanted to know if I loved you, and that sort of thing."

She was not looking at him now. Her eyes were fixed upon the burning logs in the grate.

"And finally he warned me not to try to find out about this mystery which surrounds me, and on no account to employ anyone to find out. So you see, he's guessed. I think we'd better call it all off, don't you? There's the awful risk that you run to consider, too. You insist on making light of it, but you know it exists. So I think if you don't mind we really will finish it this time."

Robin walked over towards her and stood on the hearthrug looking down at her bright head.

"I—I can't," he said suddenly.

She looked up at him, a startled expression in her eyes, a half-formed question on her lips.

Robin went on, speaking jerkily and without considered thought.

"I can't throw it up," he said. "You can withdraw your confidence from me if you like—you can even refuse to see me—but nothing will make me change my mind. I am going to see this thing through. I am going to see you free from the terrible nightmare which haunts you, and I am going to see your enemies safely under lock and key. I'm afraid there's no use arguing with me."

She rose slowly to her feet and stood there, her face raised to his. There was a half-puzzled, half-tremulous happiness in her eyes, and Robin suddenly forgot everything else in the world except her. The mysterious hints of Madame Julie, the sinister death of Tony Bellew, the attack upon his own life which had very nearly proved fatal, and now grave suspicions enveloping Sir Henry, were all wiped from his mind.

Jennifer stood very close to him.

He suddenly bent forward and, taking her in his arms, kissed her lips. He felt her stiffen for a moment, and then she sighed, an intoxicating little sound of surrender.

Before either of them could speak, voices sounded outside the door, and the next moment it was thrown open and they had just time to spring apart before Sir Henry, followed by the two inspectors, came into the room.

The old man was flushed. There were an unusual brightness in his eyes and a nervousness about his walk and gestures which might have passed for the ordinary mannerisms of a different man, but which on his part were clearly, Robin reflected, the outcome of extreme nervous tension.

He nodded to Robin graciously enough, however, and shot an almost pathetic smile at his daughter.

"Well, my dear," he said with forced joviality, "here are Inspectors Whybrow and Mowbray to see you. They haven't come to arrest us, yet."

He laughed at his own heavy joke, and the girl, shaken from her recent emotional experience and naturally unnerved a little by the sudden appearance of the two Yard men, bowed to them stiffly, a faint, scared little smile on her lips.

Inspector Mowbray took the lead.

"We haven't much to ask you, Miss Fern," he said. "Just one or two formal questions. How well did you know Mr. Tony Bellew?"

"I knew him very well," she said stiffly. "He was one of a party of us who spent a holiday on the Riviera. We all came back together a few days ago."

"You were not engaged to him?"

"Certainly not. I—I'm engaged to Mr. Grey."

"Oh, yes, so I see." Mowbray looked a little discomfited. "Well, then, I think that'll be all for the present. Oh, by the way, there's one other thing. On Waterloo Station when the boat train came in from the south, Mr. Bellew had an accident and all but lost his life on the electric rails. Isn't that so?"

She nodded, the old scared expression returning to her eyes.

The inspector said slowly: "You're sure it was an accident, Miss Fern? I mean," he went on ponderously, "you had no reason for thinking there could be any foul play connected with his fall upon the suburban line?"

"Why, no. I—I—" the girl lied with difficulty. "Robin could tell you better than I," she went on. "It was he who saved him. Why, that was the first time I saw Robin——"

She bit her lip as the fatal admission slipped out, and recovered herself awkwardly.

"The first time I saw Robin after we came back," she corrected herself.

The lie served, but Robin, catching a glimpse of Sir Henry's face, saw a half-wistful smile appear and vanish. It was as though he had been convinced of something which he had more than suspected already.

The two inspectors remained stolid. There was nothing on their wooden faces to show how much of the story they believed, or how little.

Mowbray flapped over the pages of his ragged book.

"Thank you, Miss Fern," he said. "Now, Sir Henry, there's nothing you'd like to add to your statement, is there?"

"Nothing at all, Inspector." The old man seemed anxious to talk, however, for he went on: "I repeat I did go up to Tony Bellew's flat yesterday, but I called just before lunch. I imagine about half-past twelve or a quarter to one, and not, as you seem to think, about four or half-past in the afternoon."

There was an unmistakable ring of truth in his voice, and while he was talking he seemed to have regained confidence.

"I got no reply from the flat, so I came down again," he went on. "I may have met the janitor on the stairs; I can't remember. But certainly I carried no paper parcel. Frankly, Inspector," he went on with a little grimace at Mowbray, "am I the sort of man to be seen carrying a bulky brown-paper parcel?"

"No, sir, I can't say you are," said Mowbray, shaking his head gravely. "Still, we have to check up on everything, you know. There's just one other thing, sir, while we're on the subject: Had you any particular reason for going to call on Mr. Bellew?"

Sir Henry took a deep breath. It was evident that he had been expecting this question.

"Well, yes, as it happens I had. I didn't see any reason for mentioning it until I was asked, and even now I shall expect you to regard the information confidentially. Young Bellew's father is an old friend of mine, and when the boy came to London he told me to keep an eye on him. I'd heard one or two things about the youngster, don't you know—nothing greatly to his discredit, but enough to make me feel that I'd take him out to lunch at my club and have a chat with him. As it happened, I had no engagement for lunch yesterday, so I went round to see if I could catch him. I was unlucky, and there you are. Now, poor young fellow, no advice of mine can help him."

Inspector Mowbray, who had been writing busily, glanced up.

"Thank you, sir," he said. "That'll be all now. I'm sorry to have bothered you, but you understand, sir, in an affair of this sort every avenue must be explored."

"Oh, yes, that's all right, Inspector." Sir Henry smiled wearily at the man. "I've given you a detailed account of my movements during the afternoon. If you take the trouble to go around to my club—the Junior Greys, Pall Mall—I think you'll be able to find someone there who'll tell you that during the hours between three and five-thirty I was in the smokeroom. The doorkeeper will certainly have my name on the book. But I've told you that once already, haven't I, in the other room?"

Mowbray nodded again, and there was a pause which indicated quite plainly that the interview was at an end.

Sir Henry turned to Robin.

"Well, my boy," he said, "I hear the dinner party last night was a great success."

This deliberate changing of the subject was so obvious that Robin felt in duty bound to respond to it.

"Well, yes, I think so, sir," he said. "I enjoyed it, for one. Which reminds me," he went on, as the topic showed signs of flagging, "a Mr. Caithby Fisher, an interesting-looking man in a wheeled chair, invited me to go and see him at his office this afternoon. He hinted he had some proposition to make."

"Really?" drawled a voice from the background. "You're a lucky young man, Mr. Grey. Let me congratulate you."

The little group turned to find Sir Ferdinand Shawle standing in the doorway.

"I hope you don't mind, Sir Henry," he smiled. "I told your butler I'd find my way."

This strange, tall figure with its cadaverous face and cold, penetrating eyes brought an entirely new atmosphere into the room. Robin was aware of it instantly. Sir Henry was plainly apprehensive, while the inspectors became instantly on the alert.

The newcomer went on, speaking lightly to Robin.

"You're certainly in luck, young man," he said. "I can't imagine any greater good fortune for a youngster who has to make his way in the world than to be taken up by Caithby Fisher. He is a strange personality, and his very name works like a charm in the City. I suppose he's one of the greatest financial geniuses of our time."

"Really?" said Robin with just a touch of stiffness in his tone. "I had no idea. I shall certainly look forward to my interview."

Inspector Mowbray took a heavy step forward.

"Well, I think we'll go now, Sir Henry," he said. "Thank you very much for all you've told us."

Whybrow laid a hand on Robin's arm.

"You'd better come along with us, my lad," he murmured.

There was authority in the whisper, and Robin signified his assent with a feeling of dismay. He had hoped to stay behind and catch at least a few words with the one girl in the world.

He turned to look at her now and caught her unawares. She was smiling, a curious expression of secret understanding with someone on the other side of the room.

He turned his head sharply, expecting to find her father signalling to her behind the inspector's back. But what he did see sent a thrill of horrified amazement down his spine.

The man at whom Jennifer was smiling with that look of complete understanding, that expression that told more plainly than any words could have done of some mutual secret, and who was smiling back at her with just the same expression, was Sir Ferdinand Shawle.

Robin walked out of the house between the two inspectors, his mind in a daze.

CHAPTER EIGHT
STRANGE MEETING

"Thank you. If you put me down here it will do very well."

The woman in the long fur coat and the tiny fashionable hat with the veil which half obscured her pale, still beautiful face, tapped on the window of the taxicab, and as the man drew up at the side of the crowded curb she stepped out on to the pavement with a half-frightened, half-shrewd glance about her.

It was the heart of the City in the crowded lunch hour on a foggy November day, and the busy throng were much too interested in their own affairs to take much notice of this fashionably dressed woman who looked as though she had strayed out of Bond Street rather than a City office.

Only the driver looked at her curiously as she slipped double his fare into his hand and sped off down a dark alleyway, always gloomy, but now almost lightless in the foggy atmosphere.

Madame Julie pulled the collar of her fur coat so high round her face that only her eyes peering through her half-veil were visible to the casual passer-by.

She walked swiftly, with the furtive speed of one who is desperately anxious not to be seen. No sneak thief escaping from the police could have moved more purposefully, more unobtrusively.

She passed through the alley and turned down a side street where only the great blank walls of warehouses flanked the narrow thoroughfare. These gave place eventually to a row of houses, dingy, forgotten little City offices in which it seemed incredible that any business could still take place.

Before the door of one of these she paused, and, with a swift glance to right and left to make certain that she was unobserved, stepped quickly into the narrow stuffy passage within.

The place seemed to be deserted, but the woman was completely familiar with her surroundings. She hurried up a flight of stairs and pushed open a door on her left as she reached the first landing.

She passed through another corridor, and, ignoring the rooms on either side, paused before a tiny door in the wall directly ahead of her.

Here she knocked softly two or three times.

It was opened immediately, and she stepped into the blackness beyond. The door closed behind her.

It was a mysterious entrance, and the uninitiated might well have been afraid. But Madame Julie had come this way often enough before.

She waited until the faint outlines of a huge figure showed dimly in the gloom before her and then followed it silently down a short staircase to yet another door.

The man who led her thrust back the bolts and stood aside to let her pass. As the door swung open, a very different atmosphere met her nostrils. Here was scented warmth and elegance and the faint pleasing fragrance of cigar smoke.

Madame Julie stepped into a big, brilliantly lit apartment whose walls were lined with glistening furniture and hung with choice prints. The carpet on which she trod was yielding, and her feet sank into it.

The man who had admitted her closed the door behind him, and it swung perfectly into place, so that it appeared no more than part of the walnut panelling with which the room was lined. He surveyed her gravely.

"If you will wait here a moment, Madame, the master will be with you in a moment."

She watched him striding out of the room, a magnificently proportioned figure with the shoulders of a giant and the grace of an athlete. It was typical of his master, she reflected, to employ such a man.

She had not long to wait. Almost at once the rumbling of wheels sounded from the corridor without and the main door of the room was again thrown open to readmit the young giant, now propelling an invalid chair in which reposed the twisted body and shrewd face of Mr. Caithby Fisher.

As soon as the cripple was in the room he turned on his attendant savagely and ordered him out as if he were a slave. The magnificent figure moved obediently, and the next moment Madame Julie faced the man alone.

He sat for some moments smiling at her, and even her sophisticated calm became ruffled by the intensity and malignant humour in his eyes.

"You sent for me?" she said at last.

"Yes, Madame. Won't you sit down?"

The harsh, unpleasant voice was softened to a travesty, and the woman, who knew the symptom, trembled.

She sat down in one of the big chairs by the roaring fire in the grate and regarded her host with as much calm as she could muster.

The man in the wheeled chair came closer until his face was within a foot of her own.

"Now, Madame," he said, "have you anything to report?"

She shook her head. "No," she said faintly. "Nothing at all."

One skinny hand seized her own, and the gnarled fingers bit into her flesh with intentional cruelty in their grip.

"You're lying to me again."

The voice was still pleasant, but there was an underlying note of sheer savagery which made her shrink back from him, a huddled figure in her furs.

"You think I am a fool," he went on, the grip on her hand tightening until she could have cried out with pain. "But you are wrong. Why did you go to see Robin Grey last night? Ah, that surprises you, doesn't it? Why did you buy two reservations for the *Orestes?* Don't look so uncomfortable, Madame. I don't imagine that you were trying to persuade this boy to elope with you. You tried to get him to take the girl away. You tried to persuade him to get married immediately, didn't you? Didn't you? If you were not so stupid, I should be very, very angry with you."

He threw her numbed, bruised hand down with a gesture and shot back in his wheeled chair until he was within some little distance of her on the other side of the hearthrug.

"If you were not so stupid, Madame, you would be dangerous and I should have to get rid of you," he continued. "As it is, I shall give you one more chance. Let me explain a little."

The woman stretched out a hand appealingly, and her lips opened as though she were about to speak. The terrifying figure in the invalid chair laughed.

"Do not interrupt! Let me remind you: I placed you in Sir Ferdinand's house not to interfere with matters which are too deep for you to fathom, but to collect information for me, information which would help both me and you. Now, how much do you know?"

The woman cowered. Her big dark eyes filled with tears, and her lips trembled.

"Nothing," she said wretchedly. "Nothing. I am grateful for what you have done to help me."

He swept the words aside with an impatient gesture.

"Speak the truth, or I shall expose you to Sir Ferdinand and you will be back where you started two years ago. Or perhaps you are not interested in the fate of——"

"Don't! You're torturing me!"

The words broke from the woman explosively. She bent forward. Her face had become dark with passion, and her eyes were terrible in their anguished sincerity.

"I think of him always. Always only of him. To secure his freedom I would do anything. I am where I am because of him. I would do anything—anything, I tell you. You know that."

Her voice trailed away, and the cripple sat looking at her, an indefinable expression on his twisted face.

"Well, then," he said at last, his voice adopting once again the unnatural softness which lent it so much power, "you must trust me implicitly. Remember, I am your only friend. How much do you know?"

The last words were uttered in little more than a whisper.

The woman looked round her helplessly. It was evident that she realized that she had nowhere else to turn. She was here alone in Mr. Fisher's ancient house, one of the last of the great residences of the City. Her position seemed to her to be symbolical of her whole life.

"I know," she said softly, "very little, but in the two years I have worked for you I have realized that if Jennifer Fern marries, some sort of information will be released which will incriminate Sir Ferdinand himself. Don't you see," she went on with sudden ingenuousness born of her despair, "it seemed to me that these two young people are in love and that if they married Sir Ferdinand would fall? And if he fell, surely the whole story of that terrible business ten years ago might come out. Then, surely, Jim would be released."

The cripple echoed her words. "Might come out? Might? You must be very desperate if you are catching at straws. Don't you see, you pathetic fool, if Sir Ferdinand is exposed *before* I am ready, your only hope of saving your husband will be gone for ever? You must be patient. You must trust me. Fortunately young Grey treated your extravagant proposal with the contempt it deserved. What else do you know?"

The woman shot a penetrating glance at him beneath her lashes.

"Nothing."

"Is that the whole substance of your conversation with Robin Grey last night?"

An inflection in his tone told her that he was ignorant of the final warning she had given the boy. She took the risk.

"Yes," she whispered.

To her intense relief the cripple seemed satisfied.

"Very well, then. You have been indiscreet, Madame, dangerously indiscreet. But on this occasion, because you are useful to me, I shall overlook it. Now, what report?"

The woman glanced furtively over her shoulder as if she feared that even in this windowless sanctuary she might be overheard.

"There is very little. Life has been going on much as usual. Sir Ferdinand is an inscrutable person. He never seems to lose his temper, never seems to show any sign of nerves. It is only in the things he does that one can gather what is going on in that strange, cold mind of his."

"Yes," said the cripple impatiently. "Yes. And have you noticed anything? Anything remotely unusual or mysterious?"

"Only one thing. It is so slight and yet so curious that I hardly know whether to mention it or not."

The woman was speaking cautiously now, and her dark eyes were large and candid.

"Several times lately he has received a mysterious visitor late in the evening. The man only comes at night, and he always arrives at the side or garden door. Sir Ferdinand admits him himself and takes him straight into the library. They remain there together for a long time, sometimes two or three hours."

"Yes?" The cripple's eyes were glowing with interest. "Is that all you can tell me?"

She shook her head. "Not quite all. I have found out who the stranger is. The second time he came I hid myself behind the banisters on the landing, and I caught a glimpse of him framed in the light of the hall in the doorway of the library when Sir Ferdinand was about to show him out."

"Who was it? Did you recognize him?"

The woman nodded.

"He has an unmistakable face. I have seen it in several illustrated papers."

"Who? Who? What's his name?"

Madame Julie surveyed her employer frankly.

"Gordon Frayne," she said.

"So!" It was evident that the information had come as a surprise. The cripple sat huddled in his chair, his forehead puckered, his sharp eyes momentarily quiet with thought.

For Gordon Frayne, as both Caithby Fisher and Madame Julie knew perfectly well, was one of the greatest character actors the world had ever known, the man of whom it was said that in his hands the art of make-up and disguise had reached a height it had never before attained, a man who could deceive a mother concerning her son, or a police inspector concerning a well-known criminal.

A strange guest indeed for a respectable banker in the position of Sir Ferdinand Shawle.

"Good-bye, Madame. Forgive me that I do not rise."

There was a half-bitter, half-contemptuous tone in the little cripple's voice as he nodded to Madame Julie as she stood framed in the dark doorway in the panelling.

"Good-bye, Mr. Fisher."

The next moment she was gone, and the man sat alone in the brightly lighted but windowless room, his shrewd, evil little face wearing a strange expression as he looked down into the fire.

For some time he did not move. Then he brought one skinny hand down upon the arm of his chair with a gesture of one who has arrived at a decision.

"The boy," he said softly to himself. "Of course, the boy."

He touched a bell push concealed in the marble carvings of the fireplace, and when his magnificent manservant arrived he spoke harshly and with the same ill humour that was always apparent when he addressed the man.

"When Mr. Grey arrives I will see him here. At once, you understand. Mr. Grey is a very important person to us just now. Do you understand that, Reith? Very important indeed."

CHAPTER NINE
MISS FERN REGRETS

"No, Sir. I'm sorry, sir. I don't think anyone's in, sir." Old Williamson, Sir Henry Fern's butler, stood in the doorway looking profoundly uncomfortable. Insofar as he permitted himself to have any private opinions, he was inclined to approve of the young man who had lately become so interested in his master's daughter, and he very much regretted the duty which compelled him to give his present message.

Robin, who was paler than usual and on whose round, good-humoured face there sat an anxious expression which ill became it, raised his eyebrows more at the old man's manner than at his words.

As soon as he had been able to tear himself away from a long discussion with the two inspectors, he had hurried back to see Jennifer in spite of the lateness of the hour. It was now nearly half-past two, and he was due at Caithby Fisher's office at three.

He had come, however, because he was unable to keep away. All through the inspectors' interminable discussion of the Tony Bellew case he had been haunted by the apparently inexplicable smile which had passed between those two, Jennifer and Sir Ferdinand Shawle.

Moreover, he wanted to talk to her. That hurried kiss that had passed between them, what had it meant? There was hope in his heart, and fear.

He stood looking at the old butler in astonishment.

"But surely," he said at last, "surely I can come in and wait for her? It's most important that I see Miss Fern immediately."

Old Williamson's pink face became a shade more rubicund. Evidently he found the situation most embarrassing.

"I—er—hardly know what to say, sir," he said. "Perhaps I could put it more plainly. I have received instructions to the effect that Miss Fern and her father will—er—always be out in future to you, sir."

"What?" The ejaculation escaped Robin involuntarily.

Williamson did not like to repeat his statement but stood licking his lips nervously.

A thousand thoughts were crowding through Robin's brain. This was the last thing he had anticipated, and he was a little unprepared for the overwhelming sense of dismay which passed over him at the old man's words.

"Look here, Williamson," he said at last, "is Miss Fern actually in the house at the moment?"

Williamson's mild blue eyes faltered. "Well—er—yes, sir. To be strictly accurate, she is."

Robin pulled out a visiting card from his pocket and scribbled a phrase on the back of it. He stood looking at the message consideringly. After his first moment of panic his brain had become icily clear.

"I love you. Let me see you."

The simple direct words, which gave him away so completely, were, he felt, the only ones possible in the circumstances.

He thrust the card into Williamson's hand.

"Take this up to her. I promise you shan't regret it."

Old Williamson glanced at the card and wavered. Then he nodded.

"Very well, sir. Will you wait here, please?"

The old man hurried off, and Robin paced the small outer hall which led into the big reception lounge, his heart bursting. It seemed incredible. It was only a few hours since Sir Henry had been chatting to him about the dinner party and Jennifer had kissed him.

Williamson was gone an unconscionable time, and the boy remained on tenterhooks. At last, however, he was rewarded by the sight of the portly old man coming down the staircase with more agility than usual. His colour was heightened, Robin noticed, but his face wore that peculiarly wooden expression which seems to be the special posses-sion of the well-trained upper servant.

He came straight up to Robin and took a deep breath.

"With Miss Fern's compliments, sir," he said, and dropped something into Robin's palm.

Robin looked down, and the colour gradually mounted into his face. Lying in his hand were the two halves of his own card on which the message had been pencilled.

Through the confusion of his mind he heard Williamson's dry official voice.

"Will you come this way, sir?"

Robin followed him blindly. The great hall doors swung open, the cool air of the afternoon blew upon his face, and the next moment he was stumbling down the steps, despair, bewilderment, and shame in his heart.

He walked straight ahead of him down the road for some time, and it was not until a clock with the hands indicating five minutes to three caught his attention that he pulled himself together with a start.

After his first setback his natural reaction was one of fierce determination to see the thing through. Robin was tenacious. He was also in love. Deep in his heart he felt that Jennifer, whatever she thought, would never willingly administer such a rebuff to him as the one he had received. Jennifer was innately kind, innately gentle. There was no cruelty to her make-up, no arrogance, no coquetry.

Caithby Fisher: he remembered the old man with his little wizened face, his curious bright eyes, and the faint air of mistrust which he had awakened in the boy's consciousness. Perhaps he would know something.

He hailed a taxicab and drove to the City. It was late when he arrived at Armaments House—nearly a quarter to four—and as he walked up the imposing flight of steps which led to the entrance he reflected grimly that it would be more than unlikely that the important financier would still be in the mood to see him.

To his astonishment, however, his card was taken up at once and a suave secretary conducted him to the magnificent old private house behind the modern building where the cripple lived.

Here there was no delay either, and within three minutes of his arrival Reith, the giant manservant, conducted him into the brilliantly lit windowless room where Caithby Fisher sat huddled up over the fire.

As Robin came into the room he noticed something which puzzled him. It was a faint, very faint odour of perfume which was vaguely familiar, although he could not place it. For a reason which he could not explain, it was remotely connected in his mind with danger.

Mr. Fisher's greeting, however, was warm enough to put any man off his guard.

"Well, young man," he said, looking up at him quizzically after they had shaken hands, "you're late."

Robin nodded, but his excuses were cut short by the older man.

"I know," he said, "I know. You young men in love—well, I envy you. Sit down, won't you? Smoke?"

Robin declined but sat down opposite his host in the chair Madame Julie had so lately vacated.

But Caithby Fisher was now in a different mood from that which he had adopted with his former visitor. He was smiling, hearty, unmistakably friendly, and as soon as the boy was settled he plunged into business.

"You may ask me why I asked you to come here," he began. "I daresay you know enough about business men to realize that they are not often mere philanthropists. In other words, Mr. Grey, they expect their money's worth."

Robin smiled frankly. He was doing his best to keep Jennifer out of his mind and to concentrate on the strange little man before him.

Caithby Fisher went on.

"As a matter of fact, young man," he said, "I arranged this little talk because you and I, Mr. Grey, have a mutual interest and together we may accomplish something."

He paused, and the quick bright eyes were bent upon the boy with such a good imitation of shrewd benevolence that even Robin was deceived.

He had barely time to wonder where this preamble was leading before the man's next words made him sit bolt upright, every sense in his body alert with interest.

Caithby Fisher had leant forward and inquired in a soft ingratiating tone: "I don't know if you've noticed it, my boy, but there's something damned queer worrying that future father-in-law of yours. You're walking on the edge of a mystery, and by an absolute miracle you are the only man in a thousand capable of putting things straight. Have you noticed anything?"

Experience had taught Robin caution. "I have been vaguely aware of something," he said.

Caithby Fisher appeared perfectly satisfied.

"Very well. Now look here, you and I can help each other. I shall have to tell you a short but I am afraid not very creditable story. Sir Henry Fern and I are business friends of long standing. Once, many years ago, we had an enemy."

He paused, and a far-away expression which was a miracle of acting flickered across his face.

"There was a woman in the matter, so forgive me if I am not very explicit. Let that rest. Our enemy was a famous man. His name was Blount—Morton Blount—the greatest detective of all time, and Sir Henry Fern's brother-in-law."

Robin was following this story with breathless attention. So far there was nothing to indicate that the man was not telling the truth, and on the whole the yarn sounded very feasible. Moreover, there was, so far as the young man knew, no reason for the cripple to lie.

"You will wonder why I am taking you into my confidence, but you will see," he went on. "Morton Blount had a very peculiar form of mania which made him absurdly vindictive, ridiculously cruel. Some years ago he died, and when we read of his death Sir Henry Fern and I both heaved a sigh of relief, believing as we did that the monster who had persecuted us so ruthlessly and for so long was now beyond the power of hurting us further."

He paused, and Robin nodded understandingly. After all, the story was not unlikely.

Caithby Fisher hunched his withered body more tightly in his chair.

"Unfortunately," he went on at last, his dry voice sounding oddly convincing, "we discovered that this enemy could strike from the grave." He leant forward. "Sir Henry Fern—and I, in a lesser degree, you understand—are being blackmailed from the grave."

He touched the wheels of his chair so that he moved closer and laid his hand on the boy's arm.

"Morton Blount, who begrudged Sir Henry and I something which after all it was not in his own power to attain, left documents with a firm of solicitors with the instructions that these documents be published in a book on the day of Sir Henry Fern's daughter's wedding."

Robin started. This garbled version of the truth which the man had told had just enough of reality about it to make the genuine facts fit in, and Robin, believing that he had stumbled on the truth, could not repress a movement of interest. The hunchback, seeing that he had won his battle, pressed his point home.

"Now," he said, "this is where you can help. This is where you can rid your future father-in-law of his terror and at the same time clear the path for your own marriage. You hold a curiously important position with Scotland Yard, Mr. Grey."

Robin nodded. He saw now where the trend was leading, but his quick brain had also seized upon another damning fact. Tony Bellew had been murdered; Sir Henry Fern had been seen coming down from the boy's flat; it was to Sir Henry Fern's interest that his daughter should not marry.

There were other facts that did not fit so well. Caithby Fisher admitted that he too was interested in Jennifer's remaining single; why dared he admit it?

The old man answered his question almost before it had formed in his mind.

"I daresay you'll wonder at my daring to tell this to you, Mr. Grey," he said. "But you see, I have seen you with Jennifer and I know you to be in love with her. Moreover I know that if I can convince you of the innocence of myself and Sir Henry I need not fear that I shall not have your cooperation."

Robin nodded. "What do you want me to do?"

The shrewd little eyes glinted. "Something very simple. Find out for me the name of the solicitors with whom Morton Blount was likely to leave his most important papers. It's a very little thing, one of those simple matters that lead to the most important things in the world. In your position at Scotland Yard it should be easy. There are records, private papers. Do you understand? That is all I require: the name of the solicitors."

For a long time after the man had spoken, Robin sat silent. He was not a fool, but he was very much in love, and he fancied he saw now an explanation of Jennifer's refusal to see him. On the whole he was inclined to regard Caithby Fisher as a friend.

Ten minutes later he walked out of Armaments House, having made a bargain.

The commissionaire hurried towards him.

"Taxi, sir?"

A cab appeared as if by magic.

"What address, sir?"

"Scotland Yard." Robin gave it without thinking. There was a sense of relief at his heart. At last he felt that he had found some clue, however small, which would lead him towards the unravelling of the web which kept the girl he loved from his arms.

As soon as the taxi moved, the commissionaire turned and, with the air of a man who is acting under important instructions, hurried over to the mysterious little house behind the modern building and gave the information that Mr. Robin Grey had driven straight to Scotland Yard to a wizened, terrible little creature in a wheeled chair who sat and laughed softly to himself.

Chapter Ten

Summons

"You're very secretive, my lad. What are you up to?" Inspector Whybrow put his head in at the little room in the Records Department at Scotland Yard and regarded his friend quizzically.

Robin sat at a desk littered high with papers. He looked up and grinned, but his expression was not so open as usual, and he had the uncomfortable feeling that the inspector might not approve altogether of his present occupation.

"Private investigation," he said.

Whybrow raised his eyebrows. "Really? Well, I've been doing more good than you will poking about in ten-year-old files. I've been having another little chat with Sir Henry Fern. In fact I've been down at the house for the last two hours."

"Have you, though?" Robin's heart quickened uncomfortably, and in his effort to make his tone sound casual he achieved a stilted note which he feared the inspector would recognize. "Anything fresh?"

"No. Not exactly."

The inspector was irritatingly vague.

"He's got an alibi. Fellow swears he was at the club all through the afternoon. That doesn't prove that he didn't get into the flat earlier in the day, though. Still, I'm inclined to feel you may be right. He seemed a nice old boy. Not a homicidal type at all. All the same there's something remarkably queer going on there. Something deuced queer. The man Shawle was still there when I went back, and there were doctors in the house."

"Doctors?"

Whybrow nodded. "Something about the girl."

The papers fluttered out of Robin's hand.

"The girl? Jennifer? Are you sure? Why, she was perfectly all right when I saw her this morning."

Whybrow shrugged his shoulders. "You're in love, my boy," he said. "Be careful. I've never known a detective yet who could do his work when he was in love. Old Morton Blount, the cleverest of 'em all, never looked at a woman. Some early affair put him off 'em, I believe."

Robin's eyes flickered. Here was corroborative evidence of the story at which Caithby Fisher had hinted. The broken romance, the man embittered and eaten up with revenge.

The inspector's news was disturbing, however, and Robin pressed for details.

Whybrow laughed. "There was a doctor in the house, and I had an impression it was something to do with the girl. But there's been no accident, and I may very well be completely wrong. After all, the fellow may have been attending Sir Henry. If ever a man needed a nerve specialist, I've been talking to him this afternoon. Well, I'm disturbing you. I'll go up to my own office. Look in on me before you go."

He bustled off, leaving Robin fighting with the desire to phone the Regent's Park mansion for news of Jennifer in spite of the rebuff which he had received only a few hours before.

Prudence told him to wait, however, and urged him to concentrate on the clue which Caithby Fisher had put into his hands.

He set to work again feverishly, and half an hour later sat back in his chair, regarding three pencilled names on a slip of memorandum paper.

"Knowles & Kirby, Lincoln's Inn. Faber & Washington, Cursitor Street. Rolls & Knighton, Quality Passage."

They were all solicitors with whom Morton Blount had at some time had private dealings. Yes, it must be one of the three.

He was eyeing the notes, debating on his next move, when the telephone on the desk in front of him began to ring and he lifted off the receiver mechanically.

"Is that you, Mr. Grey?"

He recognized the voice of the man on the switchboard downstairs.

"I've had some difficulty in tracing you. I wasn't sure whether you were in the building at all. It's a private call for you. Shall I put it through?"

"What name?" A ridiculous hope shot through his mind that it might be the girl herself.

"A Mr. Rex Bourbon, sir. He said you probably wouldn't remember the name, but it seems most urgent."

Robin did remember the name, however. He remembered the face too, remembered the sallow complexion, the twitching nervous hands of the man who had been present at Sir Ferdinand Shawle's dinner party.

"Yes. I'll speak to him."

Immediately came another voice.

"Is that Mr. Grey?"

The tone was nervous, the words almost inarticulate.

"I don't suppose you remember me. My name's Rex Bourbon. We met at Sir Ferdinand Shawle's. I've rung you because you're the only man I've met at the Yard, and it's most imperative that something be done at once. I implore you to come at once—come yourself."

Robin pulled a scribbling pad towards him. He had had some experience of dealing with hysterical people who wanted immediate attention, but there was something in this broken voice, with its nervous, high-pitched timbre, which told him that he was dealing with someone in genuine trouble.

"Wait a minute," he said soothingly. "Of course I remember you very well. Is there anything I can do?"

"Yes. Come at once. I've told you. Listen, can you hear me? I must speak softly. Do you understand? I'm not sure I'm here alone. The office is closed, but the street door downstairs is ajar. You must come at once. I have something of vital importance to tell you. If you don't come instantly it may be too late."

The last sentence ended in a gasp, and Robin made up his mind.

"I'll come," he said. "Wait a moment, though. You haven't told me where you are. What's the address?"

"Thirteen, Wych Street. Ash, Henderson & Fern, Limited. You know—Sir Henry Fern's office—Jennifer Fern's father. Come at once."

There was a click and all was silent.

Robin moved the telephone hook up and down eagerly, but there was no response. Thoughtfully he hung up the receiver, and then, slipping the memoranda of the legal firms into his pocket, he reached for his hat and hurried downstairs into the street.

At that hour the streets of the city were all but deserted, and when Robin reached the outside of the imposing building in Wych Street which housed Sir Henry's firm, its dark façade did not look at all inviting. The steady yellow glow of the street lamps showed the windows to be dark, and there seemed to be not even a watchman on the premises.

Robin was perfectly aware that he might be walking into a trap, but, since the office was Sir Henry's and Rex Bourbon's message had struck him as a genuine cry for help, he did not hesitate.

The great door under the ornate porch opened to his touch, and he stepped into a darkened hall, from which a flight of steps rose into the gloom above.

As soon as he entered he was aware of an atmosphere of horror. It descended upon him unexpectedly, and he reproached himself for what he felt was an unnecessary alarm.

Nevertheless he pulled out his torch and hurried up the staircase, the feeling of apprehension growing upon him at every step.

On the first landing all the doors were locked, and he went on to the next floor, the uncanny premonition growing.

The second floor was devoted to the directors' own offices. Here there were heavy carpets laid, and the doors were ornate affairs of polished mahogany and brass.

The centre door, the one which instinct told him belonged to Sir Henry Fern's own office, stood open, and he advanced cautiously.

The silence of the great building was deathlike. There was no noise from the traffic below, no creaking, no movement; only silence, thick, oppressive, and somehow terrible.

The room he entered was in darkness save for the faint light from the street lamps below shining in at the uncurtained windows, and Robin paused on the threshold, every nerve strained, every sense alert.

Still there was no sound. He allowed the beam of his torch to sweep round the room.

The next moment a smothered exclamation escaped him, and he stood looking down at the thing which lay face uppermost on the floor.

Now he knew what had caused that strange sense of something wrong which had swept down to him from this silent room the moment he had entered the building.

Rex Bourbon lay sprawled upon the thick Turkey carpet. A glance told Robin that the man was dead. He could see the thick neck, the sallow skin, the ponderous body of the broker, and recognized it instantly.

One hand was doubled beneath the man, and the other lay flung out at an unnatural angle, the fingers clenched.

Robin glanced swiftly round the room. The place seemed to be undisturbed. There was no sign of a struggle.

The boy bent over the body. He was too well trained to disturb it, but he satisfied himself that it was indeed the man who had been speaking to him over the phone less than twenty minutes before, and discovered the small round bullet hole in the dark cloth above the heart and noted the tiny burns which surrounded it.

The shot had been fired at close quarters, then. There was the revolver lying beneath the body. Robin did not touch it. There was work for fingerprint experts, members of the complicated machinery for the detection of crime.

At first sight it was almost certainly a suicide, but Robin had an uncomfortable feeling that in this case first impressions were not going to be reliable.

He turned to the telephone, but before he touched the instrument something caught his attention. The outstretched hand of the corpse lay almost at his feet, and, acting on impulse, he bent down and opened the fast stiffening fingers.

He was rewarded. A small piece of yellowed paper fell out onto the carpet. He picked it up, and a puzzled expression spread over his face.

The scrap of paper was the torn-off top of what appeared to be an old-fashioned playbill of the colonial type. Across the coarse paper were the words "Prescottville Theatre: Lessee and Manager, Eric Waterhouse," and underneath, "Monday, Dec. 3rd, 1896."

Robin stood looking at the crumpled scrap in natural astonishment. Then he glanced round the room, half expecting to see the remainder of the bill lying on the floor. But, although he searched, there was no sign of anything of the kind in the neat, well-ordered office.

The more he looked at the scrap of paper the more remarkable and incomprehensible it became. Prescottville he remembered vaguely as a little frontier town on the Canadian-American border, but how a thirty-seven-year-old playbill could come to be lying in the dead hand of a well-known City broker in Sir Henry Fern's own office was more than he could hope to guess.

But here he stood with a corpse at his feet, and Robin, always a Yard man, became his cool practical self in the emergency and picked up the telephone receiver to summon the police.

He got on to Inspector Whybrow immediately and told his story briefly and concisely.

"Suicide? Where?" He heard the older man's voice rise in astonishment. "Sir Henry Fern's *own* office? Get away! You stay there. We'll be right down. This is serious. Don't touch anything till I've come."

Robin replaced the receiver and stood for some moments looking down at the thing which lay so pitifully on the carpet.

Then he pulled himself together and wandered over towards the door. He knew Inspector Whybrow's methods and did not wish to poach on his preserves.

The atmosphere of the great building got on his nerves, and, suddenly remembering that he had closed the main door behind him when he entered, he went down to open it, deciding to wait for the police in the hall.

As he opened the door, however, and the cool air from the street greeted him, acting on impulse he stepped out and stood looking up and down the deserted road, revelling in the sense of relief which had passed over him on leaving the sinister building.

He walked to the edge of the curb and back, and finally took up his position in the porch to await the police car.

The more he thought of the man upstairs the less inclined he was to believe that it was a case of suicide.

He was so engrossed in his thoughts, so enmeshed in his efforts to solve the fantastic mystery which seemed to weave Sir Henry Fern and his daughter into a closer and more complicated pattern, that he did not notice the slight rustling sound behind him as the door of the building before which he stood, and which so far as he knew contained nothing but the corpse of Rex Bourbon, moved slowly open.

It was not until footsteps sounded on the stone behind him that he swung round just too late to save himself. A blow crashed down upon his skull. He fought to regain consciousness, but it was impossible. The blood surged up behind his eyes, the dull, sickening sensation spread through his brain, and he slumped forward to the ground, senseless.

When he came to himself he was lying on the uppermost bunk of an ambulance. His head was throbbing, and the light in the top of the car beat into his eyes unbearably.

Gradually recollection came back to him. His first thought was that his enemy had left him where he lay and that the police, arriving, had discovered him and called the ambulance.

But that sixth sense, that intuition which had preserved his life on more than one occasion, came to his rescue now.

He began to be aware of danger, imminent and inescapable. Without daring to move, he turned his eyes slightly and took in as much as he could of his surroundings.

He recognized at once that the ambulance was not of the official pattern, but belonged rather to some private nursing home. He could just see the nurse's head with its enormous white veil as she stood with her back to him looking through the little window into the driver's cab.

As he watched, she bent forward and he saw her shoulders. Something strange about them attracted his attention, and the next moment she turned her head.

Robin closed his eyes at once, but that single glance had been sufficient.

The figure in nurse's clothes was a man, powerful and barely disguised save for his unusual costume. In that brief moment Robin had seen something else also. The man's arms had been crossed upon his chest, and in the right hand something small and gleaming had flickered for an instant.

Robin did not doubt that it was the barrel of a revolver.

So he was being kidnapped. The realization came home to him slowly.

There was a window on his right, and by moving very stealthily he was able to peer out.

He was still in London; he saw that instantly. Moreover, they were in the Strand. He could not trust himself to risk breaking a window and fighting his way free. The fact that the "nurse" held a revolver alone showed that his enemies, whoever they were, meant business.

Moreover, he knew from experience how difficult it is to attract the attention of a London crowd when one is in some ordinary everyday vehicle which people are used to meeting in the streets.

Halfway down the Strand a traffic block threatened to hold them up, and the ambulance swung down into the Adelphi. It was a strange experience to lie there and see the familiar street passing rapidly by, framed like a cinematograph film by the window.

As he approached Mrs. Phipps's house he edged still further round and peered up at the windows in the wild hope that someone would see and recognize him.

As his eyes swept the windows, to his complete astonishment he caught a glimpse of a white face looking down from between the curtains of his own sitting room.

His first impression was that he was dreaming or that some malignant fate had swept him completely out of his mind. But as he stared, the features burnt themselves into his brain, and he knew that, whatever else in the world might be illusion, this one thing was true.

The face that peered out at him from the window of his own sitting room, high up above the ambulance which bore him, powerless, he knew not where, was the face of the one girl he loved: the face of Jennifer Fern, and across its loveliness, stamped so vividly that the recollection of it remained with him to his dying day, terror, naked and uncomforted.

CHAPTER ELEVEN
A WOMAN AFRAID

"Well, my dear, I don't know what to say, I really don't."

Little Mrs. Phipps, her beaky face a picture of concern, stood looking at the girl who crouched on the window seat in Robin's study.

The Jennifer Fern who, white and trembling, shrank back among the bright cushions on the leather couch, made a very different picture from the smiling, poised young woman of the morning.

Mrs. Phipps was bewildered. After Robin's experience of the night before, she had been inclined to refuse the girl admittance when she had come pounding upon the door nearly an hour earlier in the evening, but there was something about Jennifer which had touched her heart, something which told her that here at least was someone whom Robin had no cause to fear.

The girl moistened her dry lips with a feverish tongue.

"But he must come soon!" she said. "Surely he must come soon!"

Mrs. Phipps glanced at the clock.

"He ought to have been in some time ago," she said. "And he's not at Scotland Yard, because Inspector Whybrow's been ringing up every two or three minutes for the past I don't know how long."

Mrs. Phipps had salved her conscience by staying at Jennifer's side throughout her entire visit. "After all," she reflected, "nothing can happen to Mr. Robin's flat if I'm in it."

The girl's pitiable state worried her motherly heart, however, and she stood looking down now, her bright bird-like eyes unexpectedly tender.

"I expect you must think me very presumptuous, my dear," she said at last, "but I've known Mr. Robin a long time, and I've cared for him, as you might say, quite as much as if he was my own son. Just lately I've noticed that a change has come over 'im. He's not at all a one for ladies—not at all. But I have said to my husband, I have said, 'That boy's in love,' and now when I see you, my dear, I can understand it. Isn't there something I can do? You're worrying me out of me life sitting there looking so unhappy, so little and fright-ened. I've seen you watch the window, and I've seen you start and look up at the least sound on the stairs. What's the matter? Have you had a quarrel with him? And are you waiting to make it up?"

"Oh, no, no. Nothing like that. I don't even know if Robin does love me. I wasn't sure till this morning that I loved him myself."

The girl's voice was very low, and her eyes looked like dark pits of tragedy in her pale face.

"It's—it's much worse than I can tell you. You're so kind."

She stretched out her hand.

"You're such a dear that I want to confide in you. But I don't know how to begin. I came to find Robin, Mrs. Phipps, because I was in danger, because I was virtually a prisoner in my own home. It's all happened so swiftly. At first I thought

I was dreaming, but gradually the terrible reality began to force itself upon me. I saw there was nothing to be done but to run away. And so I did."

A shudder shook her slender form, and she turned and peered once more down into the street.

"If only he would come!"

The words were uttered so softly that Mrs. Phipps scarcely heard them. She saw the graceful shoulders tremble, saw the hunted look creep again into the white face.

Outside, the narrow street was deserted, but as the girl watched, the shrill clangour of an ambulance bell rang out above the dull roar of the Strand traffic and a familiar white vehicle rushed past and disappeared down the steep hill.

For some reason which the girl could not fathom, the sight of it sent yet another thrill of apprehension through her heart. She looked back into the room.

Mrs. Phipps made up her mind. "I'm going to make you a cup of tea," she said. "Mr. Robin told me only this morning that I wasn't to leave anyone alone in his suite while he was out, but thank goodness I'm not such a fool that I don't know when to use my own judgment.

"Now look here, my dear, you lie down. You're safe here and quiet. You have a little sleep. I'll bring you up a cup of strong tea, and then when Mr. Robin comes you'll be all right and ready to talk to him."

She moved over impulsively and dropped a little peck of a kiss upon the girl's cheek.

"You're nervous," she said. "I've seen nerves before. You must take care of yourself. You young girls don't eat enough, anyway. And take my advice"—she wagged a bony forefinger in front of the girl—"don't get ideas in your head. All this talk about being kept a prisoner! It's exaggeration. Who's going to keep you a prisoner? You're probably not very well, and your folks want you to rest."

The little woman was unprepared for the change which came over the girl at these ordinary, but in the circumstances apparently sensible, remarks.

Jennifer started to her feet and shrank back from the woman, a look of sheer unadulterated horror appearing in her eyes. Her hand went to her throat impulsively while the other was outstretched as though to ward off something intangible.

"Oh, not you too!" she said, her voice poignant with fear and entreaty. "Not you too! I'm all right, I tell you. I'm perfectly all right. I'm quite well. Do you understand me? Quite, quite well."

This outburst only served to convince Mrs. Phipps more firmly.

"You're certainly not at all the thing," she said, a characteristic touch of obstinacy coming into her voice. "Not at all the thing. You lie down, child. I'll bring the tea. Mr. Robin will be that frightened when he comes in if you're not ready to see him in a sensible frame of mind.

"Why, child," she went on more kindly, "you're white as a sheet and trembling all over!"

Jennifer took the old woman's hand.

"Listen," she said. "This morning, after Robin had gone, my father and Sir Ferdinand Shawle had a long talk together. I was going out shopping, and I had just got into the hall when they came out of the study, and from that moment my life has been a nightmare.

"They say I'm ill, nervous, imaginative, in danger of a complete breakdown."

Her voice was tense now, and it was evident that the relief of being able to pour out the story into unbiased ears was doing her good.

"I laughed at first," she went on, her wide grey eyes peering into the other woman's own. "I thought they were joking. But I suddenly realized that they were in earnest."

Tears came into her voice, and her grey eyes became pathetically shiny.

"I can't tell you what it's been like. The whole house seemed to enter into the conspiracy. I've been treated as though I were a child, as though I didn't understand quite what I was saying. If I tried to joke, my maid—my own maid who knows me well—looked frightened. I was locked in my room. A doctor came to see me—oh, a dreadful little man!—who talked to me as though I were a peculiarly stupid child. He frightened me, and I began to cry. And then, I don't know why, I got angry. I lost my head. I ordered him out of the room.

"Then a nurse came, a hateful woman who said, 'Yes, try to sleep' to everything I said to her.

"Finally I heard her and my maid talking outside the door."

The girl's eyes dilated with horror at the recollection.

"I couldn't stand it any longer. There's a balcony outside the window in my room. I got to it. I crept down into the street, and here I am. Oh, why doesn't Robin come? Don't you see, he's the only person in the world who'll help me now that my father doesn't seem to understand."

Her voice failed her completely, and she sat trembling.

Mrs. Phipps, who had listened to this recital in bewilderment, reserved her judgment.

"I don't know what to say," she said. "You wait till Mr. Robin comes. That's certainly the best thing you can do. Now lie down and I'll get the tea."

She bustled out of the room, leaving the girl crouching in a corner of the sofa, the indignation and bewilderment which her astounding treatment had produced giving her an oddly pathetic and disturbing air, like some wounded animal or a child punished when it had done no wrong.

Left to herself, the girl resummoned her courage and tried to thrust the fear which haunted her out of her mind. Soon Robin would come, soon she would look up into his face and be reassured.

Although he had never told her he loved her, although the pathetic message he had pencilled had never reached her, she knew instinctively that next time they saw each other they would meet as lovers, not merely as friends.

She bent forward, pressing her cool palms to her burning forehead and closing her eyes.

A draught of air suddenly passing through the room brought her to an upright position again, however, her eyes fixed eagerly on the door. It was opening slowly.

She sprang to her feet and started across the room. "Robin!"

The name froze upon her tongue. Standing in the doorway, a strange smile upon his lips, was not the man she loved, not the boy from whom she knew she could obtain comfort and reassurance, but the sinister figure of Sir Ferdinand Shawle.

Chapter Twelve
The Terror Grows

The girl stood petrified in the middle of the room, her eyes fixed upon her unexpected visitor. He did not move or speak, but stood holding her with his set, terrifying smile.

At length she retreated slowly across the room until she stood with her back to the wall, her eyes fixed on his face.

She had not seen Sir Ferdinand often, and on her first meeting had been inclined to regard him as rather a harmless if slightly eccentric individual, but now, as he stood looking at her, she was aware for the first time of something different about him, menacing, evil.

All the control which she had been summoning so bravely was swept away before that twist on the narrow lips.

"What do you want?" she said, and her voice was toneless and abrupt. "Go away. I won't go back, I tell you. I won't. I'm perfectly well. There's nothing wrong with me. I'm going to wait for Robin. I must see him. He'll know that I'm all right. He'll know I don't want to see any doctors. He'll know that I'm not on the edge of a nervous breakdown or—or—anything else. Why have you come here? Go away."

The man's smile broadened.

"Come," he said in a little sharp, dry voice, "you are being foolish. Your place is at home, by your father's side."

She caught at the words, and a new terror, not for herself this time, came into her eyes.

"What's the matter with Daddy?"

The man glanced over his shoulder as though he were afraid of being overheard.

"There has been an accident in his office. The police are questioning him. Mr. Grey is in his proper place assisting them. I came to fetch you. Your father guessed you would be here.

"I have a taxi waiting," he went on. "Will you come at once?"

In spite of her terror of the man, in spite of her fear of the home she had known and loved since a child, at this sudden news of a danger threatening her father her terrors for herself were temporarily forgotten.

Yet she could not repress a shudder of repugnance as she permitted the man to take her hand in his hard, dry palm and lead her into the darkened hall.

"I ought to tell the woman," she murmured. "She's making tea for me."

The man tugged at her hand. "There's no time for that now. Your father needs you. Come."

She went with him unsuspecting and stepped into the taxicab which waited outside in the narrow street.

"An accident?" she questioned anxiously. "What's happened? What is it?"

The man's tone did not alter.

"A friend of his has shot himself."

"Oh—oh, how terrible! We seem to be surrounded by horror, Daddy and I."

Once again the hard, dry palm was laid over hers.

"Keep quiet," said the icy voice. "Don't excite yourself. You'll need all your strength later."

The girl shut her lips, and as the taxi rocked and swayed through the streets she struggled to reconcile herself to this new development of this terrifying day.

If her father was in danger and had sent for her, that at least proved that the ghastly illusion concerning her health and state of mind under which he seemed to have dwelt earlier in the day must be dispelled.

And there had been that comforting remark about Robin. Robin was at her father's house with the police. She would see him. At least he would be there to help her, to champion her if it were necessary.

When at last the cab drew up before the familiar stone building, she noticed that the hall door stood open, and she sprang out of the cab with something of her old reassurance. She felt strong again, strong in the belief that her words would be taken seriously again, that her arguments would carry weight.

She glanced over her shoulder to look for Sir Ferdinand and saw the lean figure bending forward to speak to the taximan. He seemed to be getting change.

She burst into the house, brushed past old Williamson, who stared at her as though he had seen a ghost, and hurried into the library.

On the threshold she stopped. The blood rose in her face and drummed in her temples. Her hands felt icy cold, and there was a choking sensation of sheer terror gripping her throat.

For out of the deep chairs before the fire two men had risen and come towards her.

One was her father. She saw the surprise mingled with something she did not understand in his very blue eyes.

And the other, tall, cadaverous, and utterly unexplainable, the man she knew she had left in the street not thirty seconds before, the man who even now must be following her through the house, Sir Ferdinand Shawle.

After that first moment, when all the natural laws seemed to be inexplicably reversed and she felt that she must faint, a smothered exclamation of fear escaped her, a deep, horrible little sound which struck a chill into the hearts of those who heard it.

Then she turned on her heel and hurried out into the hall again, the two men following her in alarm.

The hall door still stood open as she had left it. There was no sign of any other entrant. She hurried on to the steps and looked about her wildly.

All sign of the cab which had brought her and the man who had accompanied her had vanished.

She turned to her father, her lips quivering, her eyes starting.

"How long has Sir Ferdinand been here?"

The old man put his arm round her shoulders. There were tears in his eyes, and his voice was none too steady.

"Why, Jenny," he said, "why, Jenny, my little girl, what's the matter? What is it, dear? Sir Ferdinand has been here with me the whole time, ever since you ran away. Come in, into the study, and sit down."

Jennifer laid her hand on his cheek and looked up searchingly into his face.

"Daddy, you don't mean this?" she said. "You don't mean the whole time? You don't mean that he didn't bring me home just now in a cab?"

Sir Ferdinand and old Sir Henry exchanged shocked glances, and the old man, yielding to a sudden impulse, took the girl in his arms and held her close to him.

"Hush, hush, my dear," he said, soothing her as though she were a baby. "You're imagining things, my sweet. Why,

Jenny, you know Sir Ferdinand. You know me. You know where we are."

"Of course I do! Of course I do!" The girl was crying now, and she permitted herself to be half led, half carried into the big, tobacco-smelling study and set down in the velvet chair before the fire.

Sir Henry was trembling violently in spite of every effort to keep himself under control.

"Now, look here, Jenny, suppose you tell us?" he said. "Suppose you tell us all about it? You're frightening me, my dear."

Jennifer poured out the whole story.

"I saw Sir Ferdinand," she finished. "I saw him with my own eyes. He sat beside me in the taxi. He told me you needed me. He told me that the police were here with Robin because a man had committed suicide in your office. I left him paying the cabman. I came in here a minute afterwards—less than a minute—and there you were."

She turned to the banker, her grey eyes staring, lips trembling.

Sir Henry Fern wiped his eyes openly. Then he rose to his feet from the kneeling position he had taken up on the rug beside her and strode down the room.

Jennifer sat trembling. Fear for herself, then for her father, and now actually of herself, of her own mind, had rendered her helpless, beaten, and bewildered.

Suddenly she became aware of a signalled conversation going on over her head, and panic seized her.

"You don't believe me?" she said, her voice rising high and uncontrolled. "You don't believe me?"

She sprang to her feet and faced them.

"Sir Ferdinand," she said, "early this morning you telephoned me. You promised me—or rather you offered —to do anything you could to help Robin. You told me you had a scheme to put up to him. You cautioned me not to tell him before you could have a word with him yourself. I am only reminding you of this to show you that this morning you were my friend. When you called here and we were all together in the morning room, you caught my eyes and smiled, as though we shared some pleasant secret, which I thought we did. You were going to help my fiancé.

"This afternoon you became my enemy. You persuaded my father that there was something wrong with me. You sent for a doctor. You had me confined to my room, as though—as though I were not responsible."

"My dear young lady"—Sir Ferdinand's tone was dry—"after your extraordinary story of five minutes ago you can hardly blame me. I've been sitting here with your father for the last hour at least, in this very room. Yet you deliberately say that you rode home in a taxicab with me. You don't inspire confidence."

"Don't try to argue with her, F. S." Sir Henry's voice was pathetic. "My poor little girl! She's not herself at all."

Jennifer clung to her father.

"Not you, Daddy!" she said piteously. "Not you! Send for the woman, Robin's landlady. She'll tell you Sir Ferdinand was there. Send for her—I implore you to send for her."

Sir Henry pulled himself together with an obvious effort. There was fear in his eyes as well as consternation, however, and the beads of sweat stood out upon his forehead.

"Now look here, Jenny," he said, still using the childish diminutive which he always employed when deeply moved, "now look here, my dear. Mr. Ash, my partner—you know him, don't you?"

"Of course I do! I'm not a child, and I'm not crazy."

He patted her hand soothingly.

"There, there, my pet. Listen to what I'm telling you. Mr. Ash has gone for a very famous doctor. We—we feel"—his voice trembled—"we feel that you ought to go away for a day or so to a nursing home, somewhere in the country where you'll be quiet, where you'll be looked after, and where I can come and see you."

She gasped at him, and then, as the real significance of his words slowly forced itself upon her, a cry of sheer terror broke from her, and she shrank shuddering into his arms.

"Don't send me away—please!—please! I'm all right, I tell you, perfectly all right. Have a little pity on me. Don't let them send me away."

The old man's face was ashen, but he stuck to his point.

"Listen, Jennifer, you mustn't be silly. And oh, my dear, you mustn't make things too difficult for me to bear. You're going to be very well looked after, my dear; very kindly treated."

He glanced at Sir Ferdinand with a half-questioning expression which told, plainer than any words could have done, the tragic question in his heart.

Sir Ferdinand nodded.

"Of course," he said. "Of course. Jennifer only needs a little rest. These—these hallucinations are the outcome of nervous strain."

Jennifer wound her arms round her father's neck.

"No—no—no!" Her voice rose passionately. "Send for Robin's landlady. At least do that for me. You're wrong, I tell you."

Sir Henry glanced over at the banker.

"Send for her," he said, and added with a touch of fire unexpected in one who had so long been silenced: "Both she and I deserve that."

Sir Ferdinand shrugged his shoulders and went out of the room.

Father and daughter faced each other. The old man suddenly rose to his feet and, going over to the girl, pushed her hair off her forehead and stood looking deeply into her eyes. In that moment there was born a strange understanding between them.

The girl heard her own voice softened to a breathless whisper.

"What is it, Daddy? What is this thing that's happening to us? What does it all mean? Can't we—can't we do anything?"

The old man sank down into a chair and covered his face with his hands.

"God help us, Jenny," he said brokenly. "God help us both."

The girl dropped on her knees beside him.

"Don't let me go. Don't let me go away from here —please—please!"

The old man raised his head, and for a moment it seemed as if he were about to pour forth the whole story, so far as he knew it, into her bewildered ears. But before the first word could leave his lips, a shadow, a flickering doubt passed through his mind and showed in his eyes.

"Jenny," he said, "that story of Shawle bringing you home: why did you invent it?"

"I—I didn't. It *was* he. The same clothes, the same voice, the same everything. The same hard, unsympathetic face."

"Jenny! My God! Don't you see what you're saying?"

The old man's fingers bit into her flesh.

"When Ash brings this specialist of his we shall have to tell him that story. Remember, Jenny. Admit you're mistaken. Think, my darling."

Jennifer swept his words aside. Mrs. Phipps was coming, and she knew she could rely on that old woman's honesty as upon her own.

Instinctively she knew that she would have very little time alone with her father, and there was something she wanted most desperately to know.

"Daddy, who sent for the specialist? Who thought of this monstrous idea? I don't need nerve treatment. Who suggested I did?"

Sir Henry Fern's arms tightened about his daughter.

"That, Jenny," he said brokenly, "please God you'll never know."

CHAPTER THIRTEEN
SHE SHALL HAVE EVERY CARE

"Extraordinary business, Shawle, the girl getting genu-ine hallucinations. It simplifies matters."

Nelson Ash stood on the hearthrug in the morning room and looked down at the man lounging in the chair beside him.

Sir Ferdinand Shawle stretched out his long thin legs to the blaze.

"Yes," he said softly, and there was something approaching awe in his tone. "I sometimes wonder if our friend the Dealer is human, or——" He shrugged his shoulders.

"The devil himself?" suggested Ash and laughed.

Sir Henry Fern's partner was the same unprepossessing figure he had been at the meeting in Sir Ferdinand's own house. His pale eyes seemed to be if anything of a more indeterminate colour than before, and his thick loose white skin looked pasty and unhealthy.

"I'm sorry for the girl in a way," he said. "After all, she's so very young. But I must say that the Dealer has pulled off a master stroke. In Crupiner's private sanatorium she couldn't be safer, from our point of view. She'll be given every care, so the chances of her dying are remote. People live to ripe old ages in such places, I believe. And she certainly can't marry. I see no reason why the box should ever be opened."

Sir Ferdinand rose abruptly to his feet. "It's diabolical," he said, and added with an unpleasant laugh, "but, as you point out, damned ingenious."

Ash took his arm. "I think we'd better be getting back to the hall. Dr. Crupiner will be finishing his interview with the girl, and I fancy Sir Henry will need a strong hand. After all, these scenes are very painful."

He got no further, for at that moment the door was thrown open and Jennifer, followed by her father, burst into the room. At first sight of the two occupants the girl was inclined to withdraw, but the glimpse of a rubicund little person in gold pince-nez following her father decided her, and she came on. Her eyes were red and tear-stained, and there was nameless terror on her face.

"I won't go. I won't go. I won't—never. Don't let them take me! Please, Daddy, please! At least give me a fair chance. You've got no grounds for thinking that there's anything wrong with me at all, except for my own story concerning Sir Ferdinand in the taxi. But wait for Mrs. Phipps. I implore you!"

The person in the pince-nez bustled forward with a sickeningly ingratiating smile on his plump face.

"Now, little girl," he said in a syrupy, irritating voice, "we don't want any fireworks. We want to get you well. You're upsetting your father. When you've had rest you'll feel better. Then we can have a nice long talk and find out just what strange ideas have got into your funny little mind."

Jennifer's gentle temper had been strained beyond endurance. She turned like a tigress on her persecutor.

"I hate you," she said. "I hate you. You're trapping me, catching me into silly admissions, destroying my faith in myself."

The plump man drew back and shrugged his shoulders, nodding to Ash and Sir Ferdinand.

Sir Henry, his face white with agony and his blue eyes dangerously shiny, put his arms round the girl.

"Quiet, Jenny, my darling. Quiet," he whispered. "Keep your head. Keep your head."

It was at this moment that old Williamson, who seemed to have grown visibly older since the morning, opened the door and announced firmly: "Mrs. Phipps."

The old lady came bustling in. In spite of the urgency of the call she had attired herself in her best black costume, her little tippet of real fur and the toque which had been considered so fashionable three years before.

She stood clutching her bag and umbrella and surveying the company with a mixture of suspicion and curiosity.

Jennifer uttered a little cry of relief as she caught sight of the kind, homely face and saw the honest eyes peering at her across the room.

"Mrs. Phipps! Oh, Mrs. Phipps!" she said brokenly. "Come and tell them it's true. Come and save me. Tell them——"

Dr. Crupiner intervened.

"Really," he said. "This is most irregular and dangerous. The patient must not be excited further. I will see this woman in another room."

Mrs. Phipps, who objected to the appellation "woman," bridled visibly and took a step closer to the girl, and Sir Henry Fern, in one of his rare flashes of authority, spoke abruptly.

"Let the child defend herself, Doctor. We must get this thing straight."

Richard Crupiner would have raised further objections, but Nelson Ash rather surprisingly came to his partner's aid. It would seem that his curiosity had been aroused.

"I agree emphatically with Sir Henry," he said. "I think the girl should be allowed to have every chance."

Though it was evident he spoke merely because his curiosity had been aroused, he received a grateful glance from his partner.

"Miss Phipps," Jennifer said suddenly, "a gentleman came to fetch me from your house about an hour ago, didn't he? You let him in downstairs."

Mrs. Phipps's puzzled expression vanished, and she smiled brightly round the expectant company.

"Yes," she said, "that's right. You were waiting for Mr. Robin, and I went down to make you a cup of tea. While I was in the basement the front door bell went. 'Now who can that be?' I said to myself. 'Pulling on the wires like a lunatic.' So I ran along to see. Such a nice gentleman stood on the doorstep. 'I'm Miss Jennifer Fern's father,' he said. 'Are you, sir?' said I, wondering what I ought to say next. Well, he got round me."

She smiled disarmingly at the little group before her.

"And in the end I said, 'Well, you run up to her. I daresay you'd rather see her alone.' I know girls are headstrong sometimes—I was when I was a child. And after all," she went on, patting Jennifer's arm, "we older people always side together when it's a question of parents' authority. So I said, 'You go straight up, sir.'

"I was surprised, I must say, when I found you'd both gone off without saying good-bye. Still, I understand. You can't always be thinking of manners."

Jennifer broke into this harangue, a sob of relief mingling with the words.

"Oh, Mrs. Phipps, I can't tell you how grateful I am to you. This was the gentleman, wasn't it?"

She took Sir Ferdinand by the arm and led him forward.

Mrs. Phipps peered into the dark face and then drew back, bewilderment on her own.

"Why, no, my dear," she said. "Of course it wasn't. I've never seen this gentleman before in all my life. I wouldn't say that the man who called for you wasn't wearing a dark suit, but he was very different from this gentleman here. Why, I'd know him again wherever I saw him."

"You've got funny ideas, young lady. You want a rest."

There was complete silence in the crowded little breakfast room as Mrs. Phipps ceased speaking. Jennifer stood as though petrified. The colour slowly drained out of her face, and her eyes had the hurt expression of a child who has been unaccountably let down by one whom it believes it has every reason to trust.

Sir Henry put his arms round his daughter's shoulders, and a spasm of pain passed over his handsome old face. If Mrs. Phipps had dropped a bomb she could have produced no more consternation in the father and daughter.

The old woman stood looking about her, a puzzled expression in her birdlike eyes. No one in the room doubted for an instant that she had spoken with perfect sincerity when she had declared that Sir Ferdinand Shawle was not the man who had come to fetch Jennifer from her house earlier in the evening.

She gripped her bag and umbrella as though they were her one mainstay in these palatial surroundings in which she found herself so unaccountably, and nodded her head emphatically.

"You go to bed and have a good sleep, my dear," she said. "You're not the first person in the world to have an attack of nerves, nor yet the last, by a long chalk. You need a rest."

Dr. Richard Crupiner came bustling forward, the smug, self-satisfied smile which seemed to be his chief characteristic very much in evidence.

"This good lady has given you better advice than she knows, Miss Fern," he said. "Now I must ask you to sit down quietly in the other room while your maid gets a hat and coat, and then we'll go for a long drive to a beautiful retreat in the country where you can rest completely undisturbed."

His tone had the soothing inflection which some misguided persons adopt towards recalcitrant children, and guaranteed to move to fury any person of sound and adult mind.

Jennifer was no exception to the rule. She clung to her father.

"There's some terrible mistake," she said, her voice rising hysterically. "Don't let that man touch me. I won't go with him. I won't—I won't—I won't! Daddy, don't you see what they're saying? Don't you see what they're hinting? They're suggesting that I'm not responsible, that my mind isn't—isn't to be trusted. Oh, Daddy, don't let them, don't let them—shut me up!"

Sir Henry Fern, his face contorted and his eyes wet with the tears he could no longer control, grasped her hands.

"Gentlemen, please," he said in a voice harsh and broken by emotion, "perhaps you would be good enough to wait for me in the other room. As you see, this is a very painful situation, and not unnaturally I wish to be alone."

The last word ended in a gasp, and Nelson Ash gripped Sir Ferdinand's arm and together they moved discreetly and silently out of the doorway.

Mrs. Phipps stood hesitating for a moment like a frightened hen in the path of a motorcar, and then, with some of the startled bird's flurry, bolted out into the hall.

Only Dr. Crupiner made no attempt to move. He advanced upon the father and daughter with the same bland, ingratiating smile, his pale eyes hidden behind his

gold-rimmed pince-nez and his warm white hands held out
soothingly.

"Now," he said, "come, come. You're not making things
easy for your father, Miss Fern. Remember, you must consider his feelings as well as your own. This is an ordeal for
all of us, and you must be as helpful as you can. Don't forget,
my dear," he went on in the same gently reproachful tone
which the girl found so unbearable, "don't forget that in a
sense you are responsible for this upheaval. We know it is
not your fault. We know better than anyone that you are not
consciously to blame for anything. But after all you must
exercise a little control. The more courage you exhibit now,
the sooner we shall get you better."

Jennifer swung round upon the little man, her eyes blazing, but her father's hand closed over her wrist and warned
her to be silent.

"That'll do, Dr. Crupiner," he said. "I don't think there's
any point in reproaching my child.

"You're not well, Jenny," he continued, returning to the
girl in his arms. "You have lots of silly ideas in your pretty
little head, lots of quaint fancies which sometimes come to
people when they are overwrought. Now run upstairs, put
on your hat and coat, and I'll come with you. I'll see you're
comfortable. Don't worry. You're going to be looked after.
You're going to be taken care of by kind people."

There was a tremor on his lips on his last words, and the
wistful glance he shot at the doctor was a passionate plea for
confirmation.

"But of course." Dr. Crupiner spoke with his usual cheer-
fulness. "Miss Fern has nothing to fear from us. It's the
effect her unfortunate illness has on other people which is
the only alarming aspect of the whole case."

"There, my dear, there, you see? Now don't worry. Don't worry at all."

The old man escorted his daughter to the door, and as it swung open both bent figures stiffened a little.

Standing in the hall, severe and businesslike in their starched uniforms, were two nurses. Both were middle-aged women, both had strong, expressionless faces.

The taller of the two stepped forward at once.

"I have Miss Fern's things in the little dressing room downstairs," she said in the quiet businesslike way which so many of her profession adopt.

"You will come with me, won't you, dear?" she went on, and her tone immediately became a replica of the doctor's when speaking to the patient.

Jennifer shot a despairing glance at her father, but she was tired, and her weariness was fast driving her into a state of apathy.

The other nurse noticed the expression in her eyes, and, hurrying forward, took out a small bottle of what appeared to be aspirin tablets from the pocket of her cloak.

"Poor lamb," she said, and, although her words and voice were kind, to Jennifer's ears at least there was something hypocritical, something vaguely untrustworthy in her tone.

She took the tablet obediently, however, and swallowed it. The slightly salty taste of aspirin did not reach her palate, but she thought nothing of it. Her mind was on her father and on the weird succession of incidents which had made him doubt her senses.

Sir Henry Fern watched her disappear down the corridor, flanked by the two strong, efficient women. Then, with bowed head, he turned and went back into the little room where Dr. Richard Crupiner awaited him.

For Jennifer life had become a nightmare. In the little dressing room which she knew so well her own maid, her face pallid beneath her make-up and her dark eyes round pits of terror, stood beside a suitcase, a fur coat and travelling hat in her arms.

"Mademoiselle, shall I be going with you?" she said as she helped the girl into the comforting folds of the long squirrel wrap. "I have everything prepared. I could be with you in a moment."

Jennifer's impulse was to cling to the girl, although she felt instinctively that it was only loyalty which made her make the offer, and she could feel her hands trembling with ill-concealed fear as she fumbled with the fur-covered buttons on the coat.

Before she could speak, the taller of the two nurses had intervened.

"Miss Fern will not require a maid. It is part of the cure that she should get away from familiar surroundings as much as possible. Sister Agnes and I are perfectly competent to look after her in every way."

"Very good, madame."

Jennifer felt a spasm of pain at the ill-concealed tone of relief in the little maid's voice. "She is afraid of me," she reflected wretchedly. "Terrified, poor child. Oh, if Robin were only here!"

She turned listlessly. Weariness was stealing over her, a strange lassitude which could not be accounted for by the emotional ordeal through which she had passed. This was something physical, something over which she had no control. The memory of the aspirin tablet came back to her, and she turned to the nurse, a last flash of energy in her eyes.

"That—that was not aspirin," she said thickly.

The woman seemed to have become very far away, and when she spoke it was as though her voice travelled from a long distance.

"Poor child, you're tired."

The next moment Jennifer's eyes closed and she stood swaying. The two nurses exchanged meaning glances, and the taller of the two put a strong arm round the slender fur-clad shoulders.

They led her out into the hall again, the maid following with the case.

Sir Henry Fern, followed by the doctor, came hurrying down the corridor from the morning room.

"Jenny, my dear," he said, "Jenny, Dr. Crupiner has almost persuaded me that it would be better for me not to come down with you now. But I shall come soon, my darling. If you want me, my child, even now, I shall disregard his advice and come with you. Why, Jenny, my darling, what's the matter?"

The girl was taking no notice of him. Although her eyes were open, their expression was dull and apathetic. Her lips were tightly closed, her cheeks ashen.

Dr. Crupiner laid a hand on the old man's arm.

"Don't disturb her," he said. "It's a normal form of collapse in cases where severe nervous excitement has been undergone. On the way down she'll drop into a natural sleep and probably remain in a condition of semi-coma for two or even three days. It's nature's way of refuelling the exhausted nervous system. There's nothing to be alarmed about. I shall write you every day and let you know as soon as it will be wise for you to see her. Nurse, take the patient along, please."

It was an old and broken Sir Henry Fern who followed the little procession through the hall of his mansion to the street, where a black car with shaded windows was drawn up outside the elaborate portico.

One nurse entered the car, and the other lifted the slight form of the patient bodily and passed her in to her colleague, who made her comfortable among the deep cushions of the limousine.

It was all over in a moment. Dr. Crupiner, his pale eyes glittering behind his pince-nez, shook hands hurriedly and sprang in beside the driver.

The car began to move, and Sir Henry, standing bareheaded in the darkening street, watched it bear the child he loved swiftly away into the twilight.

CHAPTER FOURTEEN
GATHERING SHADOWS

"I've taken the liberty of bringing you the decanter and some sandwiches, sir."

Williamson's voice trembled as he spoke, and he set the silver tray down upon the small table at his master's elbow with a none too steady hand.

The old servant was genuinely grieved, and in his privileged position of butler and confidant to the family for so many years, he went on, still with the same deference and gentle persuasion:

"You really ought to eat something, sir. Sitting brooding over the fire, it's not healthy, sir, if you'll forgive my saying so. Do eat something, sir. Just nibble a sandwich if nothing else. It'll keep up your strength."

Sir Henry lifted leaden eyes from the fire and, turning his head slowly, regarded the old man.

"Thank you, Williamson," he said. "Don't worry. Keep the servants quiet and don't let me be disturbed."

Old Williamson bowed. "Very good, sir."

But he hovered in the background until he had satisfied himself that his master had taken a sandwich from the plate.

As soon as Sir Henry Fern was assured that the old servant had gone, however, he replaced the food on the plate and turned again to his gloomy contemplation of the fire.

He had gone over the ground again and again. In his heart he believed his daughter to be as clear-minded and free from neurosis as any other healthy girl, but he could not explain away her two extraordinary lapses: first the story of her encounter with Sir Ferdinand Shawle, and then her remarkable story of the man who had committed suicide in his own office. That smacked of mania.

However his mind twisted and turned, it could not overcome a story like that. Jennifer was suffering from delusions. Perhaps, after all, he was doing the right thing in sending her away to a private sanatorium where they specialized in such things.

He was still sitting thinking when the phone bell rang, and he stretched out his hand to take the instrument from its place on the table beside the tray.

"Hallo," he said, and was startled by the hollowness of his own voice.

"Hallo. Is that Sir Henry Fern?"

He recognized the soft voice instantly.

"Madame Julie?"

"Yes." The woman's voice was as clear as though she were in the room. "I phoned to ask you if Sir Ferdinand is still at your house. There is an urgent message for him here, and I thought I might catch him with you. ... Oh? He's left some time, has he? Well, never mind. I only asked because after seeing him with Jennifer I thought that very likely you would know where they were."

Sir Henry Fern's eyes narrowed, and the hand that gripped the instrument trembled.

"What did you say, Madame? You saw Sir Ferdinand Shawle and my daughter together tonight? Where?"

"I only caught a glimpse of them for a moment."

The woman at the other end of the wire seemed surprised.

"Only for a moment. I happened to be in the Adelphi a little after seven this evening, and I saw Jennifer and Sir Ferdinand come down the steps from Robin Grey's house and climb into a taxicab. I assumed he would be still with you. Why, Sir Henry, what's the matter?"

But although she moved the hook up and down she received no reply.

Sir Henry Fern sat staring at the instrument in front of him as though it had been a living thing. Mechanically he replaced the receiver and rose heavily to his feet.

The information had been dropped so casually that he could not feel that it was not genuine. Jennifer's story had been borne out startlingly. The mystery was more insoluble than before.

If Jennifer had spoken the truth ... The bewildering idea came to him as something of a shock. If, after all, the child had spoken in good faith, then was it not himself who might be suffering from a delusion?

The world seemed to be revolving about him, and he sank down heavily into his chair.

A discreet tap upon the door, and old Williamson, obviously disturbed, came silently into the room.

"Inspector Whybrow and Inspector Mowbray are in the hall, sir," he murmured. "I told them that Miss Jennifer was ill and you were not in the frame of mind to see anyone, but I'm afraid they insist."

Sir Henry looked up dully. "The Scotland Yard men?" he said. "Oh, show them in, Williamson, show them in."

The old butler hurried off, to return a moment or so later, followed by the two inspectors.

Sir Henry turned to meet them, and even in his weary and bewildered state was able to recognize that a subtle change had come over them since the morning.

Inspector Whybrow's friendly, good-humoured smile had vanished, and there was a grim expression on his wide, good-tempered mouth.

Inspector Mowbray's face was blank. No one could have told what he was thinking.

Neither man sat down, although Sir Henry indicated chairs.

Inspector Whybrow was watching the old man's face carefully. He was quick to notice the signs of nervous strain round the eyes and the rigid set of the well-shaped mouth. In a long experience of human nature he had grown used to the signs of mental exhaustion, the traces of well-hidden despair. And all these were apparent in the old man who stood before him.

It was Inspector Mowbray who spoke first, clearing his throat and using the monotonous tone of the police officer on duty.

"Sir Henry Fern," he said, "are you aware of any mishap at your office in Wych Street this evening?"

The old man's eyelids flickered.

"Why, no," he said. "I hope you haven't come to report anything unpleasant to me, Inspector."

"That all depends." There was no good humour in the police officer's tone. "I have your statement. I take it that you have heard nothing from your office this evening and that you know of nothing untoward which may have occurred there?"

"Really, Inspector, you're very mysterious."

"I'm sorry, sir. But I must do my duty. During the course of this evening we received a mysterious telephone call from your office, giving us certain information which we thought proper to regard as serious. We hurried down there to find that the office had been broken open."

He paused significantly. Through Sir Henry's bewildered mind there ran the memory of his daughter's tortured voice pouring out the mad story he had been forced to consider the ravings of a disordered mind: "He told me that the police were here with Robin because a man had committed suicide in your office ... "

He could hear her voice now, pleading passionately to be believed. He clutched wildly at the hope held out to him. Perhaps, after all, he had misjudged her; perhaps, after all, she was the victim of some ghastly mistake for which there was some logical explanation.

The two astute criminal investigators watching him were able to follow the emotions, if not the thoughts, clearly depicted upon his face.

It was only his sudden hopefulness which baffled them.

He moved over to Whybrow and laid a hand upon his arm.

"You found something there?" he said. "Was it—was it a suicide?"

The two inspectors exchanged significant glances. Whybrow led the trembling old man back to his chair.

"I'm not at liberty to tell you yet what we found," he said. "But I can assure you that the safe was not tampered with and that no actual harm has been done to the office itself."

Whybrow poured a small glass of wine from the decanter and stood over the baronet until he had swallowed it. Then he stood back.

"Sir Henry Fern," he said, "circumstances have arisen which make it unwise for us to discuss this matter any further at the moment. Meanwhile, I must warn you that the police require you to stay in London for the next few days. Any attempt to leave the city on your part will have the inevitable result. And now, if you will excuse us, good-night."

This announcement, virtually a threat of arrest, made little impression upon Sir Henry Fern. He sat slumped forward in his chair, his eyes glazed, his mouth slack.

The two Scotland Yard men let themselves quietly out of the house. As they walked down the steps together, Inspector Whybrow whistled softly under his breath.

"Well," he said, a faint expression of wonderment creeping into his tone, "well, what do you know about that?"

Inspector Mowbray nodded. "To be poetic," he said grimly, "I think someone has put their foot on the first rung of the ladder which leads up to the scaffold. And the rest, my boy, is up to us."

CHAPTER FIFTEEN
STRANGE PASSENGER

"Still unconscious."

The words, murmured through the trap window of the driver's cab, barely reached Robin where he lay on the top stretcher in the private ambulance.

After his first glimpse of Jennifer peering through the curtains of his own sitting room, he had relapsed again into his torpor. Now the voice at the other end of the van brought him to his senses once again, and the events of the preceding hours crowded once more into his mind.

His head was hurting, and there was an unnatural stiffness in his limbs. He knew himself to be incapable of any great exertion. An attempt to fight his way out must inevitably end in disaster.

He saw the broad shoulders of the pseudo nurse bending forward as he stooped to peer through the narrow window.

Robin was not fool enough to lose his head, in spite of his frantic anxiety to discover the reason for Jennifer's terror. One thing comforted him, however, in spite of his wretchedness: Jennifer had come to him. Jennifer had visited his flat. In her terror, whatever had been its cause, she had turned instinctively to him.

He knew now that it was not she who had torn his card in half. He knew now that the kiss she had given him was spontaneous and genuine, an indication of the state of her heart.

Putting the girl from his mind as well as he could, he reconsidered his own position. The lights in the top of the van had been dimmed, and he could just see a glimpse of hedges and trees through the window at his side. They were in the country, then.

How long he had been unconscious for the second time, he could not tell, and he had no way of guessing how far out of London he had been carried.

Once or twice the powerful headlights of other cars met them as they sped on. They did not seem ever to be overtaken, and he gathered that they were travelling at considerable speed.

After a while the hedges vanished, and he guessed that they were on one of the great arterial roads, for the other traffic became more frequent.

The nurse had now turned from the window and sat down on the small seat in the far corner of the vehicle. He could only see the top of the headdress from his position, and he dared not move.

And then quite suddenly the most uncanny sensation of his life was produced by a voice which came, harsh and unnatural, from somewhere just above his head.

"Ambulance Y03," it said distinctly. "Stand by for Headquarters."

Robin lay trembling lest his involuntary movement had given him away, but to his relief he discovered that the voice had produced almost as much surprise in the nurse.

The man in the incongruous uniform leapt to his feet and moved forward.

Robin heard the metallic sound of a switch being thrust home and guessed the truth. The van was equipped with wireless, and not far above his head was situated the loudspeaker from which the man in command could issue orders, probably from some office or private house in town.

The nurse lifted an instrument from the wall, and Robin heard his voice, gruff and very masculine.

"Ambulance Y03. Patient still unconscious. Seven miles from home."

There was another click as he replaced the instrument, and then once again the mysterious harsh voice sounded from the loudspeaker.

"Search prisoner," it said distinctly. "Notes concerning the names of law firms especially required. Staff at the house have full instructions concerning this man, but I advise you to use great caution. The prisoner is above the average in intelligence and strength. It is important that you should not underestimate him. Good-bye."

Robin lay very still, his heart beating violently. The message was significant. But all the time he had been striving to recognize the voice which he knew must belong to probably the greatest enemy he had ever had in his life.

He was conscious of an odd sort of thrill as he realized it, but his excitement was coupled with despair, for the inhuman loudspeaker had robbed the voice of any distinctive quality by which he could have recognized it again.

Its message, however, woke him to a sense of the necessity for prompt action. Caithby Fisher, he knew, had no need to go to these remarkable lengths to obtain the information which he himself in his stupidity might have given him for the asking.

Therefore there were other forces at work, forces which had some particular interest in the firms of solicitors who might have been employed by Morton Blount.

In that brief instant after the mysterious and dramatic voice had died away, Robin's keen brain reasoned swiftly.

Caithby Fisher had evidently not told him the true story. At all costs he must protect the scrap of information pencilled on the little square of paper in his waistcoat pocket.

But already the nurse was advancing towards him. Since he was armed with a revolver, Robin knew he was powerless. Already he saw himself parting with knowledge which must hinder the course of justice and put some important facts, he knew not what, into enemy hands.

This time it was fate who stepped in to give him the few moments' respite he so badly needed.

Once again the loudspeaker spoke, this time in a new, official voice:

"Police car 7082 cruising in Winstree district. Look out for white ambulance. Reinforcements coming. Shadow ambulance. Crew believed to be armed."

The nurse stopped in his tracks and turned excitedly to the little window in the driver's cab. Robin heard him giving anxious instructions. He repeated the message which the wireless had picked up.

It puzzled Robin at first how they could possibly have heard a message broadcast on Scotland Yard's own private wave length, but he recollected the little metallic click which had followed the broadcast of the first mysterious voice and realized that his captors, having received their own message, had tuned in to the private broadcast of the police.

The nurse's excited conversation with the driver, however, gave him the time he needed.

Moving as gently as possible, he drew the tiny square of folded paper from his waistcoat pocket, screwed it into a ball, and forced it between the interstices of the tiny ventilator in the glass of the window beside him.

When his captor returned to him, he was lying as before, his eyes closed.

Robin was submitted to a rigorous search, and his respect for his enemies increased as he observed the efficiency of the man in nurse's uniform. No police-trained searcher from Scotland Yard could have done the job more thoroughly. All his belongings were taken from his pockets and placed in neat piles upon the shelf on the opposite side of the vehicle.

He was thankful that natural prudence prevented him from carrying any important information in his pockets.

The nurse had barely finished the task set so mysteriously by the voice over the wireless, when the boy became aware that they were nearing their destination. There was a gentle soughing of brakes, the crunch of wheels upon a gravel drive, and the car came to a standstill.

Peering beneath his lashes, he caught a glimpse of a great wall silhouetted against a paler sky.

There was a sound of excited voices from outside. Someone flashed an electric torch, and he caught a glimpse of massive iron gates which looked as though they belonged to a fortress. Then strong hands seized the stretcher on which he lay, and he was lifted down none too tenderly to the floor of the vehicle.

There he rested for a moment while the man who had driven the car spoke rapidly to someone who had come from the house.

In that brief moment Robin turned his head.

Lying on the lower bunk, exactly on the same level as he was now himself, was something stiff, unnatural, and oddly terrifying which he recognized instantly.

It was a corpse, a corpse which must have lain nodding and grinning with every jolt of the wheels directly beneath him for the whole journey.

He only saw it for an instant, but it was enough.

The body which lay beside him in the ambulance was the corpse he had last seen lying face uppermost in Sir Henry Fern's office in Wych Street, the corpse of Rex Bourbon, suicide or victim of a murderer's bullet.

It seemed to Robin now that there could be no question which.

"Which is this? The prisoner or——"

The whisper reached Robin where he lay on the stretcher, the night air blowing upon his face. He had been lifted bodily out of the ambulance, and now found himself lying on the ground in the midst of a group of shadowy figures.

The speaker stopped abruptly after the last word, and the remainder of his question hung significantly.

"This is the prisoner."

Robin recognized the second voice as belonging to the nurse who had accompanied him on the journey down. The first man was a newcomer, and he could only distinguish him by his huge bulk and ape-like arms.

The other was still in the car.

"What shall we do with it? The usual, I suppose?"

"I think so. We've had no instructions from Headquarters, but I should have it sent down to the furnace room."

The enormous newcomer, who seemed to be some person in authority, stepped forward, and he and the nurse withdrew some yards from the main group, which seemed to have increased in size within the last few moments.

Although Robin strained his ears to catch the gist of their conversation, he found it impossible to hear much. Isolated words reached him from time to time, stray phrases which told him little. He caught the words "crowded" and "inconvenient" from the newcomer and heard the man in nurse's clothes say irritably, "Anywhere'll do. He's still out. Give him a shot to keep him quiet if necessary. We've got the contents of his pockets. That's all we want for the time being."

Robin lay very still, and when a torch was flashed suddenly into his face he had the muscular control to remain still and lifeless.

"Bring him along," said the huge man who had been speaking to the nurse. "Room K will do."

Robin was dimly aware of a swaying and dangerous journey across a strip of grass, up steps, and finally into a faintly lit corridor which smelled convincingly of iodoform. Then he was thrust into a small room and the door closed firmly behind him.

As he lay listening, hardly daring to breathe, he heard two heavy bolts shoot home.

For some time he did not stir but contented himself with opening his eyes cautiously and peering around. He was in a small room, furnished as a bedroom, but which evidently had not been in use for some time. It smelt stuffy and ill ventilated. There was no window, and the only light shone through the glass transom at the top of the door from the passage without.

Carefully he climbed to his feet. His head was swimming, his limbs were stiff and cramped. Nevertheless he made a systematic tour of the tiny room.

At first it seemed to him that, apart from the door, which, besides being securely bolted, was too much in evidence to be easily negotiated, there was no other outlet from the room. But, as he was about to give up all hope, he discovered a small sliding hatch hidden behind a mirror on the dressing table. He found to his delight that it was unlocked.

Once he had removed the mirror, the hatch slipped back easily, and he found himself peering through a small grille into another and more brightly lighted apartment.

At first he did not recognize it at all. The white garments hanging upon the wall, the desk, the sinks, and the heavy mahogany cases bewildered him.

Suddenly, however, he caught sight of a white linen mask lying upon the table, and recollection came back to him. He remembered being shown round a big London hospital by one of the surgeons and seeing the little robing room off the operating theatre where the surgeon donned his coat, gloves, and helmet.

The room into which he peered was a smaller, less efficient travesty of the robing room at the hospital.

He was in a genuine nursing home, then.

But it was not this discovery which made him stiffen and brought a fresh ray of hope. In those mahogany cases not far from his hand, although so well protected by the narrow grille, were doubtless surgical instruments—weapons, certain and deadly, if he could lay hands on them.

He tried the grille tentatively and his heart leapt. Although by no means loose, it gave definite signs of yielding.

CHAPTER SIXTEEN
TERROR'S CAPTIVE

"I shall be glad if you will get me my clothes, Nurse Agnes. I'm perfectly well, and there's no point in keeping me in bed."

Jennifer sat upright among the pillows in the bleak, cheerless little room and regarded the woman who stood at the end of the bed with as much courage as she could muster. She was very weak. The effects of the drug which had been administered to her before leaving the house in Regent's Park had worn off but had left her pale and weak.

Her spirit was not broken, however, and the old imperious light had flashed into her mild eyes, and her tone was firm and vibrant.

Save for the bed on which she lay and a single table beneath the high window, the room was completely devoid of furniture, and its white walls were unrelieved by any form of decoration.

The temperature was low, and the whole place contrived to give an atmosphere of chilly inhumanity which would have quelled the heart of many hardier persons than Jennifer Fern.

The nurse, austere as the room itself in her crackling white uniform, stood looking at the girl with a faintly supercilious smile.

"Lie down," she said. "Lie down and keep quiet. You'll never get well if you don't," she added, and there was something that was almost amusement in her cold eyes.

The colour rushed into the girl's face.

"You're laughing at me," she said. "You're torturing me deliberately. You know perfectly well that I'm quite all right. You must be able to see it. You know I'm being kept here a prisoner and you're conniving at it. How can you?—How can you? If you had any spark of human feeling in you at all you'd show a little mercy and try to get me out of this place."

The woman laughed dryly.

"My dear child," she said, "did you know that I am supposed to take down everything you say, so that the doctors may see it and draw their own conclusions concerning the state of your—er—mental balance? I should be very careful how you talk, young lady. This illness of yours sometimes takes a very long time to cure. Sometimes"—she lowered her voice—"a lifetime."

Jennifer grew suddenly cold as the significance of the last words sank into her mind. "Sometimes a lifetime." She saw herself trapped, caught in the toils of a malignant fate, inhuman and relentless.

"This is incredible!" she said breathlessly. "I am well, I tell you, perfectly well. I've never been so sane in my life as I am now. You can't mean that I'm going to be forsaken here for a long time? I should go mad."

The amused expression which passed over the other's hard face caught her up sharply. Her first fears were giving place to sheer undiluted terror. She felt her control slipping. She felt that the hold she had upon herself must snap and she must give way to screaming hysteria. She felt she must spring from her bed and attack this grinning fiend who tormented her.

Fortunately, however, her better self came to her rescue, and she began to reason swiftly, her brain becoming cool, as is often the case when genuine danger threatens.

Her only chance, she knew instinctively, was to keep her head. If she gave way to her fears, she would be playing straight into her enemy's hands.

She leant back among the pillows, therefore, and forced a wan smile.

"Of course you know best, Nurse," she said, her voice sounding pathetically childlike in her attempt at subterfuge. "I feel much better, though. Perhaps if you could get me paper and a pencil I could write to my father. I should like him to know that I am quite comfortable and—and happy."

She watched the woman carefully to see the effect of this new move and was delighted to find that she was inclined to be obliging.

"Yes," said Nurse Agnes dubiously. "I think that could be arranged."

She hurried out of the room, locking the door ostentatiously behind her, and returned a moment or so later with a pad of paper and a lead pencil.

Jennifer fell upon them with the eagerness of a child.

"Oh, thank you," she said. "Thank you. I'll write at once if I may. I—I'm very fond of my father, you know. I should like him to come and see me. Dr. Crupiner did promise that he should come, you know."

The woman did not reply but stood watching her as she began to write feverishly. Her hand moved like lightning, and her confused thoughts were poured out upon the paper.

Nurse Agnes stood looking down at her, an inscrutable expression on her broad face.

She allowed the girl to write three pages, three poignant, ill-constructed pages of passionate appeal. Then she moved over to the door.

"I shall come back in an hour," she said. "I am glad to see you amusing yourself. There's just one thing, Miss Fern, which perhaps may make some difference to your enthusiasm."

Something in the mocking voice made the girl look up.

"You mean—you mean my letters won't be sent?"

The nurse's smile broadened.

"Letters of mental patients are never sent," she said quietly. "We keep them as amusing and interesting documents. Still, write away, my dear. It passes the time and does no one any harm."

Then, before the horrified girl could speak, she had hurried out of the room with a rustle of starched garments, and Jennifer heard the turn of the key in the lock as she fastened the door before going downstairs.

For some time the girl sat motionless. Then she began to cry.

She sat there sobbing in the little white bed for some time. She dared not think of her father, and Robin's behaviour bewildered her. Of course he did not know of her present terrible predicament. If he did he would never let her be taken to a place like this without first seeing her himself.

In that moment of her despair she longed for him more than for anyone else in the world.

Robin was clear-headed and intelligent. Robin not the man to be deceived by any lies told by a little gold-spectacled quack doctor. But she knew in her heart that Robin would not come. Something had happened to prevent him hearing of her troubles; she was sure of it.

She tore the letter she had been writing to her father into a hundred pieces and buried her face in the pillows. They might keep her here for life. The thought petrified her. Medical men, she knew, had strange powers. To the layman their word was law.

Her own helplessness terrified her, and she summoned to her aid every ounce of courage left in her make-up. She sat up in bed again and looked about her.

The window was high up in the wall and protected on the outside by a very heavy set of iron bars. She listened, but there was no sound from without, and presently she slipped out of bed and crept over to the table.

She was surprised to find how weak she was, and her fear of her enemies increased. She was completely at their mercy. They could drug her into insensibility if they wished. With a great effort she climbed up on the table and peered out through the narrow window.

Her room was evidently very high up in a large building surrounded by a massive wall, the top of which was liberally spiked. She could see over the wall, and beyond, instead of the quiet meadows of an English countryside, were the desolate mud flats of the East Anglian coast stretching out for a mile or more to the grey sea.

The landscape was completely flat, but as far as the eye could reach there was no sign of human habitation or even of life itself, save for myriad sea gulls wheeling and screaming over the desolate mud.

She guessed that the tide must be out and realized with dismay that when it came in it must lap against the wall which surrounded her prison.

The cold grey noon increased the dreariness of the scene, and Jennifer, trembling in the chilly little room, felt that she was surveying a picture of the end of the world.

She crept down from the table again and clambered back into bed. She was past weeping. Despair had settled down upon her.

How long she lay there staring up at the white ceiling she never knew, but she was interrupted in her reverie by the sudden unlocking of the bedroom door and the reappearance of Nurse Agnes, with Dr. Crupiner close behind her.

The little man appeared to be in a state of high excitement. There was more colour than usual in his cheeks, and his eyes behind his spectacles were glittering.

Jennifer caught the impression that there had been a hasty consultation behind her door just before they came in, and she guessed that something unexpected had occurred to alarm, or at least embarrass, the little doctor.

As he came over to the bed he had lost much of his usual good humour, and his voice when he spoke was no longer modulated soothingly.

Instead he was surprisingly brisk.

"Now Miss Fern," he said, "I can see you've quite recovered from your journey. I want you to get up and dress and go with Nurse Agnes down to the rest room on the next floor. You may be receiving visitors this afternoon."

"My father?"

The girl spoke eagerly, and the nurse and the doctor exchanged sly understanding glances.

Dr. Crupiner laughed.

"Your father would hardly come here as a visitor, Miss Fern," he said. "Hurry and dress now, and I'll see you later."

He bustled off, leaving Jennifer to ponder over the exact meaning of his last cryptic remark concerning her father.

Suddenly she turned upon the nurse.

"Do you have only one kind of patient here?" she demanded.

The woman looked up at her slyly, and Jennifer was conscious of something malignant and cruel lingering behind her shrewd glance.

"Yes," she said distinctly. "Only one kind of patient—like yourself."

Jennifer asked no more questions. Clad in her own garments, she felt more herself. But some of her fear returned when the woman insisted on her wearing a coarse grey cotton frock, which buttoned down the back, instead of her own dainty skirt and blouse.

"It's the rule of the house and Dr. Crupiner's orders," she said. "I'm afraid you must wear it. Now hurry up, dear."

It was a pathetic little Jennifer, muffled in the unbecoming folds of the hideous dress, who permitted the stalwart nurse to lead her down the corridor outside her room to a flight of stairs, chilly and uncarpeted.

When these had been negotiated they came at last to another room situated on the warmer side of the house.

Here the nurse left her and went out, locking the door.

Feeling weak and helpless, Jennifer crept in, grateful for the warmth but appalled by the hideousness of the furnishing, which was bare and unlovely as a barracks.

The one bright thing in the room was the window, and she hurried over to it eagerly.

To her relief it gave upon a garden, comparatively well kept and very green for the time of year. In the distance she could see the great wall encircling the house and grounds, but it did not seem so ugly when separated by this expanse of smooth, velvety lawn.

As she was standing there looking down, she fancied she heard a movement in the room behind her.

Turning swiftly, she was just in time to see a little observation hatch high up in the wall which contained the door spring shut.

She shivered. Even here she was being watched.

The next moment, however, she turned to look out into the garden again.

As her eyes fell upon the lawn for the second time, a cry of mingled bewilderment and delight escaped her. Walking slowly across the grass, his hands clasped behind him and his head bent, was a familiar figure. Even had it not been for a glimpse of his face she would have known him anywhere. The set of the shoulders, the walk, the characteristic droop of the head, she knew them all so well.

She beat upon the glass.

"Daddy! It's me—Jennifer."

The figure did not look up. Fearing that he had not heard her, she threw up the sash so that the cool air of the morning blew upon her face.

This window was barred on the outside like the one in her room, but she leant forward and caught the iron rods in her clenched hands.

"Daddy!" she shouted. "Daddy!"

The figure on the lawn was directly beneath the window. At the sound of her voice he turned and looked up at her. The light fell upon his face, and, although he was some twenty feet away from her, she could see his features quite distinctly.

She held out her arms to him.

"Oh, darling, I'm so glad you've come! This is a terrible place. I'm frightened here. Make them let you take me home."

The last word died on her lips, and she felt the blood in her body running slowly cold. The man on the lawn looked at her fixedly. The eyes which she knew and loved regarded her dully, uncomprehendingly.

And then, with a gesture of one who is confronted by a phenomenon he neither can nor wishes to understand, he turned away and walked slowly off across the grass, his hands clasped behind him, his chin upon his breast.

CHAPTER SEVENTEEN
THE SPRUNG TRAP

J ennifer leaned as far out of the window as the bars would permit, and her clear young voice, now shrill with terror, echoed over the sodden garden.

"Daddy! Daddy! Come to me!"

But there was no answer save the plaintive cries of the gulls circling over the mud flats.

Slowly she drew back from the window and mechanically pulled down the sash. She stood very straight and still in her hideous grey dress. She was past tears, and her wide eyes were hard and bright.

Once again the utterly incredible had occurred. She had seen her father face to face and he had not recognized her, and slowly into her mind there crept the insidious doubt of her own brain.

She sank down on the rug before the enclosed iron stove and covered her face with her hands.

She was still in that position five minutes later when the door was thrown unceremoniously open and Dr. Crupiner, a triumphant gleam in his pale eyes behind his spectacles, ushered two men into the room.

Sir Henry Fern, looking paler than usual and somehow shrunken within his heavy overcoat, was followed by the square burly figure of Inspector Whybrow. Both men looked anxious. But while the inspector was merely grave with the expression of one who has an unpleasant, embarrassing duty to perform, there was genuine grief and alarm in Sir Henry's face.

It was evident that they had not received an encouraging report of the patient's condition from the doctor, and indeed the little man wore an air of smug regret which was easily recognizable.

Jennifer lifted her head dully as they came in, and then, as her eyes fell upon her father, the swift colour came into her cheeks and she half rose.

The next moment, however, the recollection of her recent experience came back to her, and she drew back stiffly like a hurt, reproachful child who fears for its reception.

Sir Henry, whose face had lighted at the sight of her, was quick to notice the change, and the worried light in his eyes deepened.

"Why, Jenny," he said, "how are you this morning, my dear? Dr. Crupiner tells me you passed quite a good night. I've brought Inspector Whybrow down to hear your story about the man you told me had committed suicide in my office. Will you tell it to him, please?"

He was speaking nervously and jerkily, hurrying on further than he had intended because he was puzzled and frightened by the reproach in her eyes.

Jennifer, who was nearly at the end of her tether, suddenly lost her control. That he should have treated her so extraordinarily on the lawn not ten minutes before and then have suddenly confronted her with a lot of stupid questions before a police officer made her indignant, and, in her bewilderment, a little shocked.

"My dear," she said reproachfully, "why come and ask me this now when you wouldn't take any notice of me a moment or so ago? When I spoke to you out of the window you simply stared up at me without saying a word. And besides, if you were staying here, why not come and see me before?"

She stopped abruptly. Sir Henry and the inspector had exchanged swift, startled glances, and now Dr. Crupiner stepped forward and murmured a few hurried words. The two men nodded understandingly, and when Sir Henry looked again at his daughter his eyes were full of tears.

"Oh, my Jenny!" he said brokenly. "My poor little girl!"

He held out his arms to her, but before she could reach him Dr. Crupiner had intervened.

"Please, Sir Henry," he whispered authoritatively. "The patient is very hysterical. She must not be disturbed any more than can possibly be helped at this juncture. I don't know if you're convinced, sir," he went on, turning to the detective, "but it seems to me obvious that you can get no evidence of any real use from Miss Fern in her present condition."

Inspector Whybrow breathed heavily and nodded. He was profoundly uncomfortable. He was the most human of men, and he found the scene he was forced to witness eminently pathetic and distasteful.

"I agree with you, Doctor," he said abruptly. "Come, Sir Henry. We can do no good here, I'm afraid."

"Just a moment, Inspector."

The old baronet went over to his daughter and took her in his arms. She clung to him, and as her cheek rested against his the idea was slowly borne in upon her that she was the victim of some monstrous trick, some trap, some carefully engineered mistake.

Putting all her heart into her appeal, she put her arms round the old man's neck and looked into his eyes, her own as steady and clear as ever they had been.

"Daddy," she said clearly, "there's some mistake, something we can't understand. Someone or something is trying to separate us. Take me away from here. Keep me with you. Whatever happens, keep me with you."

The sincerity of her words had an effect upon both the newcomers, but while Sir Henry was deeply affected the inspector was naturally merely surprised and discomfited even more than before.

Dr. Crupiner leapt forward.

"Come, Sir Henry, come," he said and added in a whisper, "These lucid moments are the most difficult of all to understand. Don't forget it was only a moment ago that you had evidence yourself of a new and extraordinary delusion."

Jennifer continued to cling to her father.

"Oh, Daddy," she said wretchedly. "Oh, Daddy."

In response to an imploring glance from the doctor, Inspector Whybrow took Sir Henry's arm and led him almost forcibly across the room.

The doctor thrust Jennifer down into a chair. For a moment she was rendered completely breathless by the violence of the movement. In that instant Whybrow took Sir Henry out, and Crupiner followed them hurriedly.

As Jennifer flung herself against the door, beating the panels with her clenched fists, she heard a key turning in the lock from the other side.

She was left to herself for an hour. By that time her weeping had rendered her exhausted, and despair-engendered apathy had settled down on her once again.

Nurse Agnes, tight-lipped and uncommunicative, came in to her, and she was taken back once again to her bedroom, where Nurse Edith awaited them.

The two women undressed the girl forcibly and put her to bed.

But Jennifer was too weary and too completely wretched to protest very much.

When she was tucked up firmly on the narrow couch, Nurse Agnes went out of the room, to return with a hypodermic syringe.

Jennifer roused herself at the sight of it, but all her pleading and objections were in vain. The needle was thrust into her arm and the plunger driven home.

Gradually the opiate drug took its effect. The figures of the nurses by the bedside grew misty and indistinct. She strove to keep her eyes open, but the narcotic worked swiftly. She felt her lids closing slowly, slowly, and passed into oblivion.

She came to herself to find the light in the room had faded. It was now nearly dark. Her brain was still drowsy from the drug, but a sixth sense warned her to keep still. She was vaguely aware of voices in the room, lowered voices sunk to husky confidence.

At first they sounded as though they came from a long way off, but then, as her mind became clearer, words separated themselves from the monotone, and she realized that the two nurses were talking together in a far corner of the room.

She heard Nurse Agnes laugh. It was a hard, unsympathetic little sound with no amusement in it.

"He's got a nerve," she was saying. "I sometimes wonder how he dares."

Then Nurse Edith spoke, and her voice struck the semiconscious girl in the bed as being more kindly than the other.

"It's not Crupiner. It's his master. He drives him, if you ask me."

"You keep quiet. We're not supposed to notice anything that goes on here, and Crupiner's boss is not supposed to exist—and don't you forget it. We're paid our money. We keep our eyes and ears shut. That's right, isn't it?"

"All the same, it seems a diabolical thing to do."

Nurse Edith's voice was quivering.

"It's worse than murder."

Once again the other woman laughed.

"I don't suppose that worries Crupiner."

"Will he do it himself?"

The younger woman's voice was still tremulous as she put the question.

"Rather not! It's very tricky, you know. One mistake and you kill, besides the—the other thing. He's got hold of a young man from one of the big hospitals, a brilliant student I should say. Tempted by the money, I suppose. These youngsters are often inhuman. Their training makes them callous, and they haven't had time to mellow down."

"But to deliberately destroy part of the brain in a sane and healthy girl—oh, it's horrible!"

The exclamation was uttered in a half-whisper as the younger nurse made an impulsive gesture.

The other patted her on the shoulder.

"You pull yourself together. You're getting nervous. You'll never be able to stand this racket if you get squeamish. I heard Crupiner speaking after that interview this morning. 'It's too dangerous,' he said. 'One day she'll find someone who'll listen to her, and then the whole thing'll come unstuck. There's only one safe way, and by God I'll take it.'"

Jennifer lay rigid, scarcely daring to breathe. The terrible inference contained in this conversation so casually overheard forced itself slowly upon her. "To deliberately destroy part of the brain in a sane and healthy girl." The words seemed to be written across the universe in letters of fire.

Jennifer, lying quivering in her prison bed, cut off from those who loved her, deserted and without a friend, knew that the two women whispering together on the opposite side of the room discussed her own fate, the ghastly horror that her enemies had prepared for her.

Chapter Eighteen
The Wheels of the Law

"It's all very well you sitting there smiling, Inspector, but I can see that you're really as worried as I am. I've got eyes in my head and I've never been called a fool, not to me face at any rate. Mr. Robin's got to be found, and you know it."

As Mrs. Phipps finished speaking she resettled herself on the edge of the high-backed chair on which she sat, and her bright bird-like eyes surveyed Inspector Whybrow with quick intelligence.

The inspector passed his stubby fingers through his short grey hair.

"My dear lady," he began for the hundredth time, "what can I do? The boy's stayed away for a day or two before. He's principally a policeman, you know, and policemen have to take risks."

Mrs. Phipps rose to her feet.

"Well," she said, gripping her handbag and umbrella, "I thought you were a friend of his. If anything happens to that boy, Inspector, I'll have your own law on you. It's criminal negligence, that's what it is. Let me tell you something: Mr. Robin has been away before unexpected, but he's always managed to let me know, and he's always taken a few things with him, if it was only a toothbrush and a clean pocket handkerchief. Besides, he's in love with that girl. Don't you think that if he knew she was ill, and ill she certainly is for want of a better word—out of her senses, I should call it—don't you think he'd be hovering round her like any decent other young engaged fellow? Of course he would. Now I'm going, and if you don't bring him back within twenty-four hours I shall—well, I shall take steps."

What exactly these mysterious steps were, it was perfectly obvious that Mrs. Phipps had not the remotest notion. It was equally evident, however, that she was extremely perturbed, and not without reason.

So that when she bustled out of the room, leaving Inspector Whybrow looking after her, he made no attempt to call her back but sat staring in front of him, a gloomy expression on his kindly, good-tempered face.

"Yes," he said to himself after a pause. "Yes, well, where do we go to from here?"

He picked up the telephone from his desk and put a call through to another part of the building.

After he had finished speaking he got up and wandered up and down the room, his hands thrust deep in his pockets, his chin resting on his breast.

From time to time he glanced out of the window into the bare concrete yard below. His forehead was puckered, and his sharp eyes were darker than usual, and his lips pursed gloomily.

When the door opened again and Inspector Mowbray came in he looked up inquiringly, but before the other's expression his own face darkened again and he sighed.

"Anything fresh?"

Mowbray sank into the easy chair by the fire.

"Nothing at all. I was glad to get your call, though. I would like to have a word or two with you over the case. We've gone over that office of Fern's until I'm sick of the sight of the pattern on the carpet and I feel I know the intimate life history of every fly that's died on the walls. There's nothing there at all. Robin Grey's fingerprints were on the telephone, but that only confirms the telephone message you had from him—and of course there is that small patch of blood on the carpet. Apart from that there's nothing, not even a cigarette end. The whole thing's fantastic."

Whybrow sat down at the desk and pulled a pad towards him.

"Let's go over the facts," he said. "That evening I had a word with Robin in the Records Department. He promised to come and see me before he went home, but the next thing I heard of him was the phone call from Sir Henry Fern's office to say that he had discovered the body of a suicide, or what appeared to be a suicide, on the floor there. We got round in what I suppose must have been fourteen minutes, and when we arrived the place was empty, a patch of blood was on the carpet by the desk—still wet, if you remember— Robin's fingerprints were on the telephone, and a folded scrap of paper was by the instrument. That's all."

"Now"—he pulled a sheet of paper towards him—"I've gone over the list of disappearances. There are the usual number of girls, a couple of married men, one or two out-of-works, and this."

He detached an official form from the pile.

"Rex Bourbon. The inquiry only came in this morning. He's a well-known City man, and he went out about six o'clock on the evening in question and hasn't been heard of since. The inquiry comes from his valet. Apparently his master was not in the habit of going off without due warning, and the man has become alarmed."

He paused and regarded his friend solemnly.

"I think it might be worth your while to discuss this disappearance with Sir Henry. The men were business acquaintances, and I've got a hunch that the dead man, who was spirited away from the office in Wych Street, was our friend here."

Mowbray made a note on the back of an old letter, but his expression did not betray any great enthusiasm.

"I'll certainly try it," he said. "But frankly, Jack, I'm not even convinced that there was any body there at all. After all, a little blood is no proof of a corpse."

"You don't know Robin," said the inspector. "I've just had the boy's landlady here, by the way. She's worried about him, and frankly, so am I. Some of these specialty men like to trot off and do a little investigating on their own, but not Robin Grey. He's no fool, and he's got no love of kudos. This is a very mysterious, curious business, Mowbray. It began for us with the murder of Tony Bellew—the papers are getting rather sarcastic about that, I notice, by the way—and Heaven knows where it's going to end."

Inspector Mowbray rose and stretched his legs.

"We can't keep Sir Henry Fern under such strict surveillance much longer without arresting him," he said. "You saw the girl yesterday, didn't you? Her case is genuine, you say."

Inspector Whybrow grimaced at the recollection of his interview with Jennifer on the previous morning.

"Horribly genuine," he said. "Frankly one of the most unpleasant things I've ever seen in my life. A nice girl, a charming girl, but completely deranged. The father's in a terrible state. No fake about that reaction. There's an undercurrent of something very extraordinary there, something I don't understand at all.

"I may be getting old, Mowbray," he went on, "but I've got a feeling that sooner or later we shall lay our hands on the key, something quite unexpected, probably, that will unlock the whole mystery door by door. And I fancy when it comes to that even we're going to be surprised."

Mowbray laughed abruptly.

"You've been reading detective stories. Still, I hope you're right. I've had one or two black looks lately, and if the papers don't irritate you they do me. What does the public think we are? Second-sight experts?"

Whybrow grunted and, drawing out his pipe, filled it with elaborate care.

"I'd like to know that boy Robin's all right," he said. "Don't think I don't appreciate your difficulty, Mowbray," he added as he caught a glimpse of the other's face. "I do. But it seems to me everyone's in the same boat. Dennistoun was in here just now. A convict has escaped from Porchester, and there's a tremendous to-do. It's the first they've had there for ten years. A fellow named Sacret—Wendon Sacret. I don't suppose you ever heard of him."

Mowbray swung round from the window where he had been standing looking down into the yard.

"Wendon Sacret?" he said. "Yes, I remember. One of the earliest cases I was ever on. Quite a sensational little case. The wife made a dramatic appeal in court, and the prisoner's answers to the judge got him his sentence doubled.

"I remember that woman," he went on, a thoughtful expression coming into his eyes. "Julie Sacret. Very dark, very earnest. I was younger and less disillusioned than I am now, and I remember I thought the fellow was innocent after hearing her appeal."

He laughed at his own weakness, and Inspector Whybrow's comment was interrupted by the arrival of a constable who laid a card on the desk and murmured a few words in Whybrow's ear.

When he had finished, the inspector's eyes were thoughtful.

"Yes, well, I think I'll see him," he said. "Bring him in."

Mowbray turned. "I'll leave you," he said.

"I shouldn't. This is rather curious."

Inspector Whybrow was examining the card the policeman had brought in.

"Look here, what do you make of this? Mr. Ralph Knighton, of Rolls & Knighton, Solicitors, of Quality Passage. You never know—this may be the key we're waiting for."

Inspector Mowbray regarded his friend with gentle astonishment.

"Rather catching at straws, aren't you?" he inquired.

"Perhaps so." Whybrow nodded gravely. "Perhaps so. But I don't think so, and I'll tell you why. When we returned from our rather fruitless visit to Wych Street the other evening, I had the curiosity to find out what it was that Robin had been searching for so diligently in the Records Department. And I discovered that he had been looking up the solicitors with whom Morton Blount, whose name you probably remember, had ever had any private dealings. I know this may seem fantastic to you, but I know Robin well enough to know that he never works on two cases at once. He was onto something, and I rather fancy it was something pretty germane to the issue."

"Even so," said Mowbray, "I don't quite see where Mr. Knighton comes in."

"Rolls & Knighton," said the inspector solemnly, "were the last people with whom Morton Blount had any business before he died. Now what do you say?"

Inspector Mowbray said nothing, for at that moment Mr. Ralph Knighton was shown into the room.

He was a small man, approaching sixty, with a precise, somewhat nervous manner, pale, rather shy, brown eyes, and an evident distaste for his present mission. He looked from one to the other of the two inspectors hesitantly, and Whybrow stepped forward.

"Let me introduce myself, Mr. Knighton," he said. "I am Inspector Whybrow. This is my colleague, Inspector Mowbray. Can we be of any service to you?"

The visitor seated himself before replying. It was evident from his manner that he distrusted his surroundings and that he was considerably put out at finding two inspectors instead of one.

"I hardly know how to begin," he said at last. "I'm afraid my coming here is rather unorthodox, but I find myself in a quandary, Inspector, and as I said to my partner, Mr. Rolls, this morning, 'It seems to me that in a matter of this sort the open hand is the one to play. After all, if one needs information it is always wisest in the end to go to the fountain head.' Don't you agree with me, Inspector?"

Whybrow smiled faintly and tactfully refrained from pointing out to his legal visitor that he was hardly being very explicit.

Recovering from his nervousness, Mr. Knighton went on:

"In spite of forty years in the legal profession I have never before visited Scotland Yard, Inspector. I may say I find it very different from the grim, gloomy building I had expected. We might almost be in my own—er—office."

He glanced round the plain walls and neat, comfortable apartment with shy approval.

Inspector Mowbray stirred impatiently, but Whybrow, who was an adept in the art of allowing people to talk, beamed at the newcomer encouragingly.

"Very charming, isn't it?" he said. "Would it be indiscreet to inquire, Mr. Knighton, if by any chance you have called with reference to the business of an old client of yours, Mr. Morton Blount?"

The little solicitor stiffened visibly. The words had been dropped so casually, and the inspector was still smiling. It was evident that Mr. Knighton wondered if he could believe his ears. Taken completely off his guard, he sat hesitating for some moments, and then, having made up his mind, took the plunge.

"Well—er, yes, Inspector," he said. "Although why you should have guessed it I can't possibly imagine."

Inspector Whybrow permitted himself a smile of owlish omnipotence.

"Ah, we get to know things up here, Mr. Knighton. Mr. Blount, you know, was one of the greatest servants the Yard ever possessed. Inspector Mowbray and I both remember him well, and anything we could do to be of any assistance to you we shall consider a favour granted us."

Inspector Mowbray listened to this avowal of disinterested enthusiasm with frank astonishment, but a faint smile passed over his face when he saw the lawyer brighten and a gratified expression appear in his eyes.

"Well, that's very fortunate, very fortunate indeed," he said. "Because, frankly, it makes my position so much easier. At first I was not at all sure how the etiquette of our two professions was going to be affected, but since you are both friends of my deceased client it makes the whole thing much simpler."

Inspector Mowbray continued to look dubious, but Inspector Whybrow's kindly smile did not alter.

"Suppose you tell us about it," he suggested.

Mr. Knighton fidgeted. It was evident that he was loath to come to his point. Finally he took a deep breath.

"Our agents, whom we have to employ from time to time on very secret and confidential matters, inform us that Miss Jennifer Fern went off in a motorcar the day before yesterday to a destination unknown. They also suggest that you, Inspector, would probably know where she is at the present moment, and also——"

He paused.

Inspector Mowbray's face had become an inscrutable mask, and even Whybrow was finding it difficult to maintain his genial disinterested smile. The mention of Jennifer's name had been a complete surprise to the two policemen, and their interest had been instantly whipped to fever point.

Having gone so far, evidently Mr. Knighton decided to take the plunge.

"Frankly, Inspector," he said, "what principally interests our firm is to find out the exact condition of Miss Fern at the moment. In other words, is she alive or dead. You see," he went on rapidly, "while we knew where she was it was perfectly easy for us to keep a check on the state of her health. For reasons which, naturally, I cannot go into at the moment, it is tremendously important to us that we should know instantly if anything should happen to Miss Fern, if she should die, or"—he hesitated—"get married, for instance."

"This information is important to you as the executors of the late Morton Blount?"

"Executors in a certain matter, yes." Mr. Knighton sighed. "This procedure is not very professional, I'm afraid, but in these circumstances I hardly see how I can tell you any less. Oh, dear, this is very awkward! You must forgive me, Inspector, but you see my difficulty. It is imperative that we should know immediately, if not the whereabouts, at least the condition of Miss Jennifer Fern. I came to you, Inspector, because I understood from our private inquiry agent that you would be most likely to assist me in this matter."

Inspector Whybrow's eyes had narrowed, and he did not speak for some moments. At last, however, he turned round slowly and addressed his visitor.

"I'm afraid I can't help you very much, Mr. Knighton," he said, "unless you feel disposed to tell me very much more than you have done at present."

"Oh, dear me, no, I've said too much already."

The little man's tone was horrified, and the inspector knew from experience that here was a wall of professional prejudice which he could never hope to break down.

He did not attempt it, therefore, but shrugged his shoulders.

"I see," he said. "Well, Mr. Knighton, I can assure you to the best of my knowledge that the lady is still alive and unmarried. But apart from that I'm afraid I cannot help you. Is that all?"

Mr. Knighton rose.

"Yes," he said. "I thank you for your information, Inspector, and believe me I appreciate your difficulty, which I take it is very much the same as my own. Unfortunately we're both professional men who cannot afford to discuss our clients' business with the frankness which it sometimes requires.

"Oh, there is one other thing. Of course I've reported this to our local police in the ordinary way. But last night an attempt at burglary was made upon our office. The safe was untouched, but our papers were rifled. Fortunately our more important dispatch boxes are kept elsewhere, and an old ledger containing the names of our clients of the past ten years or so was the only thing taken. Very odd and very irritating. Well, now, since I have your assurance, Inspector, that Miss Fern is all right at the moment, I will not trouble you any longer."

As soon as the formal good-byes had been said and the little man had been conducted to the lift by the constable on duty outside the door, Inspector Whybrow met Mowbray's inquiring glance and nodded.

Mowbray reached for the telephone and called a house department.

"Inspector Mowbray speaking," he said. "A Mr. Knighton has just left this office. Set a good man onto him. Oh, and by the way, he reports a rather interesting burglary at his office in Quality Passage. I want it cleared up thoroughly. Inspector Whybrow and I feel it may have an important bearing on the Bellew case. ... Thank you. Good-bye."

As he put down the receiver he stared at his colleague in amazement.

"What are you looking so infernally pleased about?" he demanded.

Inspector Whybrow's eyes were dancing.

"I believe we're onto it," he said. "I believe we've found the two keys that are going to lead us to the heart of this labyrinth. One is that infernal ass who has just gone out of the room. No one steals a ledger like that without some very good purpose. And the other——"

He opened a drawer in his desk and took out something in an official folder.

"—and the other is this. This little scrap of paper which we found by the telephone in Sir Henry Fern's office."

Inspector Mowbray regarded it with interest. It was not often that Jack Whybrow became so enthusiastic.

It was a torn and yellowed scrap, crudely printed and much crumpled, the mutilated playbill which Robin had taken from the dead hand of Rex Bourbon.

Chapter Nineteen
The Mind of a Demon

"**M**y dear young lady, you're rambling."

Dr. Crupiner spoke sharply as he stood looking down at the girl who sat upright in the narrow bed, her curls clinging to her damp forehead, her eyes dilated with fear.

"Rambling," he went on, waving his hand with an airy gesture. "You've had a nightmare. You are being very well cared for, and I had thought until this moment that you were making satisfactory progress. But if you persist in taking up this absurd attitude, well"—a faint smile passed over his insignificant face—"we shall have to resort to other treatment."

Jennifer sat staring at the man. She could see his eyes behind the thick gold-rimmed pince-nez, and something in their pale depths sent a thrill of concentrated horror through her slender form.

Suddenly she realized what it was that had so frightened her about the little doctor from the very beginning.

He was mad!

The thought shot through her brain and left her cold and numb. He was insane with the awful insanity of a man of brilliant brain turned by cruelty into something inhuman.

"But I heard," she began, "I heard them talking. I am not a lunatic—you *know* I am not insane—and to suit some foul purpose of your own you are going to operate on me. You are going to destroy my reason. Don't you see, you monster, I'd much rather you killed me!"

They were alone in the little room with the high window looking out over the desolate mud flat. It was growing dusk, and the air had become unaccountably cold. Jennifer knew herself to be helpless, knew that however loudly she might scream she could never be heard by the outside world, knew that however piteously she might implore she could never hope to dissuade the smiling figure before her from his project.

Suddenly he began to laugh. His smug round face became contorted, and as the sound of his laughter rose higher and higher and its echoes were thrown back from the walls of the little room, Jennifer felt that she must faint.

The experience was indescribably horrible. Her terror had almost left her now. It had become so great that her nerves could not stand it, and instead she felt exhausted and strangely impersonal, as if the whole hideous nightmare were not happening to her but to some other person whom she did not know.

Dr. Crupiner seated himself on the end of the bed.

"So you overheard the nurses talking, did you?" he said. "What did they say? Eh, what did they say?"

His playful mood changed suddenly, and as he repeated the question he shot out a hand and caught her wrist, twisting it with sudden viciousness which made her cry out with pain.

"Can you remember the exact words? Tell me—tell me!"

His face was very near her own now. She felt his breath upon her cheek and saw the hot, angry, lunatic eyes peering at her from behind the thick lenses.

She wrenched herself free from him and sprang out of bed, to fling herself screaming against the door.

There was a commotion in the passage outside, and Nurse Edith's voice was heard demanding anxiously if anything were amiss.

Instantly Dr. Crupiner straightened himself, his eyes softened as though a veil had been drawn down behind the pupils, his bland, rather foolish smile returned, and he stepped forward to open the door.

"I'm afraid our patient has a bad attack of nerves, Nurse," he said, and went on in the same soothing voice which had nevertheless an undercurrent of something sinister in its tone: "Apparently she has been troubled by dreams, dangerous dreams about overhearing two nurses talking somewhat indiscreetly."

Jennifer saw the woman's face grow grey with fear, and as she bustled forward to take the girl's arm her hand was trembling.

"Poor child," she said with a certain amount of real feeling in her tone. "Come and lie down now, my dear. You'll need all the sleep you can get."

Jennifer permitted herself to be helped back into bed, and as the nurse straightened the coverlet she glanced across the room to see Dr. Crupiner standing in the doorway.

It was only for an instant, but as she looked at him she saw the veil slip once again from behind his eyes, saw the hot, red, mad-dog light appear in them. Then he caught sight of her and smiled as blandly as ever.

"Good-night, Miss Fern," he said. "Let me wish you pleasanter dreams."

As soon as the door had closed behind him, Jennifer turned to the nurse.

"What are they going to do?" she begged piteously. "Tell me, what's going to happen to me? That man's mad. I know it. I saw it in his eyes. What I heard you say to Nurse Agnes isn't true, is it? They're not going to destroy my mind? If they kill me I could bear it. It wouldn't be so bad. But this is inhuman. Tell me—tell me!"

She caught hold of the woman's hand on the last word. It was trembling and icy cold.

"Tell me!" she persisted.

The woman moistened her dry lips with her tongue, and her eyes wandered towards a panel in the heavy door.

Jennifer followed her gaze, and once again the thrill of horror shot down her spine. A tiny plaque which she had not noticed in the door before had slid back silently, and through it there peered two sharp eyes.

Nurse Edith settled down on a chair at the far end of the room, while Jennifer lay quaking in the narrow bed.

How long she remained there she did not know, and she had passed into a fitful sleep, disturbed by horrifying visions of the mad doctor and his assistants, when the moment she most dreaded arrived.

Suddenly the room was flooded with a blaze of powerful light and she sat up in alarm to find it thronged with white-coated figures, chief among them Dr. Crupiner himself.

A strangled cry escaped the girl, and instantly he turned to her. Beckoning to Nurse Agnes, who had followed him to the bedside, he took a hypodermic from the tray she carried.

"Just a little," Jennifer heard him murmur. "Just enough to make her drowsy, or we shall have difficulty in getting her to the theatre."

Before the girl could protest, a swab of iodine had been dashed upon her arm and she felt the swift stab of the needle. She was conscious of a strange, numbing sensation which, while it prevented her from any acute realization of her terrible position, did not impair her powers of observation.

The rest was no more real than one of the dreams from which she had been so violently awakened. She felt herself being lifted onto a wheeled stretcher and covered with thick blankets.

Then she was wafted down the corridor, followed by the white-coated figures whose features seemed to have become shadowy and indistinct, although she knew that somewhere amongst them was the horrible little doctor with the thick pince-nez behind which his eyes glowed, hot and dangerous like those of a rabid dog.

They did not descend the staircase but went on to an apartment on the same floor, but at the other end of the house from her own bedroom.

The air was very dry, the atmosphere warm, and there was an overpowering smell of disinfectants.

Jennifer struggled to overcome the powerful drug which held her prisoner. She knew where she was now. She recognized the great arc lamps, the faint sickly smell of ether, and then, as she was brought quickly forward, she saw the table itself.

She was in the operating theatre of Dr. Crupiner's infamous establishment on the east coast.

She strove to sit up. She saw the anæsthetist with his gruesome paraphernalia, the hooded and masked figures in their white coats and rubber gloves. They pressed about her.

She was lifted off the stretcher and put on the table. The blankets still covered her.

The drug which held her was becoming more potent in its effect. She felt she must lose consciousness. She could not even raise her hand. And then there was a slight rustle in the room as the white-coated forms turned to look at another of their number who had just entered by the small door on the other side of the room.

Jennifer caught a glimpse of him coming towards her. She saw the white overall which enveloped him from head to foot, saw the long rubber gloves pulled up high over his wrists.

As he came nearer she saw the cap covering his hair and the tight cloth bound over his nose and mouth, leaving only his eyes visible.

She remembered the conversation she had overheard between the nurses: the young student…very brilliant…a diabolical thing…Crupiner got hold of him.

Jennifer struggled to speak. This man was young; probably no older than herself. Surely she could appeal to him. Surely she could shake off this numbing drug which overpowered her and kept her still and silent.

She stared into the eyes, her own dark with agony and appeal.

And then, as she stared, something that was half bewilderment and half incredulity swept over her. She would know those eyes anywhere. She would recognize them in any circumstances, at any time as long as she should live.

She knew they recognized her, too. She saw the look of startled horror come into them as he saw her face.

Jennifer's senses slipped away from her. This last shock was too much for her battered nerves.

But as she slid into oblivion it was delight and not fear which flooded her heart, for she knew that the eyes which had peered down at her above the surgeon's mask were the eyes of Robin Grey.

"Jennifer!"

Robin's lips formed the word beneath his linen mask. He stood looking down at the still form on the grim operating table. She was the last person he had expected to see when he had entered this brilliant, terrifying room with its vivid lights and crowd of strange, white-robed figures.

His own story was simple. Left to himself in his prison, he had at length been able to force his way into the robing room, into which at first he had only been able to peer.

Even so, his escape from the building had been impractical, since he had discovered that the robing room led directly into the theatre, which was always securely locked when not in use.

He had been planning a sensational dash for freedom when his chance had come.

A young man had been shown into the robing room, and while Robin watched him from the temporarily re-erected grille he had observed that the newcomer, a dissolute-looking youth very much of his own height and build, was very much under the influence of drink.

It was then that the scheme had occurred to him which had brought him to his present dramatic situation.

It had not been difficult to overpower the man and to adopt the overall and mask, which disguised him completely.

As he looked back upon it his hair rose. It had never occurred to him for a moment that the clever but intoxicated youngster might be the actual surgeon in charge of an operation. At worst he had supposed him to be an assistant attending upon some more reliable man, and he had hoped in the tension of the moment to be able to slip out of the theatre unobserved.

His alarm had known no bounds, however, when, the moment he opened the robing-room door, he was confronted by a nurse who led him directly across the room to the table where a patient lay silent and terrified awaiting the knife.

The next moment he had looked down and seen Jennifer.

Robin's brain froze. He had been in many tight corners in his life, but this was simply beyond the scope of his experience. He had no idea where he was, save that it was some distance from London, and he fancied he had at times noticed the tang of the sea in the air.

He had known, of course, that he was in the hands of enemies, but not until this moment had he quite realized how desperate were the hands into which he had fallen.

He had no notion what the operation on Jennifer might be, but he knew enough from that one agonized glance he had received from her to realize that she was in mortal danger, that she was surrounded by fiends, by unscrupulous enemies who wished her definite harm.

But apart from his first feeling of relief and delight at the knowledge that he had come in time, his next sensation was one of despair. At any moment now he must be discovered.

He glanced sharply round the room. There were six men and four women present. Unarmed as he was, he knew he could not hope to be a match for such numbers.

Jennifer lay white and very still. Just for an instant the horrifying fear that she was dead shot through his mind, but he breathed again when he saw her eyelids flutter and her lips move faintly.

The anæsthetist stepped forward.

Robin's forehead grew cold and damp beneath his linen cap. He had no weapons, nothing save the gruesome implements of the profession to which he was supposed to belong.

He shrank from touching these, since he knew that any false handling, any show of ignorance, would immediately arouse the suspicions of those about him and he must be discovered.

Since he had found Jennifer it had become imperative that he should escape. He was not fighting for his own freedom now, but for hers.

He did not know how she had come to be in such an amazing situation, nor did he waste time to consider it. The fact that she was lying before him, obviously in danger, was enough.

A short figure in glistening gold-rimmed pince-nez came up. His bland, soft voice sent a chill down Robin's spine.

"We are ready if you will give the word."

Robin's throat was dry. His tongue stuck to the roof of his mouth. It had come, then. In another instant his chance of saving the girl would be gone for ever.

Instinct told him to play for time. He glanced at the lights as though to make sure that the great arc lamps set at equal distances all round the table were in their right positions for his purpose.

How long, he wondered feverishly, how long before they began to realize that something was wrong?

Then it was that the impulse to look up into the roof seized him, and he glanced up to catch sight of something so startling that the expression on his face would have betrayed him had it not been for his mask.

As in many operating theatres, the main portion of the roof of the room was composed of glass, and Robin, looking up, caught sight of a face pressed against one of the panes.

He stared at it, fascinated, and it seemed to him that the eyes looked straight into his own.

Then it was that recognition came to him, and his heart turned over. He had seen those great dark eyes, that plaintive scarlet mouth before. It was Madame Julie who was peering down with such strained intensity at the slim figure lying so helpless and so pathetic upon the sinister table.

Even as he looked at her he heard smothered exclamations from the two at his side. They had followed the direction of his glance and caught sight of the woman peering down upon them.

Robin was aware of a tremor in the group in the big theatre. Excited whispering broke out.

It all happened very quickly. Robin stood protectingly over the girl, still staring up into the roof.

The next moment he saw the flash of a white hand, the gleam of a revolver barrel, and an instant later a shot rang out and one of the great arc lamps smashed into a thousand pieces.

The effect was instantaneous. There was a spurt of flame and the room was plunged into darkness as the wire fused and the lights all over the theatre went out.

"The emergency lighting!"

Robin heard a strangled voice at his side which he scarcely recognized as belonging to the small figure in the gold pince-nez.

A nurse bustled through the gloom. There was the click of a switch, and once again the room was flooded with light from a second apparatus above the table.

Robin became galvanized into action. He swung round, seized the heavy sterilizing basin from the tray at his elbow, and hurled it at the lamp.

It happened so suddenly that the crash occurred and the darkness returned before two thirds of the people in the room realized that this apparently lunatic act was committed by the young surgeon whom Dr. Crupiner had procured to attempt the work he dared not face himself.

As the darkness descended once again, Robin gathered up the still, light form of his love and made a dash for the door.

He reached it and burst through, slamming it behind him.

The lights in the corridor were still on and, carrying Jennifer over his shoulder, he turned the key in the lock.

Already hammer blows from within were splintering the wood. He had no time to lose.

He sped on down the corridor, very bare and dazzling with its white walls and brilliant lights after the darkness of the theatre.

In spite of her slenderness the girl was heavy on his shoulders, for she hung limply. Nevertheless, he was grateful for her unconsciousness and dreaded lest she recover before he had time to get her out of the building.

He was halfway down the staircase when one of the things he most dreaded occurred.

A man in the black coat of an upper servant paused at the foot of the stairs and glanced up. His first expression of astonishment was soon superseded by one of suspicion, and the next moment he came charging up towards the boy and his precious burden.

Robin's right arm was free. His left clutched the girl. He steadied himself halfway down the staircase and waited for the onslaught.

It came, and Robin had the satisfaction of feeling his right fist crash into the heavy face speeding up to meet him.

It was a tremendous blow which caught the man squarely on the point of the jaw, lifted him bodily from his feet, and hurled him down the flight of stairs onto the stone flags below.

He rolled over and over and lay for a moment twitching convulsively.

Robin sped on. The noise of the man's fall had been considerable, and from other parts of the house he could hear doors opening and the murmuring of excited voices.

Far above him he could hear the hammer blows on the door of the operating theatre. At any moment now the whole pack would be on his heels, wresting the girl from him, dragging her back to the terrible fate from which he had snatched her only just in time.

His mind went back for an instant to the real surgeon he had left tied with what hasty bonds he could improvise in the robing room. Sooner or later he too must get free and join the howling mob which pursued the fugitives.

Gaining the ground floor, he stood for a moment irresolute, not knowing which direction to take. From the left he heard the sound of footsteps pattering towards him on the stones. He must turn to the right, then: it was his only chance.

Holding the girl more tightly to him, he charged down the corridor.

A woman barred his path just as he reached the main hall, but before she could recover from her horrified astonishment at seeing such an extraordinary figure, for Robin still wore his mask and surgeon's overall, he had thrust her out of his path and had gained the great front door.

To his relief it was unlocked, and he swung it open and felt the cool night air upon his face.

He had just slammed it behind him when a revolver shot splintered the solid wood above his head, and he realized that one of his pursuers at least was armed and did not hesitate to shoot.

A wide flight of stone steps led to the gravel drive, and he sped down these, the fainting girl hanging over his shoulder.

His feet had just touched the gravel when a figure rose up out of the darkness before him. It was a woman, and he was just about to brush her out of his path, as he had done the other, when something familiar about her form and bearing stayed his hand.

It was Madame Julie. He saw her bewildered expression, saw the gleam of fear in her dark eyes. Then with an impulsive gesture he wrenched the mask from his face and heard her quick intake of breath as she recognized him.

"You! Quick, before it is too late!"

Already the commotion in the house behind them could be heard all over the grounds. Any second now the great door must burst open and they must be recaptured.

Madame Julie seized Robin's hand, and he followed her blindly. There are moments when important decisions have to be made, when one must make up one's mind whether to trust or whether to fly.

In that instant Robin knew that, whether the woman was his own friend or not, at least she was not Jennifer's enemy.

She led him swiftly down a narrow path among the thick laurels which bordered the drive. The screening leaves had only just hidden them when the front door of Dr. Crupiner's mysterious nursing home swung open and a crowd of figures armed with torches and revolvers burst out into the grounds.

Robin heard the woman panting at his side as they sped through the shrubbery.

"This way." He heard her sob on the words. "There is just one way. If we take it now we have a chance."

While the grounds around them were alive with angry voices and pursuing beams from the powerful torches,

Madame Julie, a dark and mysterious form in her long fur coat, led him swiftly over the rain-soaked ground to a tiny gate in the high wall which surrounded the place.

"Here," she said. "Here's our chance."

The door gave at her touch, and Robin stepped onto the hard road, just escaping the beam of a torch which had picked up their trail.

The night was very dark, but fine for the time of year. Just before them, a pace or so down the road, Robin caught a glimpse of the dark shape of a big saloon car with its lights out and its engine running quietly and smoothly. Its powerful but subdued purr was very comforting, and for the first time a ray of hope shot through the boy's heart.

"Here—climb in the back."

Madame Julie wrenched open the door, and between them they lowered the now half-conscious girl into the corded cushions in the interior.

Robin climbed in after her while Madame Julie went in front and the car began to move.

Their wheels had just begun to turn when from the grounds behind them there was a roar and the scream of a revving engine.

Almost instantly the long, dangerous-looking body of a roadster swung out of the great gates some five hundred yards farther up the road and hesitated as the giant headlights swept round this way and that.

The next instant the fugitives were in the full glare of the blinding lights.

The saloon leapt forward like a springing panther, and its own headlights, two great white beams, stretched out along the narrow road, lighting up the hedges which separated it from the saltings and the sea till they stood out like pale ghosts lining the way.

For the first time Robin noticed that Madame Julie was not driving herself but that there was a fourth person in the car. From where he sat he could just make out the emaciated but still powerful form of a man crouching low over the steering wheel.

He was hatless, and at first Robin thought he was bald, but the faint glow from the cigarette between his lips showed his hair to be grey and very finely clipped.

Madame Julie was leaning back over the seat, peering out of the window behind Robin at their pursuers.

At first the dashboard light in the roadster had been going, but now it was switched out and Robin heard her murmur, a little low sound, half surprise, half bewilderment.

But there was no time to analyze it, for now the chase had begun in real earnest.

The man who bent over the wheel in front of him was driving like a maniac. The engine screamed as though for mercy, but he flogged it and the car roared on through the night with the deadly speed of an express train.

At first it seemed that the roadster must gain upon them, although, so far as Robin could judge, there was little to choose between the two cars.

But suddenly the thought occurred to him that the pursuing car was probably more heavily laden.

Neither Jennifer nor Madame Julie was particularly heavy, and although Robin and the mysterious driver of the car were both big men, the aggregate load of the four of them was probably not so great as that of the five or six men in the car behind.

Still, for some time the space between them did not alter, and in front the road stretched on, straight and very white in the glare of the lights.

A bullet, followed by another, spattered in the road behind them. Madame Julie laid her hand on the driver's arm.

"They're firing!"

The man at the wheel nodded, and a low soft laugh escaped him.

"We'll beat 'em to it yet," he said. "Right or left?" he added swiftly as a fork in the road appeared.

"Left," she said heavily. "Left, and then right. And then—the open marsh."

Robin peered out through the window behind. Jennifer had recovered consciousness and was clinging to him, her soft arms round about his neck.

A reckless and terrible anger against the inhuman brutes who had tortured her rose up in the boy's breast, and he longed for a weapon with which to fire back at the oncoming car.

Madame Julie seemed to read his thoughts.

"I've only one more bullet," she said softly, "and we may need that—later."

They turned sharply to the right. The car swung round on two wheels, and their pursuers, in trying to follow at equal speed, skidded badly. Robin saw the reeling headlights and thought for a moment that the car had been upset. A moment later, however, it righted itself and came on.

The delay gave them a further lead, however, and they continued to gain in spite of the fact that their pace was necessarily slackened by the winding, water-logged lane through which they passed.

Suddenly the ground beneath them became violently uneven, and the headlights picked out a great rolling expanse of salting. The turf was short and springy and com-paratively dry, but Robin knew from experience that these marshes are always interspersed with great dykes, and his heart misgave him.

Glancing behind him, he saw that the other car had slowed down almost to a crawl. It was evident that their pursuers fancied they had missed their path and ran into a trap, and were preparing for a showdown.

Madame Julie urged the driver on.

"Pull up just in front of the dyke," she said. "This is the Echo Way. I've known it since I was a child. If we can make it we're safe."

There was something eerie, something supernatural about the lonely salt marsh. Far in the distance came the roar of the sea, and now and again the shrill cries of disturbed seabirds rang through the startled night.

Suddenly the car stopped with a crash of brakes, and Robin's heart shifted uncomfortably. A great dyke lay before them. Over six feet deep and eight feet wide, it was absolutely impassable by any car made.

Madame Julie opened the door near her and emitted a long-drawn-out, wailing cry, high and scarcely human in the ghostly atmosphere. Bewildered, Robin held his breath.

Then the miracle happened. From the right the cry was echoed, thrown back by some trick of acoustics, reproduced faithfully in every detail.

The woman gasped with relief.

"There," she said, "you heard it. Follow the echo."

The great car turned and ran along the side of the dyke for some two hundred yards. Then there was a bridge, rough but strong, made out of immensely thick planks.

The car passed over safely, and they raced on to the next dyke.

Here the performance was repeated. Again Madame Julie called, again the echo led her unerringly to the next bridge. The marsh seemed interminable.

Four times this strange ritual was carried out, and four times the dykes were surmounted.

Then, as they climbed up onto high ground, at a touch from the woman the driver pulled up, and the four looked back across the treacherous marsh.

Far in the distance they could see the giant headlights of the pursuing car streaming out across the ground like signals of distress. They were not moving.

Madame Julie sighed.

"I think," she said, "the mud has caught them. Near the dykes it is very treacherous. Not so dangerous, of course, as the quick patches which surround the coast, but quite strong enough to hold a car there until it is dragged out by a tractor."

She stopped abruptly. As they watched, a new phenomenon occurred. Far away, and just behind the headlights of the stricken pursuing car, another pair of powerful lamps had appeared.

The newcomer appeared to be working its way carefully across the grass to the roadster. It was very dramatic, the great beams of light cutting through the darkness.

"What is it?"

Robin hardly recognized his own voice.

"More of them?"

Almost in answer to his question, a volley of revolver shots came faintly through the gloom. The stranger in their midst sprang back to his place at the wheel.

"The police van," he said in a curiously sharp, dry voice. "Get in. We're not away yet."

Once more they sped on, striking a lane some five hundred yards farther on. Madame Julie seemed to know her way, and directed them with never-faltering skill through winding country roads until they pulled up at last before a cottage half hidden in a copse of giant elms.

At the sound of the car the door was thrown open and a woman appeared on the threshold. Robin caught a glimpse of her squat figure silhouetted against the yellow light within.

"Mary!"

Madame Julie's voice cut through the night.

"Yes, ma'am. I've been waiting."

Robin climbed out of the car and carried Jennifer, who was still very weak, in his arms. He followed Madame Julie into the house while the driver of the car took it further into the shadow of the protecting trees.

CHAPTER TWENTY
IN THE COTTAGE

"Set the poor young lady on this couch, sir. Poor lamb, a drop of hot milk will do her good."

The old woman Madame Julie had addressed as Mary hovered round the boy, and as soon as he set Jennifer down upon the old patchwork-covered couch, she bent over the girl with motherly concern.

Robin's chief thought was Jennifer, and it was not until he had convinced himself that, although weak and frightened, she was almost herself again that he looked about him.

Then he discovered himself to be in the main living room and kitchen of an old-fashioned cottage. The brick floor was covered with a rag carpet, the uneven walls plastered with a faded paper. There was a bright fire in the stove, and the brasses and china dogs on the mantelpiece shone with cleanliness.

It was a homely and a comforting room, and after his recent experiences Robin felt that he had never seen anything more friendly in his life.

Jennifer clung to his hand. Her face was very pale at first, but as she sipped the hot milk the colour gradually came back into her cheeks and some of the terror died out of her eyes.

Madame Julie stood by the cottage doorway waiting for the man who had driven them to return. As she stood there, there was a strained expression on her keen, still beautiful face. Her dark eyes were lowered, and her head was bent a little. She was listening, listening, Robin knew instinctively, for the sound of a car on the desolate muddy road.

But although she stood there for some time, there was no sound above the roar of the wind in the trees and the fire hissing in the stove behind her.

Presently Jennifer began to speak. Bit by bit she poured out the whole amazing story, her mysterious illness, her removal to the nursing home, her interview with her father, first on the lawn and then in the reception room.

When she had finished, there were tears in her eyes.

"Oh, Robin, you do believe me?" she said breathlessly. "Tell me—you do believe me? You don't think I've had hallucinations? You don't think I—I'm out of my senses?"

Robin took her in his arms, and she nestled close to him, her face hidden in his neck.

The story she had told was fantastic, but in Robin's experience truth was often fantastic, and he knew, too, the signs of a disordered mind. None of these was apparent, he thanked God, in the girl he loved.

"Yes," he said gently. "Yes, my dear, I believe you. We're up against something so diabolical and ingenious that I should not have blamed you if you had doubted your own senses. You have been deceived, and, as I believe, deliberately deceived, in order to give your father and those who love you the horrible suspicion that your mind was not to be trusted."

The girl sighed, and her arms tightened about him. The relief at discovering that someone really believed in her at last was almost too much for her. She began to cry, and the tears rolled down her cheeks.

Robin kissed them away.

"Don't, sweetheart," he said gently. "You're with me now, and I shall never let you go again. I love you, Jennifer, and I'm going to take care of you."

He had spoken oblivious of any presence but her own in the room and now glanced up to see Madame Julie looking at him, a strange, almost pleading expression in her dark eyes.

"Robin," she said slowly, coming towards him, "when I came to look for Jennifer tonight I had no idea that she was not alone among her enemies. When I saw you smash the emergency light in the operating theatre I thought you were a madman. I was trying to get into the house to attempt to rescue the girl myself when you came out with her in your arms. I have brought you to a place of safety."

Robin looked puzzled. He did not understand the note of appeal in her voice. She seemed to be asking him something, imploring him to take pity, to have a little mercy. He was bewildered.

"Madame," he said, "I cannot tell you how grateful I am to you. Had it not been for you the escape would have been an impossibility. You and your friend saved us. I shall be in your debt till I die. You have saved my life once before, but this time you have done more."

A half-smile passed over the woman's face.

"You don't understand," she said. "Although I am fond of Jennifer, she is almost a stranger to me. My motive for taking the tremendous risk I did in order to save her was not purely disinterested.

"Listen," she went on rapidly, laying a hand on the girl's arm. "You are young, both of you, but you know what love is. Already you have experienced some of the sweetness and the agony of it. You know its strength, its depth. Let me tell you a story.

"Once there were two young people who loved quite as passionately, quite as desperately as you two. They lived very happily. They had their flat in town, their cottage in the country—terribly like this one—and then one day, when they had been married some years and their love had grown so strong that they were almost welded together as one human person, tragedy overcame them.

"The husband was accused of a crime he did not commit. His enemies piled up evidence against him. The woman appealed, even in the court, in public, but all to no purpose.

"The man, her man, whom she loved even more than life itself, was condemned to a long term of imprisonment."

Madame Julie was speaking passionately now. There was fire in her eyes, and a new colour in her cheeks. Her words poured forth in a stream of unquenchable eloquence.

"The woman worked and schemed to save him. Gradually she discovered the hint of a clue to the mystery which surrounded his accusation. She stumbled upon a plot diabolical and fantastic, a plot in which her beloved husband was an instrument sacrificed for the sake of much larger game.

"In her relentless efforts to probe this mystery and clear her husband's name she became many things. Finally she acted as a spy in the house of her employer, who was none other than her husband's accuser.

"At last it seemed that she was stumbling upon the truth. Another woman was about to be sacrificed by the same men who had destroyed her own life. She determined to save her.

"She was just setting out on this mission alone when the unbelievable occurred. Her husband, the man for whom she would give her life gladly, escaped from prison.

"He was hunted up and down the country. Every hand was turned against him. Yet, instead of flying with him to one of the ports, with his consent—or rather, with his insistence—she turned aside and they went together to the rescue of the girl."

The woman paused and looked at Robin.

"Now do you understand?" she said.

Robin looked at her wonderingly. His eyes were very grave.

"I think I understand," he said. "You need not be afraid of me, Madame."

The woman sighed, and the colour flooded her face. From the doorway, where he had been standing during the latter part of her outburst, the man who had driven them to safety over the treacherous marsh stepped forward.

Robin saw the close-cropped hair, prematurely whitened, the strong, kindly, emaciated face, the eyes burning with a sense of long-suffered injustice, and his heart went out instinctively to the man who came forward cautiously into the room.

Madame Julie turned to him. Her eyes were dancing like a girl's. In spite of her anxiety there was happiness and a new youth in her face.

"Robin and Jennifer," she said, "this is my husband."

The man bowed stiffly, and as he spoke his mouth was twisted into a faint ironical smile.

"Wendon Sacret," he said. "Wanted by the police, escaped convict from Porchester. Shall we close the door?"

The old woman darted forward, but before she could reach the door the man had closed it quietly behind him.

Robin glanced meaningly at the woman, and Madame Julie interpreted his unspoken question.

"I have known Mary nearly all my life," she said. "When she left my service to marry, I never lost sight of her, and when her husband died she took over this cottage of ours and has lived here ever since. I am not afraid of Mary, Mr. Grey."

Robin nodded understandingly, and the old woman, who had been regarding the convict with real affection in her faded eyes, smiled faintly. Robin understood. Wendon Sacret was among friends.

He turned again to Jennifer. She was still in her night-clothes and wrapped only in a light woollen blanket.

Once again Madame Julie interpreted his thought.

"Mary will take Jennifer upstairs," she said. "There are some clothes of mine which although a little large for her will at least keep her warm until she can get others. We must hurry," she went on. "We have no time to lose."

The woman nodded and, putting a supporting arm round the girl's shoulders, led her out of the room.

When they had gone, the three faced one another, the anxious wife, the escaped convict, and the detective who owed them both so much.

Robin had time to examine the man's careworn features. He had at one time been very handsome, he decided, and even now, in spite of the lines which want and hardship had carved upon his features, his face was by no means ignoble.

"Madame Julie," Robin said, "what are the chances of Dr. Crupiner and his friends finding us here?"

She hesitated and glanced at her husband.

"None," he said grimly. "But," he added abruptly, "from my own point of view he is the least person I have to fear."

Robin looked up sharply. "You mean the police?"

"Yes. At the moment every man's hand is against me. That is to be understood. Did it occur to you, Mr. Grey, that the second pair of headlights which we saw hovering near our pursuers probably belonged to a police van which I know is scouring the neighbourhood for me?"

Robin eyed him gravely. "That had occurred to me," he said. "However, you are safe for the moment. The police will get no information from Dr. Crupiner, even if he suspects that it was you who drove our car."

The man bowed his head without replying, but Robin fancied he was on the alert, listening always for the sound of wheels in the lane, and the realization that this man was hunted, an outcast in constant danger of losing his liberty if not his life, came to him with overwhelming force.

The atmosphere in the room was tense. Robin glanced at the man.

"Why did you do it?" he demanded simply. "Why did you run the extraordinary risk you did in order to save a girl who, after all, must have meant very little to either of you? I don't think I shall ever be able to tell you how timely your assistance was, and I shall certainly never be able to express my gratitude sufficiently. But I don't understand why—I don't see what it was that made you take such a dangerous chance."

Wendon Sacret glanced at his wife as though asking her permission before he spoke. She signalled to him to continue, however, and when he looked again at the boy, Robin was astounded to see the passionate light in his eyes, the burning sincerity in his expression.

"I came," he said slowly and distinctly, "because Miss Fern's destiny and my own are linked. The same force which threatens her was responsible for my own wrongful imprisonment and disgrace."

He was speaking rapidly now and with such conviction that Robin found it impossible not to believe him. He leant across the table and listened intently to the other man's story.

"Our persecutors," Sacret went on, "Dr. Crupiner in Miss Fern's case and Sir Ferdinand Shawle in my own, are in turn controlled by a personality of fiendish cruelty and power. Have you ever heard of the Dealer, Mr. Grey? Ah, I see you haven't. I myself know very little of the story, but at least I can tell you something."

He went on talking rapidly, and now Robin heard the truth concerning the mysterious box deposited by Morton Blount with a firm of solicitors, to be opened only when Jennifer should die or marry.

As the extraordinary tale was unfolded to him by the hunted man in the little cottage, much of the amazing happenings of the past few weeks were explained to the young man, and he listened aghast as bit by bit the mysterious shapes in the jigsaw fell into place.

"I cannot tell you where the box is," the man went on. "Nor can I tell you exactly what it contains. Nor do I know if the whole of this story is true. But I assure you I have learnt my facts in a hard school. My information has come to me through much suffering.

"All I can tell you further," he added, "is that as matters now stand, should Miss Fern marry or die, information would come to light which would imperil the liberty, if not the lives, of at least half a dozen wealthy and influential men, one of whom, horribly enough, is her father."

Robin drew back. His face was pale, and there were beads of sweat upon his forehead. Bit by bit he saw himself dragged out of his official capacity and forced to work upon the side of those who were, temporarily at least, on the wrong side of the police.

Suddenly an idea came into his mind, and the thought of it sent a thrill of apprehension down his spine. He stared at the ex-convict. The man did not look a desperate criminal, but after all there was no telling to what lengths a man

might not go when driven to it by the piling up of circumstances which had overpowered Sacret.

The convict suddenly smiled.

"No," he said. "No, Mr. Grey, I did not seek out your
fiancée with the intention of killing her, although I admit
that that would be one way of forcing the issue. I meant
to get hold of the girl to explain to her the truth of the
situation and to persuade her to marry. After all, my wife
assured me that Jennifer was in love, and I felt sure that
after my story a run-away match would not have been hard
to arrange.

"I must admit," he added with sudden candour, "that
I might not have told her that her father's name would be
implicated in the revelations which would follow the opening of the box."

"I see." Robin spoke quietly. "And do you still intend to
press forward this suggestion?"

"No."

The vehemence of the man's reply startled him. Sacret
was pale, and there was an underlying note of disgust, if not
of fear, in his tone.

"It was not until tonight," he said, "that I realized just
how desperate my enemies were. After Miss Fern's story I
see clearly, as you must yourself, that these men will stop
at nothing. Had Morton Blount's instructions provided for
the box to be *destroyed* on Miss Fern's death, I cannot think
that she would have been alive at this hour. Having failed
in their project, which seems to have been to keep her in a
state of helpless lunacy to an advanced age, I feel sure that
they would have taken the only other course left to them,
and that is to have killed her and disposed of the body so
secretly that death could not be presumed for at least a considerable number of years.

"Forgive me for speaking so bluntly," he went on, catching sight of the boy's face, "but this is a time for plain speaking. The danger is by no means over."

Robin remained silent. He was no fool, and he knew that the man spoke the truth. Now that he had time to think, the story of the box did not seem so strange as it had done at the first hearing.

After all, he himself had proof of the interest of those powers against them in the solicitors with whom Morton Blount had been in communication before his death, and he shuddered when he thought how glibly he might have handed over the precious information to Caithby Fisher.

"No," Wendon Sacret went on, "the mere act of marriage is not now sufficient. We must find another way. I know the solicitors with whom Morton Blount is most likely to have left these all-important proofs. If that box were destroyed, even if it meant that our enemies would go free, at least they would have no further cause to persecute us."

He saw Robin's expression and laughed.

"You are a policeman," he said, "and you have your duty to consider. The question of ethics arises in your case, but not in mine."

Madame Julie laid a hand upon his arm.

"Be careful," she urged. "Oh, my dear, be careful."

He smiled down at her tenderly.

"Don't be afraid, my dear," he said. "I have lost so much already that at least I can afford to take this risk. Once the box is in my possession the tables will be turned. With such a weapon in my hand it would be possible to mete out to those who have tortured us a punishment which no law could give them. There are times when the law is inadequate."

Robin did not speak, and at this moment the inner door opened and Mary and Jennifer returned.

The girl was clad in a long brown woollen dress, but even its voluminous folds could not hide her beauty.

Sacret glanced at her admiringly.

"Now I understand how you come to be in this affair, Mr. Grey," he said. "May I congratulate you?"

Jennifer went over to Robin's side, and old Mary busied herself by laying a meal on the narrow table at the other side of the room.

In the moment when Robin put his arm round Jennifer's shoulders and felt her lean against him, some of the strain of the past forty-eight hours seemed to have slipped away from them. The warmth and homeliness of their surroundings brought an air of something that was almost gaiety into the little party.

Madame Julie watched her husband with the hungry admiration of one who once again sees a happiness which she has long since thought dead to her for ever.

Outside, everything seemed very still and peaceful, and it was not until they had settled down to the meal that the incident occurred which swept aside their sense of false security and brought them back with a jerk to the grim realities which surrounded them.

Madame Julie was laughing with unaffected happiness, and the colour had once again returned to Jennifer's cheeks when footsteps sounded in the lane, followed by a vigorous knocking on the cottage door.

Instantly everyone rose. The colour drained out of Madame Julie's face, and the old hunted lines reappeared round her husband's eyes.

Old Mary motioned them all to be seated, and with the remarkable calm which old women sometimes show in times of emergency she went over to the door and threw it open.

From where they sat behind the table, Robin and Madame Julie could just see the unwelcome visitors picked out in the light streaming from the cottage doorway. Madame Julie caught her breath, and her dark eyes were wide and frightened.

Yet the newcomers were no more than a labourer and a village constable, good-humoured, red-faced people no less friendly and kindly than others of their type.

"There's a car on the woodland path, Mrs. Bourne." It was the constable who spoke.

"There aren't any lights on it. I know that's hardly a thoroughfare, but it's a public way and it seems to me it ought not to be there."

He was peering past the woman into the room with the bright-eyed curiosity of his calling, and the old woman turned and looked over her shoulder at the occupants of the room. If she was afraid, she did not show it. Her expression was calm, her voice matter-of-fact.

"It's the policeman, ma'am, about the car," she said.

"Oh. Is the owner in there? Then I'll step in for a bit if you don't mind, Mrs. Bourne. It's powerful cold out here."

Realizing that it would be dangerous to attempt to get rid of him too ostentatiously, the old woman stepped aside, and the man walked into the room. The labourer did not follow but shouted that he would wait outside.

The constable proved to be a rubicund soul with the naïveté of a child and a complete inability to make up his mind to leave the comfortable fire and light of Mrs. Bourne's room for the cold lanes without.

The tension in the room grew. Madame Julie was plainly terrified, and even the imperturbability of the old woman became hard and unreal as time went on.

Both Jennifer and Robin felt the strain growing almost unbearable, and Sacret himself, his nerves keyed to fever pitch, constantly betrayed his agitation by little nervous tricks which might have given him away to a more acute observer than the smiling village policeman.

The man hung about until he had satisfied himself that Madame Julie's driving license was in order, and then he seemed anxious to stay and make conversation.

At length, in despair, old Mary gave him a cup of tea and he sat on the edge of his chair sipping it happily.

The talk had become fitful, to say the least of it, and old Mary, anxious to divert her latest visitor's attention as much as possible from her other guests, switched on the wireless.

They heard the end of a vaudeville turn through the somewhat nasal loudspeaker, and no audience ever listened to a comedian in a less appreciative frame of mind.

Then the clock on the mantelpiece struck the hour, and at once the music faded and the academic voice of the announcer filled the little room.

"Before reading the news tonight I have here two SOS's and a police message."

The moment the announcement was made they realized what was coming, and a cold chill of alarm passed down the spines of at least five people seated round the fire. Mary made a half-movement to turn off the instrument but realized just in time that to do such a thing would call attention to the announcement rather than detract from it.

Meanwhile the impersonal voice continued.

"The police of the Metropolitan and East Kent districts ask the assistance of the public in tracing the whereabouts of James Wendon Sacret: height about five feet ten inches, thin build, greyish hair, grey eyes, heavily lined face, good teeth. When last seen this man was wearing a dark blue or grey suit, brown raincoat, and trilby hat. This man has escaped from Porchester Prison and is believed to be hiding in the eastern-counties district. Any person knowing the whereabouts of this man is asked to communicate at once with Scotland Yard, telephone Whitehall 1212, or any police station.

"This is the first SOS. Will Gladys West, last heard of at..."

Robin never heard that SOS. His eyes were fixed upon the village constable. The man sat, his cup half raised to his lips, staring thoughtfully upon the white face of the convict, and as Robin watched, the man seemed to take in every detail of his face and dress.

Then his eyes wandered to the peg in the corner where the brown raincoat hung beside Mrs. Bourne's old black plush coat.

The next moment the constable had risen to his feet. Madame Julie's nails dug into her palms as she watched him, and Jennifer was pale with apprehension.

The constable seemed to be sizing them up, and apparently he decided that if it came to a scrap they would be too many for him. He appeared to determine to use subterfuge, therefore, and turned towards the door.

"Well, thank you very much," he said in a tone that was only a thin imitation of his bluff greeting when he had first entered. "I think I'll be getting along if you don't mind. Thank you for the tea, Mrs. Bourne. Goodnight, all."

He opened the door and was gone.

Madame Julie sprang to her feet with an exclamation, but her husband silenced her. Moving cautiously over to the doorway, he peered out and, having satisfied himself that the constable had really gone, he turned back into the room.

Robin took the initiative. He had now definitely made up his mind upon the only course left to him. One good turn not only deserved but demanded another.

"You take the car, Sacret," he said. "That man'll go to the village. He'll phone up his superior anyway, and if he's a conscientious man he'll come back himself with volunteer assistants. I don't think he was sure of himself or he would have made the arrest on the spot and risked it. If you take the car and drive away from the village you've just got a chance. But you'll have to hurry or the roads will be blocked."

Madame Julie clung to her husband. "I'll go with you."

The man kissed her upturned face.

"No, my dear," he said gently. "Not this time. The risk is too great. Besides," he added softly, "he travels fastest who travels alone, you know."

This argument carried more weight with her than any other could have done, and, dry-eyed but white-lipped, she helped him into his coat and urged him to hurry.

They went with him down to the car. Just before he climbed in he turned to Robin.

"I'll remember this," he said. "If I win through this time I know what I'm out for, and if I succeed you will hear from me again. Good-bye and good luck to you both."

Robin shook the man's hand and then stepped back as Madame Julie flung herself into the arms of the husband she adored and kissed him passionately.

Robin left her staring out in the night, watching the disappearing tail light of the great car as it shot off down the lane in a wild bid for freedom.

When she returned to the cottage, Robin and Jennifer were standing on the hearthrug. They looked up as she came in, and there was something majestic in her grief and her courage.

"There's a second car," she said. "Not a very good one, but it'll carry us to a railway station at least. We must get to London."

She turned to Robin.

"Don't go to the police for twenty-four hours. Promise me that. If you see them you'll feel it's your duty to tell them the whole story. If you don't see them, that temptation will not arise. Besides, there's Jennifer to think of. We must hide her. I shall go back to my post in Sir Ferdinand Shawle's house. I feel I can do more there than anywhere else."

Robin looked at her squarely.

"Is Sir Ferdinand Shawle the Dealer, Madame Julie?" he asked softly.

The woman's pallor increased as she glanced nervously behind her, as though even here she were afraid of being overheard by that mysterious being whose power seemed to be so enormous.

"I—I don't know," she whispered. "Sometimes I wonder."

She was silent for a moment, but a minute or so later she had pulled herself together again.

"We must go quickly," she said. "At any moment those people may come, and they would question us and we might give something away."

Their adieux were quickly said, and less than five minutes later they were trundling through the narrow roads towards the nearest railway station in an old Morris-Cowley whose battered sides and halting engine told of hard work done in the past.

Robin drove, and Jennifer sat beside him, while Madame Julie leant forward in her seat at the back urging them on ever faster.

"You must hide, Jennifer," she said again as they turned on to the main road. "At all costs they must not get you back, my dear."

The girl hesitated.

"I want Robin to take me to my father," she said at last. "He can convince him that I'm perfectly all right, and with them both to look after me surely I should be all right."

They heard Madame Julie catch her breath, and when she spoke her tone was vehement.

"Oh, no, my dear!" she said. "Whatever you do, don't do that. Hide her somewhere else, Robin, somewhere safe."

Jennifer caught at the tone in the woman's voice.

"Why?" she said. "Madame Julie, you know something. You're keeping something back! What is it? Tell me—I implore you to tell me!"

Madame Julie hesitated. Then she seemed to make up her mind.

"D'you remember," she said softly, "when we first saw the pursuing car turning out of the nursing-home gates? They had the dashboard lights on then, and I saw the man who sat beside the driver quite clearly. I shall never forget his face—never."

Robin's jaw set in a hard line.

"I can guess what you're going to say, Madame Julie," he said. "And in that case I shall take your advice. My landlady has a married daughter living in the heart of Bayswater. Jennifer, I know, will be a welcome guest there, and no one will ever find her."

"But I insist that you tell me."

Jennifer's voice had a ring of command in its childish depths.

"I insist," she repeated. "Who sat beside the driver in the pursuing car, Madame Julie? Whom did you see?"

Still Madame Julie hesitated, but at length, as the girl insisted, she spoke, and her voice was very low and unmistakably severe.

"Jennifer, my dear, you must be very brave and face this thing. It was your father, Sir Henry Fern."

CHAPTER TWENTY-ONE
THE MAN OF POWER

"I tell you, Sir Ferdinand, this is serious. Crupiner blundered, and blundered badly."

Nelson Ash leant across the desk in Sir Ferdinand Shawle's luxurious office and spoke forcefully. There was an unwonted touch of colour in his white face, and his indeterminate eyes had something in their depths that might almost have been fear.

Sir Ferdinand Shawle leant back in his chair and surveyed his visitor thoughtfully. He was not a man who showed emotion, and his eyes were cold and hard.

Ash went on, his high voice sounding even more reedy than usual in his indignation.

"Think of it," he continued. "He locked that young blackguard Grey in a room next the robing room of the theatre, not realizing that the youngster might overpower his reprobate surgeon, and then stood calmly by while the boy recognized her and carried her off under his very nose.

"He had assistants, though, and I don't think they were the police. We must go into that.

"Then there was Crupiner's ridiculous story of the escape across the marsh. Why, the fool had to be pulled out by a police van searching for an escaped convict and very nearly had a scrap with them. They were led away by marsh lights. I think that fellow Crupiner loses his head.

"Now think of it," he went on with animation. "Consider the position. The girl's gone, and the boy with her. They may get married at any moment. I expect to hear that the police have raided the nursing home any second now. What's the matter with you, man? You ought to be off your head with anxiety."

Sir Ferdinand Shawle smiled grimly.

"Don't worry, Ash," he said. "Grey has not gone to the police, and Jennifer has not gone to her father. And that puts us onto a rather interesting point. I believe those young people have found out about the box. I believe they're after it. Moreover, I know where they are."

Ash looked at him incredulously.

Sir Ferdinand nodded.

"Mrs. Phipps, Robin Grey's landlady, has a married daughter, and I rather fancy that it is there that our two youngsters are hiding. Very well, let them stay. I have a rather clever intelligence system of my own devising and I rather fancy that we can make use of this pair. Let them go after the box. Let us watch, and then at the psychological moment step in and get it. D'you see where that puts us? Completely on the top and out of the Dealer's clutches for ever."

Ash stood looking at the other man, a mixture of admiration and surprise on his strange, unhandsome face.

"I think I've always underestimated you, Sir Ferdinand," he said at last. "I was not going to bring up the subject of the Dealer, but since you raise it, I think I may mention a fact that has occurred to me. Since Bourbon disappeared, our ranks have become thinned. There are only four of us now. One of those four is the man who holds the others in such complete submission.

"Shawle, suppose that the Dealer were dead. Suppose that, unknown to us, this burden had been lifted.

"Think of it," he went on quickly. "Since Bourbon vanished no one has heard from the Dealer, so far as we know. Suppose this ghastly business were like a railway train that goes on for a little after its driver is dead. Suppose that, without realizing it, we were all free men. After all, who is left? You, I, Caithby Fisher, Sir Henry Fern."

A strange expression had come into Sir Ferdinand's eyes. It almost seemed as though the proffered relief had already been seized by that queer, unemotional mind.

"Ash," he said hoarsely, "that's a great thought, but a dangerous one."

"Well"—the other man was frankly defiant—"why not? It is a point to be considered. Once we had the box, at least we should be safe. And—who knows?—perhaps it may be within our grasp. None of us has attempted even to get hold of it before because, frankly, we were afraid of the Dealer, but with the Dealer out of the way, what is there to stop us?"

Sir Ferdinand Shawle rose from his seat and walked slowly up and down. His feet sank into the thick pile of the carpet. When he spoke, it was almost as though he were chatting to himself.

"Caithby Fisher and Sir Henry Fern," he said aloud. "Both men of unexpected powers and resource."

He looked at Ash sharply.

"Fern's love for his child," he said—"that's always struck you as being perfectly genuine, hasn't it? As his business partner, you know him better than I do."

Ash hesitated.

"It's queer you should ask me that," he said. "It's a subject that has been worrying me for some time. Sir Henry Fern has a dual personality. There are times when he seems the most gentle, natural father in the world, but there are others when I have doubted his sincerity. He has strange, sullen moods which last for days, and those trips abroad that he is supposed to make for the firm—I may be indiscreet in saying so, Shawle, but I sometimes wonder if he ever leaves the country."

Sir Ferdinand swept aside these revelations with a gesture: "Even so," he said, "Sir Henry Fern is not the type of which men like the Dealer are made.

"Then there's Fisher. Caithby Fisher is a weird personality. In that crooked little body there hides a most courageous spirit and a mind as warped as the body itself. I wonder... If what you suggest were only true, Ash, if the Dealer were out of our way, life would be very different."

He was interrupted by the ringing of the phone on his table. He picked up the instrument casually and, after a moment's conversation, turned to his visitor.

"It's for you, Ash," he said. "Personal call."

The other man looked surprised. "I didn't know anyone knew I was here," he said and took the instrument from his host's hand.

As he listened, an extraordinary change passed over his face. Every tinge of colour seemed to vanish, his jaw dropped, and his eyes widened.

"A message?" he said huskily. "Where? Under the door? My God, Shawle, look!"

He dropped the instrument and turned towards the heavily curtained door on the other side of the room. Darting over, he swept the hanging aside, and there on the floor, projecting a little into the room, lay an envelope.

Sir Ferdinand Shawle, who had had some experience of these mysterious phone messages, hurried after his friend, nearly as white as the paper itself.

"The Dealer?" he inquired.

Ash nodded. He was shaking, and his pale, contorted face was not a pleasant sight to see. The man had abject fear written in every line of his countenance.

"Yes," he said hastily. "He said 'under the door.' "

Sir Ferdinand snatched up the envelope and threw the door open.

Save for an inoffensive-looking clerk who came hurrying down the corridor, it was empty.

Shawle stopped the man.

"Wilkinson, has any stranger been down this corridor this morning?"

"Why, no, sir. Certainly not, sir."

The young man looked scandalized.

"I haven't left my desk by the half-glass door all the morning. I should have seen anyone who passed."

"I see. Thank you, Wilkinson."

Sir Ferdinand went back into the room and with trembling fingers tore open the mysterious note. The message consisted of only a few words:

"These private conferences will do you no good, my friends. Remember the sad story of the mouse who took the sleeping cat for dead. THE DEALER."

The note dropped from the man's nerveless fingers.

Ash pounced upon it and read it through.

Sir Ferdinand Shawle spoke the words which must have been uppermost in his mind:

"Sir Henry Fern or Caithby Fisher ... which?"

Ash echoed the last word, his voice barely rising above a whisper:

"Which?"

CHAPTER TWENTY-TWO
POLICE TRAIL

"Ah, Inspector, will you sit down? It was very kind of you to come."

The frail elderly lady in the stiff grey silk dress and the priceless lace fichu swathed round her bent shoulders held out one tiny blue-veined hand for Inspector Whybrow to take.

He touched it with his own and accepted her invitation to be seated.

When he had first made up his mind to comply with Miss Alice Bourbon's request that he should call on her at her house in Belgravia, he had somehow not expected Rex Bourbon's sister to have such a definite personality, or the air of gracious elegance which would have distinguished any duchess.

He judged her to be little more than sixty, a good twenty years older than her brother, but in spite of all the affectations and helplessness of a woman of her class and era she had nevertheless something strong and determinate in her bright, very blue eyes and her sharp, well-chiselled features.

She sat down opposite him in one of the brocaded rosewood chairs.

"You have nothing to tell me about my poor brother yet?" Her eyes watched his face anxiously.

He shook his head.

"No, madam, I'm afraid I haven't. I told you," he went on gently, "that on the receipt of any information at all concerning your brother we would communicate with you immediately.

"I'm a very busy man, Miss Bourbon," he went on with just a touch of reproach in his kindly voice, "and although I appreciate your concern at the continued absence of your brother I'm afraid I shouldn't have come down here this morning if in your telephone message you had not promised me something in the nature of a revelation. All I can tell you is that we're doing everything that can possibly be done in our efforts to trace Mr. Rex Bourbon.

"As far as we know, he left his home about five o'clock on the evening of the seventeenth and has not been heard of since."

He glanced up and was surprised to see a grim little smile playing round her mouth.

"Don't be afraid, Inspector," she said. "I'm not quite a foolish old woman who is simply out to waste your time, although I may look like one. My brother, as you know, is a good deal younger than I am, and, although we've drifted apart in later years, when he was a boy and a young man I looked after him very much as a mother might have done.

"Under the will of an uncle we both came into considerable fortunes, his larger than mine. Since his disappearance I have made it my business to go into his affairs.

"There's no need to look shocked, Inspector," she added briskly, and the old detective got a glimpse of the forthright personality which made her bank manager and her agents respect Miss Bourbon's temerity and determination.

"I've gone through all his private papers," she went on calmly. "You may think I've taken this step rather hurriedly, but, although neither a fool nor a sentimentalist, Inspector,

I am a person of strong instincts, and I have an unshakable conviction that my brother is dead.

"You can regard this as old woman's chatter if you like, but the fact remains that I myself, being convinced of his death, am particularly anxious to know the cause of it, so that if there should be any person in this world who is to blame, that person may be mercilessly punished."

A gleam of ferocity had appeared in the blue eyes, and the Inspector reflected that he would not like to cross this indomitable old lady if it could be helped.

She sat regarding him coldly, no trace of emotion on her finely chiselled face.

"In the course of my investigations," she went on, her clear businesslike voice sounding odd in the delicate femininity of her surroundings, "I have made one or two interesting discoveries. My brother was very near to financial ruin when he disappeared, so near that I should not be surprised—although naturally such a discovery would shock me considerably—if I learned he had committed suicide.

"Moreover," she went on, her voice sinking, "I have discovered, and I have got documents to prove, that during the last ten years he had been bled white by a firm whose name would astound you were I to tell it.

"I do not wish to speak too strongly, Inspector, and I know enough about the law of libel to realize that I am putting myself in a delicate position by saying this much to you, but I want to give you every assistance in your search for my brother, and I think it is only right to tell you that from information which I hold I have formed the opinion that it is a corpse for which you must seek.

"My brother either committed suicide or was murdered. The documents which I hold show a record of something suspiciously like blackmail. My brother may have been killed when, driven to desperation, he threatened to make public the whole story of his dwindling fortunes. Or he may have died by his own hand, but in that case I assure you, Inspector, there are men in London today who are as guilty of his death as if they had struck him down with their own hands."

The inspector, listening to this peroration, could not help but be impressed by the almost passionate sincerity in the old lady's voice.

Moreover, her last announcement had interested him considerably.

He hesitated and then embarked upon the first of the unprofessional things which were to mark that strange day's adventures.

"Miss Bourbon," he said, "just for a moment, I wonder if you could forget that I am a police officer and regard me as a professional man in whose discretion you can trust? Let me know the name of this firm of whom you speak, and I promise you that you will never regret your confidence."

She hesitated, and he saw her looking at him closely, sizing him up, her shrewd blue eyes fixed thoughtfully upon his face.

"Inspector," she said softly, "have you ever heard of a man called Sir Henry Fern?"

Whybrow's wooden face did not move a muscle, but the old woman was not to be deceived.

"I see you have," she said. "Well, Inspector, there are documents among my brother's papers which prove that during the past ten years he has paid over eighty thousand pounds to the firm of which Sir Henry Fern is the head, and there is absolutely nothing to show that he ever obtained anything in return. Except, of course," she added, significantly, "silence."

Some minutes later the inspector rose to take his leave. The quiet voice with its damning accusation was still ringing in his ears.

"Of course," he said, "should the question ever arise, the documents could be examined by our own experts?"

"The documents can be examined by anyone," she said. "They are in a safe deposit at the moment, pending further developments. Good-bye, Inspector. Thank you for coming. I shall hold you to your promise and trust to your discretion."

The inspector took her hand.

"You won't be disappointed, madam," he said. "The information you have given me is very valuable and may lead to the unravelling of one of the most extraordinary stories of crime which has ever been told."

As he drove back to the Yard he remained deep in thought. Gradually the net seemed to be closing round white-haired, good-tempered-looking Sir Henry Fern. So far there was nothing definite, but the circumstantial evidence was piling up.

Inspector Whybrow was puzzled. Never had his instincts and his intellect been so much at variance. His brain told him that even if the powerful machinery of the Yard could not fix the guilt of at least one murder upon Sir Henry Fern's shoulders, the man was assuredly responsible.

Yet his instincts told him that Sir Henry was more sinned against than sinning. His natural impulse was to trust, even to like, the man. He could not understand it.

On reaching the Yard he hurried up to his room. For days now he had been expecting a cable from the Canadian police. As his eye lighted upon his desk his face cleared. There was the familiar form spread out to catch his eye when he came in.

As he read the crudely printed lines his satisfaction grew:

"PLAYBILL BELIEVED LOCATED, COPY COMING FIRST MAIL. SANDERSON."

Whybrow screwed up the message and hurled it into the fireplace. That was that, then. Soon that avenue would be explored.

He turned to the other documents on his desk that had accumulated during his two-hour absence.

One of them caught his eye, and he pounced upon it. It was a neatly typed copy of a letter which had come to him from the Post Office branch of the C. I. D.

It is generally known that when the police are watching a suspected person his correspondence is examined before being delivered at his door. This is usually done unostentatiously, and very often the suspect is completely unaware of such surveillance.

The letter which the inspector held was a copy of one which had been delivered to Sir Henry Fern that morning. For days now all his mail had been searched, but this was the first missive which the careful watchers at the other end had thought fit to send on to the inspector.

"Dear Fern," it began, *"I am anxious to have a word or two with you in private somewhere soon. Acting on the instructions of our mutual correspondent, I am therefore writing to make an appointment with you, as I feel there are several points which we ought to discuss. As I know you will agree with me that it would not be advisable for us to meet openly either at my house or yours at the present time, I have decided that the lounge of the De Rigueur Hotel, at four o'clock tomorrow afternoon, the 20th, will meet our purpose.*

"As you have probably heard, this place is already in the hands of the receivers and is closing its doors early next week.

"I hear from the City that they have done little or no business since they opened, and therefore we shall be, I imagine, completely alone.

"Sincerely,
"CAITHBY FISHER."

The inspector read the message through slowly for the second time. Then he glanced thoughtfully at the calendar on the wall opposite him.

A big red "20" glared back at him from the printed page.

"Four o'clock at the De Rigueur. … Caithby Fisher, the head of Armaments, Limited."

He threw the letter down upon the desk again. There was a chance, of course, that it referred to an ordinary business appointment which had nothing to do with the dark matters which Whybrow was investigating.

But there was an undercurrent of command in the tone of the note which put that idea out of the inspector's mind.

He thrust the copy into his private file and glanced up at the clock. It was now five minutes to two. In an hour and a half, he decided, he would set out for the De Rigueur.

For some moments he toyed with the idea of persuading Mowbray to go along with him, but decided against it. After all, it was something of a wild-goose chase.

Caithby Fisher was a new angle on the case as far as he was concerned. He wondered how many more important men would be found to be linked up with the mysterious business.

Wise old man that he was, however, he put the matter from his mind until it was time to act.

Later on in the afternoon, Detective Sergeant Dennistoun, a keen-eyed, red-headed junior of whom great things were expected, dropped in for a chat.

"We can't locate that fellow Sacret," he said. "We had a very likely call from a local bobby down on the east coast. I believe they had some sort of a chase, but it didn't amount to anything. I'm working on the wife angle at the moment. I've been reading up the trial, and if we can only trace that woman we shall find him. I'm sure of it. Still, he's giving us a run for our money."

"Poor devil," said Inspector Whybrow unprofessionally, and added as he saw the shocked expression on the younger man's face, "When you get as old as I am, my lad, you'll find yourself being sorry for people more often than not. There's something terrific about the efficiency of the Yard. We always win in the end."

"I'm glad to hear it. Any news of the Bellew murderer?"

Dennistoun could not resist the dig, and had the satisfaction of seeing his senior's face grow a shade more rubicund.

"No," said Inspector Whybrow. "Not yet. But we'll get him in the end. We always do."

"I wish I felt as sanguine as you do about our friend the convict."

Dennistoun went out grinning, and Inspector Whybrow reached for his hat.

As he went down the staircase to the street he reflected that he was growing old. Personal considerations, he knew, should never enter into business, but the thing that was really worrying him more than his professional reputation or anything else was the fate of his young friend Robin Grey, of whom he had heard nothing for too long.

Much too long, he decided, as he strode down the pavement, and there was a gloomy, worried expression at the back of his eyes.

CHAPTER TWENTY-THREE
THE INCREDIBLE OCCURS

"Perhaps you'd care to sit over here, sir? You'll be well out of a draught."

The head waiter conducted his guest across the vast empty lounge, which for all its magnificence was badly lit and somehow very forlorn.

The Hotel De Rigueur had been one of the most sensational failures of recent speculative business. A huge company had been floated to pay for its site, its ornate steel and granite facade, its thousand bedrooms, its gilded salons, and its stupendous opening night, but the public had not responded and the shareholders had lost their money.

There were many reasons given for the fiasco. Some blamed the slump, others the vicinity, and some more superstitious spoke of the bad luck which had attended it from the day a workman had broken his neck in falling from a scaffolding during its erection.

But the fact remained that the place had not caught on, the receivers had stepped in, and within a week the magnificent doors were to be closed to the public.

Save for the waiter and the rather haggard but still handsome-looking old man who followed him, the lounge was empty.

Sir Henry Fern allowed himself to be settled in a corner protected by a huge draught screen and a modernistic pot of giant flowers.

The waiter went away, his lank drooping form looking singularly lonely and pathetic as it traversed this wealth of unwanted splendour.

But Sir Henry Fern had no thought for his surroundings. His eyes were fixed on the gilt clock over the ornate fireplace, and his heart was beating uncomfortably fast.

On the other side of the screen, and arranged in a position from which he could see the face of the old man reflected in a mirror opposite, as well as overhear anything he might say, Inspector Whybrow also waited.

He was a little conscious of the lack of dignity of his present position, but his profession, he reflected gloomily, was not a dignified one, and if justice was to be served he knew from experience that it was useless to be too squeamish.

Sir Henry Fern made an interesting study. He sat hunched up, his arms resting upon the table in front of him, his head bowed. He had grown much whiter in the past two weeks, and the inspector was surprised to see that he looked shrunken. His clothes hung upon him loosely, and there were deep circles beneath his eyes.

While he was waiting, the policeman had time to admire Caithby Fisher's choice of a rendezvous. Had he not seen the letter and made his arrangements with the waiter, no one might ever have known of this strange meeting.

His attention was distracted by a little commotion at the far end of the room as a figure in a wheeled chair appeared in the doorway.

The hunchback was even more repellent swinging along in his mobile little chair, a grey plaid rug tucked well round his knees, than he had ever seemed before, and Whybrow was conscious of a sense of dislike as he caught sight of him.

On catching sight of Sir Henry the cripple had waved the head waiter aside and now came speeding up the aisle, one hand outstretched.

He settled himself at the table, and Whybrow was irritated to find that the position he had taken hindered the inspector's view of Sir Henry's face.

Both men were now reflected in the mirror, but only fitfully as they moved or bent closer to speak more confidentially.

From where he sat, however, their conversation was easily overheard.

The cripple seemed in excellent spirits. He began with a torrent of small talk about the weather, the hotel, and everything else, but as soon as the waiter had brought them coffee and each man had lighted a cigar, the talk suddenly took a more interesting turn.

"You have news for me from the Dealer?"

It was Sir Henry who spoke, and his voice was colourless with the apathy of one who already has had too much to bear.

"Well"—the hunchback spread out his gnarled hands, and his dry voice sank a tone or so lower—"in a way, yes. The Dealer is particularly anxious about the fate of Rex Bourbon, who, as you may know, disappeared some few days ago. He thought you might know something."

Sir Henry sat up with what the inspector felt sure was a genuine start of surprise.

"I? Why on earth should *I* know?"

The cripple bent nearer.

"You've had no inquiries? No interviews with relations, friends, secretaries? No one has come to your office?"

"No one. Why should they? I didn't know Bourbon very well, you know."

Sir Henry did not seem to be at all aware that he was treading on dangerous ground, and the listening inspector was conscious of a sense of bewilderment. Either Sir Henry Fern was a remarkable actor or the accusations which Rex Bourbon's sister had made against him only that morning were monstrously untrue.

"I see."

The man in the wheeled chair seemed satisfied.

"I am sure the Dealer will be interested."

A convulsive shudder went through the older man, and neither his companion nor the listening inspector was prepared for the change which came over him.

"The Dealer!" he burst out, raising his voice unconsciously in his exasperation. "I can't stand it any longer, Fisher! Death, imprisonment, torture, anything is better than the life I'm leading now. I'm at the end of my tether."

The cripple's palm was laid over his hand, and Whybrow caught the whispered words of warning.

"Hold your tongue, you fool. Not so loud. D'you realize what you're saying?"

Sir Henry shrugged his shoulders.

"I have nothing to hide," he said, lowering his voice obediently. "I'm just finished, that's all. Do you know, Fisher, there's only one thing I care about in this world, and that's my daughter? And they've got her, the fiends! They've driven her out of her mind. By some devilment which I don't pretend to understand, that sweet lovely child has become—become——"

His voice faltered, and he did not finish the sentence.

"I can't even see her now," he went on pathetically after a pause. "They say she's too ill for me to see her. They say the sight of me might so incense her that I should ruin the chances of her ever getting well again. I tell you I'm helpless. I don't know what to do. I think I shall go mad."

"Pull yourself together, Fern."

There was something menacing in the cripple's tone, some underlying power which made the inspector stare hard at his reflection in the mirror. In his long experience he had heard that tone once or twice before, and it had always boded trouble.

After remaining silent for some moments Sir Henry got his voice under control and began to speak in the soft, penetrating monotone of one who has been driven to the last verge of despair.

"I'm through with it, Fisher," he said. "Death may be better than disgrace, but this life is unendurable. To go on living in my present circumstances is more than I can face."

"Suicide? Surely not."

Whybrow scarcely heard the whispered suggestion, but it struck him that there was a faint tinge of hope in the tone.

The baronet's reply was unexpected. He laughed savagely.

"No," he said. "I'm not a coward—or at least not that sort of a coward. I'm going to the police with all I know of the story. Let the whole thing come out, and if the Dealer gets me, then he does. But at any rate my girl will be safe. She'll be able to marry the man she loves, if they haven't half killed her already. This thing's got to stop, Fisher, and the sooner the better."

The cripple leant back in his chair, and for the first time the inspector got a clear glimpse of his face in the mirror. It was some distance away from him, and the features were slightly blurred, and also the light was not good. But he saw enough to put him on the alert.

The cripple was regarding the man opposite him with an intensity that was terrifying, and when at last he spoke his voice was redolent with that same forceful quality which had so startled the inspector before.

"Fern, you're a fool," he said. "A dangerous fool."

Once again the old baronet laughed.

"The results may be the same, but your diagnosis is wrong, Fisher," he said. "I'm a desperate man. Even a worm turns, you know. I've been pretty much of a coward in my time, but that was for the sake of my girl, my poor Jenny. But now they've driven me too far. I'm being harried to death. But that fiend shan't get me and live. I'll put him where he belongs, if it's the last thing I do."

The cripple continued to sit motionless in his chair, his lids drawn down over his eyes, his chin resting upon his pigeon breast.

"Fern," he said, "can you guess who the Dealer is?"

There was something so uncanny in his tone, something so soft and yet so sinister, that at the risk of giving himself away the inspector leant further back in his chair and peered through the crack between the screen and the wall.

He was now barely a couple of feet away from the cripple's right side, and his attention was arrested immediately by a stealthy movement of the man's right hand, which was hidden from his companion's sight by the ledge of the table.

Meanwhile Sir Henry, his blue eyes distended and his lips drawn back, sat staring at the evil creature before him.

"You!" he said thickly. "You are——"

"Yes, my friend. Interesting, isn't it? Do you know you are the first person with whom I have ever shared this fascinating confidence?"

The menace in his tone was unbelievable, and as he spoke the man leant forward out of his chair and the thing he held in his right hand came slowly into sight from the crack in the screen.

The inspector saw and recognized it just as the final threat left the twisted lips.

"How sad that you will never be able to betray my confidence, Sir Henry."

Inspector Whybrow sprang to his feet and sent the screen crashing to the ground with one lion-like movement. A moment later his great hand descended upon the weapon which the cripple had drawn and snatched it from his grasp.

The whole thing happened so swiftly that both men were taken completely off their guard. The inspector held the thing he had taken at arm's length. He knew well enough not to bring it anywhere within range of his mouth or nostrils.

It was a syringe, a delicate glass affair fitted with a plunger and a tiny spray and half filled with a colourless liquid.

At the first glimpse, Whybrow guessed what it was. The practice of spraying poison of the prussic acid or cyanide variety into the mouth and nostrils of an unsuspecting victim was a form of crime with which the inspector was becoming too familiar.

Coma, followed by death, would, he knew, be almost certain, and it would take an astute doctor some time to locate the cause.

These things raced through his mind, however, and he had no time for further consideration, for, before the sound of the crash had brought the few hotel servants in the vicinity hurrying to the scene, the first incredible incident occurred.

The man in the cripple's chair became suddenly galvanized into action. His arm shot out, and he vaulted across the table onto the parquet floor.

The inspector felt his scalp rising. If the man had vanished into thin air, Whybrow would not have been more surprised.

On reaching the ground, Caithby Fisher fled.

The vast dim lounge, peopled so gloomily by its empty chairs, seemed to have become a place of fantasy as the figure sped down the wide strip of carpet to the open doors in the main vestibule.

As he ran, an extraordinary change took place in the twisted frame. The shoulders straightened, the legs seemed to grow longer, and, although the head was still hunched upon the shoulders, and the face and hair were those of Caithby Fisher, there was something unreal about him, a creature from another world or a nightmare.

The inspector rushed after him, but he was gone. As the policeman reached the vestibule, he caught a glimpse of the grotesque fugitive disappearing down the steps into the crowded street.

When he reached the pavement, there was no sign of the man. A swiftly moving limousine threaded its way in and out of the traffic, but there was no way of telling whether its passenger was the man he sought.

The inspector's first feeling was one of frank astonishment. He was more than bewildered. His breath had been taken away literally. But then, as his sane common sense gradually reasserted itself, his next reaction was one of intense anger.

The man he most wanted to lay hands upon in all the world had disappeared from under his very nose.

The whole thing was ridiculous and absurd. He knew that the bare facts set down on an official form would look like a fairy tale. And yet it had happened. He had seen it with his own eyes.

He sent an excited hotel servant to fetch Sir Henry and then settled himself at the telephone in the manager's office and began to give clear if slightly irritable orders to minions at the other end of the wire.

There was much to be done. Statements would have to be taken from all sorts of people who might have seen the flying figure; someone would have to take charge of Sir Henry; while he himself must proceed at once to the home of the chairman of Armaments Limited.

It was as he came out of the manager's office that the second bewildering incident occurred, the thing that made the inspector doubt his own sanity for days to come.

The first person he saw in the vestibule was his own detective-sergeant, Mayhew, an intelligent officer with whom he usually worked. The man came up to him eagerly.

"I'm glad I found you, sir," he said. "I didn't like to phone you in case you hadn't given your name to the people here, and it might be inconvenient if they disturbed you. An important development, sir. Inspector Mowbray feels you ought to hear about it at once. The body of Caithby Fisher, the chairman of Armaments Limited, has just been taken from the river at Chelsea. Seems to have floated down from some point considerably higher up. It's been in the mortuary since eleven o'clock this morning, but he's only just been identified. Good heavens, sir, what's the matter?"

Inspector Whybrow was staring at his subordinate, his mouth hanging open, his bright eyes wide and incredulous.

"Caithby Fisher taken from the river? Are you sure? Who identified him? What evidence have you got?"

Sergeant Mayhew bridled.

"His doctor, Sir Humphrey Peeler, has seen the body. So has his personal valet, name of Reith. They both swear to him. He's not a difficult person to identify, sir. He's a cripple."

Inspector Whybrow passed a shaking hand over his damp forehead.

"How long had the body been in the water before it was discovered?"

"I'm not quite sure, sir, but in the opinion of two doctors it couldn't have been less than twenty-four hours and not more than forty. What's the matter, sir? Anything up?"

CHAPTER TWENTY-FOUR
INSPECTOR WHYBROW WONDERS

"Well, Whybrow, I hope you're convinced it really is Fisher. You've seen the body, you've seen the doctors. There doesn't seem any avenue of doubt to me."

Inspector Mowbray glanced across the famous windowless room in the old house behind the great offices of Armaments, Limited, and spoke somewhat dryly to his old friend, who stood by the fireplace looking more like a Scotch terrier than ever, his head slightly on one side and his eyes puzzled beneath their shaggy brows.

Inspector Whybrow passed his stubby fingers through his short grey hair.

"Oh I admit it, I admit it," he said testily. "I'm not an obstinate fool. But I tell you, Mowbray, I've had a shock. When your own eyes deceive you, the feeling is most unpleasant. Whoever the man talking to Sir Henry was, his acting was magnificent.

"Of course," he went on, speaking more to convince himself than to explain to the other man, "I didn't know Fisher personally. I'd seen him once or twice, but that was all. Still, the illusion was perfect as far as I was concerned, and, of course, the extraordinary thing is that Sir Henry seemed to be satisfied also.

"I tell you, Mowbray, when that fellow sprang out of his chair and raced across the entrance lounge, I felt the hair rising on my scalp, and I thought my knees were going to give way. I haven't had such an experience, not in thirty years."

Mowbray was inclined to be amused, but he tactfully refrained from showing it.

"Well, we're getting along gradually," he said, deliberately ignoring the slightly comic figure of bewilderment which the older man presented. "We've established the fact that Fisher was shot before his body entered the water. He had only been missing twenty-four hours, and his valet does not seem to have considered it worth while to notify the police of his disappearance. Apparently he was in the habit of going off by himself like this from time to time.

"I'm holding that man Reith on suspicion, by the way. He doesn't seem to have been very fond of his master. He's a fine-looking chap, but bone from the neck up."

"Oh, Reith wasn't in this."

Inspector Whybrow spoke with conviction.

"We're up against something much more important than Reith could ever account for. You'll find, Mowbray, that this murder is part and parcel of all the others. As soon as Sir Henry can talk we'll have the whole story out of him. I rather fancy we've got our hands on the right man at last. These lunatics are very clever sometimes."

Inspector Mowbray considered this suggestion.

"I must admit the question of insanity had not crossed my mind," he said. "But of course the girl, his daughter, is not normal, or she wouldn't be where she is. You've got Sir Henry at his own house, I hear?"

Inspector Whybrow seated himself on the edge of the shining table which filled the centre of the room, and glanced round the panelled walls before replying.

"Yes," he said at last. "I didn't want too much publicity until we get the whole thing straightened out. If we arrest a man of his calibre before we are ready to formulate the charge in its entirety, we shall have the press howling at our heels, and the others involved in this business will get clear.

"Sir Henry's an old man, Mowbray," he added, "and if I had a shock this afternoon, his must have been trebly strong. I saw him afterwards when he recovered consciousness, and I should have called him a maniac. He's quite safe, however. There's a strong police guard in his house and three good doctors in attendance, Sir Gordon Woodthorpe among them. He tells me we can't hope to question the man for at least another twenty-four hours, and then, my boy, we shall get one or two revelations."

He mopped his brow vigorously.

"I shall be glad of it. It's getting on my nerves."

There was no doubt of the truth of this statement, but Mowbray's comments were cut short by the sudden arrival of Detective Sergeant Verity, the young expert whom Mowbray had brought down from the Yard to assist in the search for evidence among Caithby Fisher's papers.

He was an eager, plumpish youngster whose round face and brown eyes were at the moment alight with excitement.

"I say, sir," he said explosively, "I believe I've stumbled on something really interesting."

He planked an old brown-paper file down upon the table as he spoke, and went on as the older men gathered round him:

"I found this in a most ingeniously hidden little safe built into the wall above the head of the bed. No one seemed to know of it, and even Reith seemed flabbergasted when he saw it. I haven't examined these very closely, but I've seen enough to know we've got hold of something really interesting. There's enough evidence here to show that Fisher was in the Camden Gun Scandal —in fact, he and another man seem to have engineered the whole thing."

"The Camden Gun Scandal?"

The words dropped from Inspector Mowbray's lips involuntarily.

Less than eighteen months before, all England had been stirred by the dramatic discovery that armaments were being shipped out of England for the ultimate use of her enemies. Public feeling had run high, and although Scotland Yard had succeeded in tracing and bringing to justice all those immediately concerned, they had not been able to lay hands upon the actual instigators of the affair.

Eventually the hue and cry had died down, but hitherto there had remained a blank space in the secret documents at Scotland Yard which related to the crime.

Whybrow pounced on the papers. He was no expert, but his experienced eye told him that Verity had not been exaggerating. Here indeed was evidence which would have sent Fisher to prison had he not at that moment been lying, a terrible, mangled, shapeless thing, in the mortuary in Seeker Street.

"But that's not all," Verity continued. "D'you see this name, sir?"

He turned to Mowbray as he spoke, and the other inspector leant forward.

"If Fisher is dead," the younger man continued, "at least we can get his colleague. Look, here it is, the whole thing. Just imagine what a great K. C. could make of a charge like that!"

"Sir Henry Fern?" said Whybrow quickly.

Verity looked at him blankly.

"Why, no, sir," he said. "This is a very different person."

"Sir Ferdinand Shawle!"

It was Mowbray who spoke, and there was an expression of frank bewilderment on his face, for there, lying before him on the table, was evidence which involved the famous banker in probably the greatest scandal of post-war years.

Old Whybrow sat down in the green leather armchair in which Madame Julie had listened trembling to the little hunchback's questions only a few days before.

"Well, this beats the band," he said. "This case is getting me out of my depth. Perhaps they're all in it," he added, brightening.

But Verity shook his head.

"No, sir. There's no other name. There's nothing here even to suggest that Sir Henry knew anything about the Camden case."

Inspector Mowbray had become brisk and businesslike.

"Well, at any rate," he said, "there's enough evidence in our hands to send Sir Ferdinand to prison. Shall we pull him in, Whybrow? What do you say?"

The elder man held up his hand.

"I don't think so. In my opinion, Mowbray, our best plan is to keep him under strict surveillance and wait. First we must get Sir Henry's story, and then I shall get that information from the Canadian police that I've been waiting for so long. There's more of value there than you dream of, Mowbray. I'm certain of it."

His colleague shrugged his shoulders and smiled. He had a very real opinion of Whybrow's gifts, not least among which was a sort of intuition which made him often place his finger unerringly upon the truth even when it seemed the most unlikely thing in the world.

At the moment, however, he was inclined to be skeptical.

"I don't want to damp your ardour, Jack," he said, grinning, "but I must say the faith you're putting in that dirty bit of paper you found by the telephone in Fern's office the night we had the spoof call from young Grey strikes me as being a bit trusting. You're not beginning to put your faith in magic in your old age, are you?"

Whybrow looked at him gravely, and the expression in the bright blue eyes was so serious that for a moment even Mowbray was silenced.

"The longer I live," said Inspector Whybrow solemnly, "the more remarkable human nature seems to become. When I was a lad about Verity's age"—he smiled at the boy with that easy friendliness which earned him his popularity at the Yard—"when I was a kid," he repeated, "it seemed to me that there were only half a dozen crimes in the world, only two or three dozen types of men and women, and that Scotland Yard knew all about the lot.

"But since I've grown older, and especially since my experience in the lounge of the De Rigueur this afternoon, I'm beginning to wonder if the phases of human nature are not as many as the stars in the sky.

"And as for that spoof call from Grey, as you call it, Mowbray, I tell you I recognized that boy's voice on the phone, and if any of these swine has murdered him, I'll have 'em strung up and watch the execution myself with pleasure."

Mowbray grunted, and Verity shot a swift glance at his superior, his brown eyes alight with interest. "The Old Man" was definitely rattled, he told his friend Sergeant Ferguson afterwards, and there was a vigorous, not to say vindictive, case brewing against someone. He was sure of it.

Chapter Twenty-Five
In Hiding

"Robin, I feel I ought to get to Daddy. I've got a sort of feeling that he's in serious trouble."

Jennifer spoke hesitantly. She was kneeling on the hearthrug in the pleasant little front room of the flat owned by Mrs. Phipps's married daughter in Bayswater. The girl looked very frail and white after the terrifying experiences of the past few days. There were dark rings under her eyes, and her lips were tremulous.

The lights were low in the little room, and Robin stood by the side of the window well out of sight of the street but in a position from which he could peer through a crack in the blind at the wet pavements below.

In the past day or so he seemed to have become older. The bland expression had faded from his face, his eyes were hard and anxious, and the line of his jaw had become grim and determined.

"Not yet, Jennifer," he said softly. "Not yet, my dear. We're not out of the wood by any means yet."

The girl looked up at him. Her eyes were grave and steady.

"Robin," she said at last, "you love me, don't you?"

Quick colour came into the boy's face.

"Oh, my dear," he said helplessly, "you know I do."

She slipped her hand into his, a simple gesture of such complete confidence that he felt as though his heart must burst.

"Why don't you tell me the truth, then?"

The calm, childlike eyes were still peering into his own.

"You think that Daddy is my enemy, don't you? I mean, you think that he's the—the Dealer that Madame Julie spoke about? Oh, Robin, why don't you tell me the truth?"

The boy sat down in the old basket chair before the fire, and, because it seemed the most natural thing in the world to do, drew the girl close to him so that her head lay on his shoulder and his arms closed round her protectingly.

"My darling," he said, and his voice sounded helpless and tortured, "I don't know about your father. Heaven help me, I don't know. There's only one thing I'm sure of, and that is that it's not safe to let you out of my sight even for a moment."

She clung to him.

"You don't know Daddy," she said. "Oh, Robin, I love you so, and I believe in you as implicitly as I do in myself, but you're wrong about Daddy. Something monstrous, something evil has got hold of him. Don't laugh at me! It's the way I feel, only I don't know how to put it any better. But when I saw Daddy in the garden at that dreadful place, although it was he, although it was his face, there was something different about him, something I can't explain. It was like—yes, it was like the thing that was strange about Sir Ferdinand Shawle when he came to fetch me from Mrs. Phipps's house. I can only describe it by saying that it was something different, something strange, something wicked."

Robin held her very close to him. She was trembling violently, and he could feel her heart beating against his own. His own desire at that moment was to protect her, to save her from the menacing horror which hovered over her.

He was also wildly and ridiculously happy. Whatever the future had in store for them, whatever terrors the past had contained, she had said, "I love you." She had said it and she had meant it, and she lay in his arms with her head heavy and warm against his shoulder.

They sat there for some time in silence. The little brass clock on the mantelpiece ticked noisily, and the old house creaked and groaned around them.

Robin was listening intently. The period of waiting was getting on his nerves. Besides, there had been that unusual coster barrow with its attendant outside the house all day.

Robin had noticed him the first thing in the morning, and for that reason had not gone out. He knew from experience that the man was not an ordinary police watcher. His disguise was just a little theatrical.

But of one thing he had been certain. The man was watching the house, and who else could there be in that quiet little establishment to interest any spy save Jennifer and himself?

He had not mentioned the matter to the girl for fear of alarming her unduly, but his heart was uneasy. If their hiding place was discovered, Jennifer was in danger again.

He was so engrossed in his thoughts that he started violently at the soft knock on the door panel, which disturbed them eventually.

But it was only Mrs. Phipps's daughter, a thin-faced, bright-eyed young woman who put her head round the door.

"Mr. Robin," she said, "there's a lady to see you. Shall I show her in?"

Robin turned to Jennifer and motioned her to take refuge through the other door which the room contained. But he was too late.

A tall figure brushed past the woman, and the next moment Madame Julie, smartly dressed as usual but pale and wide-eyed, hurried into the room.

"Oh, Robin, I had to come. You're the only person in the world who can help me."

She spoke impulsively, crossing the room towards the two young people, her hands outstretched.

Mrs. Phipps's daughter tactfully withdrew, and Jennifer clung to the newcomer's arm. Robin remained grave. He had arranged with Madame Julie that she should not visit the house save in a case of extreme emergency, lest she bring the place to the notice of anyone who might be shadowing her.

She seemed to sense the thought that passed through his mind, for she spoke quickly.

"I took every precaution, Robin. If anyone followed me here, he was a wizard. I doubled back on my tracks a dozen times, and finally, when I stepped out of my taxi at the door, I'm sure there wasn't a soul in sight."

Robin had not time to speak, for Jennifer cut in.

"What is it, Madame?" she said. "You look terrified."

The woman nodded. "I am."

Glancing about her as though she feared that even here she might be spied upon, she opened her handbag and drew out an envelope addressed to Robin.

"It's from my husband. He wanted me to send it by post, but I knew you couldn't get it before the morning. Oh, Robin, I helped you once! It's your turn now."

The boy tore open the envelope and read the hastily pencilled note within.

"Dear Grey," it ran. *"By the time you get this I shall have succeeded or failed utterly, I have discovered that Rolls & Knighton are the solicitors with whom Morton Blount dealt late in his life. In the old days before I went to the service of Sir Ferdinand Shawle, I had a friend who worked with Rolls & Knighton, and I remember he told me that the firm had an ingeniously hidden stronghold for their clients' private papers, which obviated the use of safe deposits.*

"One Saturday afternoon he showed me the place. We were both boys at the time, and I remember the notion struck me as being old-fashioned and amusing. I did not dream then that his information would ever be of service to me. I am now pretty sure that Morton Blount knew of this hiding place and it was that which decided him to use the firm.

"I am going out after that box tonight. Its discovery will bring to justice one of the greatest villains unhung. It will also free little Miss Fern from the menace which hangs over her, and I hope and trust will furnish evidence which, in bringing down the scoundrel who framed me, will clear me for ever from the charge of which I was so wrongfully convicted."

As Robin finished reading, he glanced up from the paper and met the dark, panic-stricken eyes of his visitor.

"Have you read this?" he inquired.

She nodded, white-lipped.

"I begged him not to go, but he's made up his mind. Oh, Robin, don't you see? He'll be caught and taken back to prison, and this time he won't even have right on his side. Stop him—please! You're in with the police. You can go anywhere. You can even take the box. It's different for you...But for him it means the same terrible business all over again."

She looked from one to the other of the young people piteously, and then, in spite of herself, her iron control broke down and the tears welled up in her dark eyes.

"I can't lose him again," she said brokenly. "I can't! I can't!"

Robin glanced from the letter in his hand to the two women on the sofa. There were two deep furrows across his forehead, and his eyes were hard and bright with anxiety.

"When was he going to make his attempt? Do you know?"

"I think he said something about eleven o'clock."

"But it's almost that now."

Robin glanced at the clock on the mantelpiece in alarm. "I know."

Madame Julie's voice was muffled. She looked suddenly much older. There were lines beneath her eyes and at the corners of her mouth.

Jennifer went over to Robin and put her arms round his neck.

"Please—please, dear," she whispered. "We must pay them back somehow for what they've done for us. Don't you see?—this is our chance."

"You'll have to hurry," Madame Julie pleaded. "You'll have to hurry. But it's perfectly safe. No one followed me. I'm sure of it."

Robin did not appear to hear. He walked slowly across the room and, taking care to keep himself hidden as much as possible behind the window post, moved back the blind an inch or two and peered out.

The mysterious coster with his barrow had disappeared.

He stood for a moment peering down into the empty street. Then he turned back into the room.

"Look here, Madame Julie," he said slowly, "I shall go down after Sacret now. If possible I shall persuade him to change his mind. At any rate the whole story of the box must go before the police. You must rely on me to do what I can in engineering a new trial for your husband. But in return I want you to do something for me."

"Anything—anything!"

It was impossible to mistake the urgent sincerity in the woman's tear-filled voice.

Robin regarded her steadily.

"I want you to stay here, Madame Julie. Don't let Jennifer out of your sight for a moment."

"But Robin, this is ridiculous," Jennifer began.

"My dear, you must let me be the best judge of that," he said gently and went on speaking to the elder woman. "In the case of any—well, of any emergency, I want you to ring up Scotland Yard. Ask for Inspector Whybrow and tell him the story. I can rely on you, can't I?"

The dark eyes met his gravely.

"Implicitly," she said.

Robin glanced at the clock. It was a quarter to eleven and he was some distance from the city. He turned again to Jennifer and kissed her cheek.

"Good-bye, dear," he whispered. "Stay where you are. Don't go out under any pretext whatsoever. Good-bye, my darling."

Madame Julie and the girl stood listening in the little room to his departing footsteps hurrying down the stairs.

CHAPTER TWENTY-SIX
THE FACE

"**G**ood-Night, sir."
The constable looked curiously at Robin as the boy, his collar turned up, hurried down the broad dark street whose tall houses contained numberless legal offices. Bedford Row is not a busy thoroughfare at eleven o'clock at night, and the policeman turned his head to look after the swiftly retreating figure who had hailed him with such brusque familiarity.

He did not know Robin by sight, but he guessed that the young man was a detective, and he wondered casually if anything was afoot.

Robin walked halfway down the Row and then turned abruptly to the left and entered the narrow cul-de-sac known as Quality Passage, where the old established firm of Messrs. Rolls & Knighton had their offices.

The little court was forlorn and ghostly in the light of the single street lamp of old-fashioned pattern which hung from a bracket at its farther end.

Robin began to tread warily. His intention was to take up his position in the dark doorway of the lawyer's offices and wait until the man he sought should come along.

Instinct told him that he should have put the whole matter before Inspector Whybrow first, but there had been no time, and his primary object was to save the convict from an act of folly which would certainly endanger his chances of regaining his permanent freedom.

The houses in the court were old-fashioned Georgian residences converted in the last century into offices. Their basement areas were protected by giant spiked railings which shed strange shadows on the glistening pavement, wet after a recent shower.

Robin glanced round him. There was not a light in a single window, and the loneliness of a big empty city, which is like no other loneliness in the world, seemed to close down upon him.

He found the office he sought at last. An old-fashioned doorway at: the far end of the court housed a board covered with faded gilt letters.

"Rolls & Knighton," he read. "Solicitors and Commissioners for Oaths. Second Floor."

He stepped into the shadow of the doorpost which swallowed him completely and stood waiting.

He remained there for some moments and was startled to hear a clock somewhere over in the city strike the first quarter. He was much later than he supposed. Perhaps Sacret had already arrived and was even now engaged upon his dangerous business.

Robin stretched out a hand and pressed the door behind him gently. It moved.

For a moment he stood hesitating. His own position was questionable, and he knew that he was doing a very dangerous thing in entering enclosed premises at such a time of night.

Gradually his caution gave way beneath the weight of his reasoning. He thought of Madame Julie, of Jennifer's appeal, and of the foolish but well-meaning Sacret racing headlong into prison in his attempt to free himself and Jennifer from the fate which hovered over them.

Robin moved cautiously. The little yard was still deserted. Not a breath of wind stirred in its narrow precincts.

The door swung open silently, and the boy's feet sank into a rough, old-fashioned doormat. A wave of musty, tobacco-scented air came out to meet him, and he became aware of that rustling, lively atmosphere which suffuses all very old houses at night.

He drew the torch from his pocket and swept it over the scene.

He was in a broad, old-fashioned hallway with doors on either side and a flight of stairs winding up into the darkness above. These were uncarpeted, and their surface was highly polished.

At this moment, somewhere high above him in the house, he heard a sound. Someone had moved a chair or other piece of furniture across an uncarpeted floor. The little sound, so ordinary and unexciting by day, took on a strange significance in that ghostly, silent house.

Robin, who had snapped off his torch instinctively at the first movement, was conscious of an odd, sinking sensation in his heart, and he reproached himself angrily for his nerviness.

Hastily thrusting all emotion from his mind, he reviewed the situation coldly. It was evident that someone was in the building. Ninety-nine chances in a hundred it was Sacret carrying out his avowed project.

But there was a hundredth chance that the other occupant of this otherwise deserted building was not Sacret at all, but some clerk working late, perhaps not even in Rolls & Knighton's own office.

In this case it behooved Robin to advance with caution. He did not fancy having to explain his business to the police, should they be hastily summoned by a burglar-fearing tenant.

He continued to move very quietly, therefore, keeping his torch dimmed by his handkerchief and shining it only upon his immediate path.

The stairs creaked abominably. Even by walking on the extreme sides, the noise they made seemed to be loud enough to wake half the inhabitants of London.

Robin plodded on.

On the first floor everything was silent as the grave, and he ascertained that each door was locked. As he stood there listening, one foot upon the second flight, he again heard that faint but terrifying sound which told of other human occupation in the building.

Yes, there was no doubt about it. The sounds came from the second floor.

He crept on, turning his torch out completely now and pulling himself upwards by the banisters.

As he reached the top stair he paused. He could tell by the current of air streaming out in his face that one of the doors in this hallway stood open. His eyes had become accustomed to the darkness by this time, and gradually he made out the faint grey rectangular shape of the opening directly facing him.

A faint light from the street lamp in the court below was so diffused by the time it entered the grimy windows of Messrs. Rolls & Knighton's outer office that it shed only the faintest possible radiance in that gloomy apartment, a pale grey stain in the darkness, no more.

Holding his breath, Robin crept forward.

He was aware now of the presence of another being somewhere in that dusty room. It was not even that he could hear a breath, but rather he could feel that some other entity was existing a few feet from him.

He reached the doorpost, laid his hand upon it, and peered into the darkness that was only slightly more dense than that from which he had come. Gradually the bulky shapes of furniture became visible to his eyes.

And then something moved.

He saw a shadow pass swiftly and silently across the room and drop into position behind something that he supposed was a desk, a shadow that was only visible by its movement.

Robin waited. The uncanny sensation which had seized him down in the hall had now returned a hundred times more strong. He felt his collar tightening, and he was aware of a prickling sensation beneath the band of his hat.

He was straining his eyes, forcing them by very will power to penetrate that greyish darkness.

At last he made out what it was at which he peered, and the discovery quickened his heart painfully. He was staring straight into the face of someone who sat not ten feet away from him, the eyes, he knew, looking directly into his own.

Robin whipped up his torch. The blinding beam of light stabbed the darkness like a dagger and fell directly upon the figure at the old-fashioned flat-topped desk.

Robin's jaw fell open. His eyes dilated, and blood surged into his temples and drummed madly in his ears. The world seemed to reel about him, the building rocked and trembled beneath his feet, for the face that peered into his own with eyes cold and malicious in their intensity was the face of the man whom he had last seen lying on the under bunk of the ambulance which had taken him to the nursing home, the face of the man he knew to be dead, the face of Rex Bourbon.

Robin stood staring at the figure peering at him across the desk.

As he stared, the figure moved.

The apparition was so startling and awe-inspiring after his ghostly journey upstairs that the shock temporarily paralyzed him, and the hand in which he held the torch focussed on that dreadful, leering face was steady, frozen into immobility.

As he stared, cold fear gripping at his backbone, he felt rather than saw a black iron-bound box lying on the desk beneath the figure's hand.

The whole incident only took a moment. A second later the figure had moved. Robin caught a gleam of steel, and before he could duck something struck him with overwhelming force.

There was a muted explosion in the dusty room, the torch clattered out of the boy's hand, rolled along the floor, and went out, and Robin pitched forward on the boards, a thin trickle of blood oozing from his temple and creeping down his face.

CHAPTER TWENTY-SEVEN
THE SAFE

When Robin opened his eyes he was conscious first of a sickening pain in his head and then of the glaring light of day forcing its way in through the grimy window. Gradually the events of the preceding night returned to his mind. He found he was very cold and stiff, and the left side of his head, which ached so intolerably, felt as though it were held in a plaster cast.

He put up his hand and touched his forehead gingerly. There was a long groove-shaped wound across his temple, and he guessed what had happened. The bullet which had been fired at him had struck obliquely and in glancing off the frontal bone had had precisely the same effect as that of a tremendous blow. He had been, in fact, literally stunned.

He knew himself to be amazingly lucky to be alive after such an attack, and he scrambled cautiously to his feet and stood swaying dizzily, clutching at the desk for support.

The main office of Messrs. Rolls & Knighton looked much like any other old-fashioned solicitors' in the chill light of morning. It was gloomy, dusty, and shabby without being poverty-stricken.

Slowly the boy turned his head and looked down at the desk. The box was gone. He forced himself to consider the situation coldly. Of one thing he was certain: it was no ghost who had peered at him across the desk.

Robin's belief in the supernatural had never been very strong, and the revolver shot, to say nothing of the removal of the heavily bound box, did not aid the theory of ghostly manifestation.

Yet the face had been the face of Rex Bourbon, and Rex Bourbon was dead.

His mind shied away from the problem, and he began to consider the more practical questions confronting him.

He glanced out of the window and guessed it was about an hour after dawn. The sky was still faintly rosy in the east, and as yet there was no movement in the little court.

He turned to move towards the door, and as he did so became aware for the first time of a muffled scratching sound which had been slowly forcing itself upon his consciousness for the past two or three minutes.

He stood listening.

For a moment he conceived the wild idea that his enemy had returned, but as the noise increased in strength it dawned upon him that it emanated from the far corner of the room, and glancing over he saw something that in his excitement he had not noticed before.

A big roll-top desk had been pushed aside, and a trap-door, upon which it usually stood, was disclosed. Moreover, the door of the trap stood open, its corner just visible round the edge of the desk.

He walked unsteadily across the room towards it. He was still very dizzy from his wound, and the room reeled about him.

He reached the desk at last, however, and stood clutching it for support. The sight which met his gaze astonished him.

Beneath the trap, clearly exposed and looking remarkably odd in that position, was the face of a large old pattern safe.

The hiding place was so elementary and yet so efficient that he was lost for a moment in admiration. This, then, was the ingenious cache of which Sacret had spoken in his letter.

It was while he stood looking down at the iron door at his feet that the scratching sound began again, and he realized with a little thrill of astonishment that there was some living thing imprisoned beneath the heavy slab of steel.

Stooping down, a gesture which made his head swim painfully, he knocked three times on the safe.

Three raps answered him instantly, and he straightened his back and stared about him in amazement.

There was an intelligent entity imprisoned in the safe below him, of that he was certain. The discovery was amazing. There seemed scarcely room in the steel cupboard for anything human to be confined.

He saw at a glance that the lock was a combination one, and he realized that it was hopeless for him to try to release the safe's prisoner, especially in his present weak condition.

His eye lighted upon the telephone on the top of the displaced desk, and with a sigh of relief he reached out for the instrument.

Within five minutes he was speaking to a sleepy but interested Inspector Whybrow newly aroused from bed.

Robin had called him at his private house and had been lucky in waking the old man without much difficulty.

Robin told his story breathlessly.

"I know I'm in enclosed premises," he finished, "but there's someone imprisoned in the safe here. It's a very small safe and the signals are weak. I'm afraid whoever it is will suffocate. Can you do anything?"

"Robin, that really is you, my boy? Thank God for that! I thought you were dead."

Robin touched his forehead thoughtfully.

"So I am—save for a miracle," he said. "For heaven's sake come along, Whybrow, and bring someone to open this damned coffin."

Inspector Whybrow arrived from his house in Maida Vale in an incredibly short space of time, considering he had called at a Bloomsbury Square house on the way and had brought a somewhat dishevelled but excited and definitely friendly Mr. Knighton with him.

The old lawyer hurried into the office in front of the inspector and looked about him in amazement.

Robin, his face still covered with blood, sat white and exhausted in the chief clerk's chair. The trapdoor and desk remained as he had found them.

Whybrow was plainly overjoyed to see Robin. He hurried over to the boy, his hand outstretched, his kindly face a picture of concern.

"Good heavens! What's happened to you, Robin? H'm—a bullet graze, I see. Come, my boy, we must have the full story of this. However, as I said on the phone, thank God you're alive. Did you see your man?"

Robin shuddered.

"Yes," he said in a curiously dull voice which made the inspector look at him sharply. "Yes, I did."

The older man had no time to make further inquiries, for Mr. Knighton, who had been bending over the safe, straightened his back suddenly and pulled up the heavy iron door.

The next moment a shrill ejaculation escaped him, and both Robin and the inspector leant forward. Whybrow bent down and began to haul up a limp human figure which had been wedged in between two of the great steel shelves.

He dragged the man out into the light, and the morning sun fell upon a face blue and distorted, but still recognizable and startlingly familiar.

"Sacret!"

Robin breathed the name, and Whybrow glanced at him sharply.

"The convict? Good God, this thing becomes more complicated every moment!"

"Is he dead?"

It was Mr. Knighton who spoke, his pale face grey with alarm, his tongue moistening and remoistening his parched lips.

Whybrow was tugging at the man's collar.

"No, he's all right. We came only just in time, though. Get the window open, will you? What he wants is air."

Robin moved over to obey the old man, but the effort of raising the sash proved to be the last straw and he lurched forward and collapsed upon the floor again, the mists closing over him.

He did not recover consciousness until he was in the taxi speeding on its way towards the Yard. The inspector had rendered first aid and had decided that a visit to hospital was unnecessary for either of his two charges.

Mr. Knighton, flushed and excited by this strange adventure which was disturbing the slow, even tenor of his uneventful life, supported the drooping figure of Sacret, who was too weak to put up any show of resistance even had he desired to do so.

Robin's lips moved.

"Jennifer," he said weakly. "Someone must get to Jennifer."

Whybrow laid a hand upon his arm soothingly.

"All right, my boy, all right. You save your energy. We've got a tremendous morning ahead of us. You'll want all your strength."

Robin's eyes closed again, but he could not get the girl out of his mind.

On the other side of the cab Sacret was staring at him dully, his eyes smouldering, a strange reproachful expression lurking in their depths.

Mr. Knighton was pouring out his troubles, his thin dry voice cracking in his agitation.

"But, Inspector, the box has gone. There's been a burglary. You don't seem to be taking this seriously. Morton Blount's box, a relic which I may say was left to us in the nature of a sacred trust, has been stolen. It's got to be found, I tell you. It's got to be found."

Inspector Whybrow regarded him wearily.

"All in good time, my dear sir," he said. "All in good time. Surely," he added plaintively as he indicated the two wounded men in the cab, "surely we've got enough to go on with? For one morning, at any rate."

CHAPTER TWENTY-EIGHT
JIGSAW PIECES

"Don't worry yourself, my boy. Take it gently. It's an astounding story, but thank heaven I think we're getting to the bottom of it at last. There's nothing to get worried about as long as you don't make yourself ill. We need you, Robin, if we're to get our man."

Inspector Whybrow spoke with genuine concern as he stood on the hearthrug confronting the boy who sat in the armchair, his head swathed in bandages.

The morning sun was streaming through the window of the inspector's bare little office in Scotland Yard. The room was not quite so speckless as usual, the cleaners having been disturbed at their work, but there were an air of suppressed excitement and a foretaste of coming victory occasioned by the story which Robin had just told, a story more strange than even that room of strange secrets had ever heard before.

Inspector Mowbray, hastily summoned from his home, sat at Whybrow's desk, a pad and pencil under his hand. The three men were alone. Mr. Knighton and Sacret had been accommodated in different parts of the building.

Robin, looking very white beneath his bandages but still resolute and very much alive, glanced up at the inspector gratefully.

"Thank you, Jack," he said. "I think I've made a clean breast of everything now. You see why I couldn't come to you before."

Whybrow glanced at Mowbray, and there was a twinkle in his eyes.

"It seems to me, Bill, that we've got a very good case against this lad for assisting an escaped convict to elude the emissaries of justice," he said.

Inspector Mowbray grunted. "Let's get on with the job. We must keep our eyes on that nursing home down on the east coast, although now we've got hold of the big fish I think the little fellows will automatically slip into the net."

Robin glanced from one to the other of the two men searchingly.

"Sir Henry?" he questioned.

Mowbray nodded, and a grin of satisfaction passed over his face.

"It's certain, I think. The fellow's probably insane, of course, but I don't think there's much doubt that he's at the bottom of things. At any rate we shall know soon, for certain."

Robin opened his mouth to speak. There was a curious expression in his eyes. But his observation was never uttered, for at that moment the phone rang and Mowbray took off the receiver.

He listened for a few moments, consternation and irritation on his face.

"All right," he said at last. "All right. No, you can't do anything."

He rang off without another word and, rising to his feet, went over to the door, beckoning Whybrow to follow him.

The two inspectors were gone for some moments and, left to himself, Robin's mind went back immediately to the one subject which worried him more than any other. He wanted to get a word through to Jennifer. Mrs. Phipps's daughter's house was not on the telephone, and he did not want to send a messenger. He was convinced that the fewer people who knew of the girl's hiding place the better.

Moreover, his head was aching intolerably, and he was finding clear thought increasingly difficult.

The two inspectors returned almost immediately. Whybrow's good-natured heavy face had clouded visibly, and there were deep lines of worry across his forehead.

Mowbray looked frankly angry, and Robin caught the muttered words "damned incompetence" as the two men came in. It was evident that something had occurred to check the inspectors' triumphant progress towards the end of the case, but as they quite obviously did not intend to take him into their confidence Robin did not press them.

Whybrow shrugged his shoulders.

"Oh, well," he said. "We shall have to leave that to Mayhew, that's all. We must get straight here first."

He turned to Robin.

"I've sent for Sacret," he said. "We've taken a deposition from him already, of course, but this is to be in the nature of an informal chat."

Robin nodded gloomily. Things had not panned out as he would have wished.

"I'd stake my oath that that man was innocent on the charge on which he was imprisoned," he said.

"Would you, now?" said Inspector Mowbray cheerfully but without malice.

Sacret was brought in almost immediately. He was now very much recovered from the effects of his imprisonment in the safe, but there was a sullen expression in his eyes, and he did not look at Robin.

The uniformed man who had accompanied him laid a sheaf of typewritten pages upon his superior's desk. Whybrow nodded to him.

"Thank you, Robinson. You'll wait just outside the door, please."

"Yes, sir." The man saluted and went out, and Whybrow turned the full force of his bland, kindly smile upon the newcomer.

"Sacret," he said, "I just want you to sit down over there. There are one or two points I want to go over with you."

The convict took the chair the inspector indicated and sat down. He was very quiet and seemed to be resigned to the situation.

"I realize I've made a tremendous mistake, Inspector," he said. "By breaking into the lawyer's last night I've ruined my chances of ever proving myself innocent of the charge for which I served part of my sentence. I realize there's not much to be said. I'll answer anything you want to know."

Whybrow shot him a sharp, approving glance from under his bushy brows. Ever quick to recognize intelligence when he saw it, the inspector was inclined to approve of Wendon Sacret. He made no comment, however, but merely nodded and turned over the pages of the deposition.

"I see here," he began, "that you say that you entered Messrs. Rolls & Knighton's office about a quarter to eleven last night in order to obtain an iron-bound box which you believed to contain evidence that would prove your innocence of the eleven-year-old charge on which you were convicted. You entered by a lower window, I understand? And yet Mr. Grey here, who followed you in at a quarter past eleven, found the door on the latch. You're sure about the window?"

"Yes, sir. I climbed over the area railings and pushed up one of the ground-floor windows which was unlatched. I went straight up to Messrs. Rolls & Knighton's office on the second floor. I pushed back the roll-top desk and disclosed the safe hidden beneath the trapdoor, and I got it open."

The inspector raised his eyebrows.

"That was very extraordinary, wasn't it?" he said. "It was a combination lock, I understand."

Sacret smiled grimly.

"I was extremely fortunate—or unlucky, whichever way you like to look at it. I remembered years ago that the same friend who showed me the hidden safe told me that the combination word was always the first in the firm's name. The safe was so well hidden, you see, that it was really not necessary at all for there to be a lock of any sort upon it.

"I remembered that the firm was so old that it was notorious for its adherence to the traditions of the founder, and I tried the word 'Rolls' therefore. My success was immediate."

"I see." Inspector Whybrow nodded. "Did you find what you were seeking?"

"Yes. Almost at once." The convict's voice trembled. "It was a large square box, infernally heavy, made, I think, of tin or some other metal and bound with iron. The name 'Morton Blount' was painted across it in white letters."

"What did you do then?"

The man shivered, and it was apparent by his expression that the full recollection of his experience still lingered with him.

"I put the box on the floor beside me and bent down to close the lid of the safe. As I did so I suddenly realized that I was not alone."

His voice sank to a whisper.

"I can't tell you how ghastly it was. The place was very quiet, there was hardly any light at all, but I suddenly became aware that there was something or someone standing just behind me. I looked up. I didn't see a face, but two hands seized me by the throat and I was forced downwards. Whoever my assailant was," he added grimly, "he had the strength of an ox. I was forced down into the safe and the iron door closed upon me. The rest of the story you know."

The inspector nodded. There was silence in the room for a few moments, and Sacret suddenly bent forward.

"I suppose you're going to hand me over to the prison authorities?"

Whybrow looked him squarely in the face.

"I've already informed them, naturally," he said. "But," he added after a pause, as with a gesture of helpless resignation the man sank back into his chair, "since this is an entirely unofficial conversation, and since you have brought us certain information concerning this box of Morton Blount's, I think it's only fair to tell you that in our investigations into the death of a Mr. Caithby Fisher new evidence has come to light which will justify a new trial for you. I can't say any more than that at present, and I only mention it now because we are extremely grateful to you for the help you've given us."

Sacret darted to his feet, a light of hope in his eyes, which died out, as a new thought occurred to him.

"But the attempted burglary?" he began.

Inspector Whybrow glanced at Mowbray, who was studiously ignoring what he frankly considered was his old friend's very unprofessional behaviour.

"I rather fancy, Sacret," he said, "that that incident might come under the head of 'work for and on behalf of Mr. Robin Grey,' who is, after all, attached to the staff.

However," he went on, "I shall have to send you back to the waiting room for the moment, although we may need you again later."

As soon as the door had closed behind the convict and his escort, Inspector Whybrow plunged into the details of the case without giving Mowbray time to express any opinion.

Robin knew the old man well enough not to say any word of thanks, but a glance passed between them which was sufficient.

"That settles that," said Whybrow. "You're not suffering from hallucinations, Robin, and it was no ghost who attacked you up in Knighton's office. I'm sorry to put you through this all over again, but we must get the matter clear.

"You say you saw Rex Bourbon last night, and he fired at you. You also say that you know Rex Bourbon to be dead— in fact that you saw his dead body several days ago."

Robin rose to his feet.

"I know that sounds like the statement of a lunatic," he said, "and you may think I'm crazy. I may be, for all I know. But I tell you that is exactly what happened."

Whybrow and Mowbray exchanged glances, and it was Mowbray who spoke.

"No need to look so alarmed, Robin," he said. "Whybrow here has put his finger on the whole secret, I believe."

Robin laughed abruptly. "I'm glad to hear it. I suppose you're thinking that the man I saw last night was a man in disguise? I tell you you're wrong. I only saw his face for an instant, but I could have sworn it was Bourbon himself."

Whybrow beckoned to the boy.

"Come here, Robin," he said. "With my post this morning I received a letter from Canada. I've been waiting for it impatiently for over a week. The man you saw last night was not actually in disguise, and yet he was not Bourbon. The man we're dealing with, the man who is responsible for the most cold-blooded set of crimes which it has ever been my lot to investigate, has one very amazing gift. Had he chosen to exploit it on the stage he would probably be one of the most famous men in the world.

"Just as Houdini was recognized as the master magician of the age, so this man has a gift for mimicry. But whereas the ordinary mimic is only able to imitate walks, gestures, inflections of his subject, this man was able to imitate the very faces of certain men. Some actors have this gift in a lesser degree, but this man is a past master at the game. Given certain broad physical resemblances, such as age, height, sex, and so on, he was able by very slight recourse to artificial aids to assume the outward appearance of at least half a dozen men, each of whose peculiarities he has studied carefully over a number of years."

Robin was listening spellbound, a light of hope in his eyes.

"This is my theory," he said. "This is what I've been thinking ever since I heard Jennifer's story. But after last night I can hardly believe it. I tell you the man was incredibly like Bourbon."

Mowbray leant forward.

"How often had you seen Bourbon, Robin? Three or four times at most, and then at a distance?"

Robin nodded.

"That's true," he said. "But how *you* got onto the idea, I can't possibly imagine. You hadn't even Jennifer's story to go on. Besides, this is amazing if it's true."

"Oh, it's true all right." Whybrow's tone was grim. "What do you make of this, Robin?"

As he spoke he drew an envelope from his pocket and extracted two pieces of yellow paper, which he laid down upon the desk. One was the torn playbill which the inspector had taken up from beside the telephone in Sir Henry Fern's office on the night that Rex Bourbon met his death, and the other was another copy of the same playbill, identical save that the sheet was in its entirety.

"There you are," said Whybrow triumphantly. "We set the Canadian police a pretty hard task, but they did it. Cast your eye down that, my boy. It may not be actual evidence, but it's a pretty strong clue to my way of thinking."

Robin followed the inspector's stubby finger down the list of turns advertised on the bill. It came to rest beneath a single name, *"CHARON,"* in inch-high letters, and beneath, in smaller type. *"THE MAN WITH A DOZEN FACES. See him change before your eyes into someone else. The most remarkable show ever staged. Any test gladly given."*

Robin stared at the inspectors in amazement for a moment. Then the truth slowly dawned in his eyes.

"So this is why Rex Bourbon phoned me that night?" he said. "He'd stumbled on the truth. Don't you see, when I found him lying dead in Sir Henry Fern's office he had this torn playbill clasped in his hand. The murderer must have snatched it from him either before or just after he shot him and did not realize until too late that he had torn the paper.

"This explains everything," he went on slowly. "The man on the railway station—the man who Jennifer thought was Sir Ferdinand Shawle in the taxicab—the man on the staircase of Bellew's flat—good heavens! It's probably even the explanation of the man in the nursing-home garden who Jennifer thought was her father."

Mowbray nodded. "The whole thing's so ingenious that it takes one's breath away," he said. "You see, this fellow they call the Dealer—and I must say that but for you, and Sacret, Robin, we should never have cleared up this point—having got half a dozen rogues in his power, proceeded to blackmail them most ingeniously. He was able to force them to do several swindles on his behalf, and even to convince them that certain of their numbers had committed murder at his instigation.

"Of course what he actually did was to commit the murders himself—no man's going to trust another man to do a crime like that for him—but always when he had disguised himself, or transformed himself if you prefer it, to look exactly like one of the others.

"You must realize," he went on, "that he had studied this half-dozen for years. He knew their every trick, their every mannerism, so it wasn't so difficult as it sounds.

"By this method he had a complete alibi for himself and a scapegoat in whose guilt at least five other men believed should the occasion demand it."

"The one fly in the ointment was Morton Blount's box. Jennifer Fern had to be kept alive, and at the same time prevented from marrying. Quite a pretty little business, don't you think?"

Robin sat staring at the playbill.

"Charon," he said softly. "Charon. But *who?* Even now you can't be sure."

Inspector Whybrow regarded him kindly.

"My dear boy," he said, "I see the awkwardness of your position, but I'm afraid there are one or two unpleasant revelations coming. Remember," he went on, "the ranks are getting thin. Caithby Fisher is dead. So is Rex Bourbon."

He got no further. The little conference in the austere office was brought to an abrupt close by the arrival of a flustered constable.

"A lady calling herself Madame Julie outside, sir," he said. "Says it's a case of life or death. Seems to mean what she says."

"Madame Julie!" Robin was already halfway across the room, and the next moment Madame Julie herself, white and haggard from loss of sleep, appeared upon the threshold.

"Where is he?" she said, her voice trembling. "Oh, Robin, where is he? They—they haven't caught my husband?"

Tired as he was and racked by nervous strain, Robin found time to reassure her.

"It's all right. Don't worry. Where is Jennifer? You swore you wouldn't leave her."

The woman stared at him in astonishment, and Inspector Whybrow came forward.

"Calm yourself, Madame," he began, and stopped abruptly before the expression of blank bewilderment in the woman's eyes.

"Inspector Whybrow," she said. "But—but—you're different!"

Robin, with a sudden inkling of the revelation to come, caught the woman's arm, his face distorted with fear, his eyes blazing.

"Where's Jennifer?" he repeated. "For God's sake, Madame Julie, what is it?"

It was Inspector Whybrow who assisted the trembling woman to a chair, and the two inspectors and the distraught boy bent over her while she stammered out her story.

"I don't understand. ... It's like a nightmare. Very early this morning, Robin, before it was dawn, Inspector Whybrow—only it wasn't this Inspector Whybrow, it was someone very, very like him, someone a little taller, a little less—oh, how shall I say?—less kind-looking—came to fetch Jennifer to bring her here to you. He explained that she wasn't arrested, but that she'd got to come at once, and that I was to stay where I was and not to attempt to get in touch with you until I heard from you first."

"But I told you," said Robin huskily, "I told you not to let her out of your sight."

"I know. But this was the *police.*"

Inspector Whybrow forced Robin gently out of the way. His face was very grim and his blue eyes had lost much of their kindliness.

"Let's hear about this man, Madame. You had seen me before, and yet you thought the stranger who came for Jennifer *was* me?"

The woman nodded. Her lips were white, her eyes staring.

"I'd seen you only once before, Inspector, and, although I see now that there are differences, I could have sworn at the time that it was the same man.

"I went down to the car with her myself," she went on. "It was a big saloon car. There was a man in chauffeur's uniform driving. Jennifer sat at the back beside the man who looked like you.

"I—I was convinced," she went on helplessly, "because— well, because——"

"Because what?"

Robin bent over her, as though already he knew what she was about to say.

She met his eyes, frantic appeal in her own.

"Because," she said wretchedly, "there was an iron-bound box on the seat between them, and I hoped——"

Robin's frantic laugh of sheer despair silenced her.

"Well," he said, turning to the inspectors, "there you are. That shows one great flaw in your theory. Sir Henry Fern is under lock and key at his home, and yet a man disguised as

Rex Bourbon shot me at half-past eleven in Quality Passage, and a man like Inspector Whybrow arrested Jennifer at dawn this morning."

The two inspectors exchanged glances. Then Inspector Whybrow stepped forward and laid a hand on the boy's shoulder.

"I didn't tell you before," he said. "The news came through on the phone this morning when we were sitting here. D'you remember? Sir Henry Fern escaped some time last night. When the detectives went to his room this morning they found the nurse who had been left in charge of him had been locked in a cupboard in the bedroom since ten o'clock yesterday evening. The boys are out after Sir Henry now."

"I won't believe it of Sir Henry. I can't."

It was Robin who spoke.

The two inspectors looked at him dubiously, but before either of them could speak the telephone bell had again rung. Whybrow bent over and took the instrument.

After a hurried conversation he hung up the receiver and turned to the others.

"Things are moving fast. Sir Ferdinand Shawle slipped out of his house last night. He eluded our men but came back this morning, called his car, and has motored out of town. Our men are following him. That message was from a callbox on the London to Ipswich Road."

"The east coast!" said Robin eagerly. "He's making for Crupiner's nursing home. And that's where you'll find Sir Henry, too, Whybrow. He's gone down there to find his daughter. He doesn't know she escaped. Shawle's the man we want—I'm sure of it. Some accomplice of his has probably got Jennifer."

Startling confirmation of Robin's suggestion came within the next five minutes when a secretary entered with a confidential report which had just come through by phone from the special squad who, aided by the local police, were keeping an eye on Crupiner's establishment.

"Unusual activity down here," the inspector read. *"Phone instructions."*

He handed it silently to Mowbray and, receiving his colleague's nod of assent, scribbled a few words on a pad of paper, handing it to Mowbray for approval before he gave it to the secretary to despatch.

"I think you're right, Jack," said the younger inspector as their subordinate departed. "We'll go down right away. You'd better stay here, Robin," he added kindly. "You're in no condition for a trip of this sort."

The boy did not appear to hear him. There was a puzzled expression in his eyes and he stood hesitating.

"Why," he said at last, "why should he go there? It's a god-forsaken place, and he had the box." He answered his own question, still in the same musing tone. "Of course it might have been anything—to pick up documents, perhaps, evidence that he was afraid to leave behind. And yet, why should he take Jennifer? If he's got the box himself he can't have any interest in her any longer."

Old Whybrow's face clouded.

"I don't want to alarm you unduly, Robin," he said, "but I think there's one little point you're rather overlooking. Hasn't it occurred to you that Jennifer Fern and yourself are the only two people who knew the whole truth of that business in the nursing home when they proposed to operate?"

Robin turned to him, the fear which had been lurking in his eyes suddenly leaping into prominence.

"Of course," he said. "And he probably thought he had killed me last night. My God, Whybrow, we've got no time to lose! I'm coming with you. We must go at once. He's got a good start."

No one knew better than Whybrow how important it was to avoid delay, and he did not attempt to argue with the younger man.

Mowbray gave a few curt instructions over the telephone, and they prepared to depart.

"Where is this place?" said Mowbray suddenly as they reached the door. "It's out beyond Colchester somewhere, isn't it? On the marshes?"

A wave of helplessness passed over Robin. The only time he had approached the lonely nursing home from London had been in the ambulance, and he remembered with a touch of despair those narrow winding lanes in the pitch darkness.

Now there was no time to lose. By the time they had gone to the local police headquarters and picked up a guide, the Dealer would have been able to escape and to dispose of Jennifer and any other evidence he wished to hide.

Suddenly the boy's eye fell on Madame Julie, sitting white and silent in a chair. Her eyes sought his, imploring him to let her help.

The inspector followed the direction of his glance and read the thought which had passed through his mind.

"Of course," he said. "She knows. Take her. Have you got a gun on you, Mowbray?"

He took his own from a drawer in the desk as he spoke, and the next moment the four anxious people sped down the concrete staircase to the car waiting below.

Both the inspectors were keen. They were nearing the finish of the most sensational case of their career. Madame Julie had private reasons for wishing to help the police in every conceivable way in her power, since it was only through them that she could hope for her husband's ultimate salvation.

But Robin was moved by the strongest force on earth. The girl he loved was in danger. Upon their swiftness now depended everything that mattered in the world to him.

CHAPTER TWENTY-NINE
THE DEALER

"Your instructions have been followed closely, sir. We have men on every road. That is to say, there's another police trap like this one on the north road, and a third on the byway which runs west. We didn't go too near for fear of alarming them, as you suggested."

The sergeant of the local police saluted as he finished speaking and stepped back from the car.

It was now nearly noon, and yet a grey haze still hung over the rain-soaked marshes which stretched on either side of them as far as the eye could reach.

Whybrow nodded to the man and climbed out upon the road, ignoring Robin's impatient signals for him to go on.

They were about a quarter of a mile from the nursing home, and the mass of shrubs and trees which surrounded it was just visible ahead.

"Every exit has been covered, then? What's that lane over there? Isn't that a way along the coast?"

The old man pointed to a strip of green running behind the nursing home along the sea border.

"That's a cul-de-sac, sir," said the sergeant. "It leads down to a broken pier left over from the days when they tried to develop this part of the world into a seaside resort.

The pier's derelict—rotten through and through. There's no way of escape there, sir."

This conversation was interrupted by the arrival of a constable on a motor bicycle. He pulled up at some little distance upon observing the car, but came forward when the sergeant beckoned him.

He made his report in a brief and workmanlike fashion. Dr. Crupiner, three nurses, and four members of the nursing-home staff had been held up on the northern road.

"We're holding them, pending inquiries, sir," he finished. "That's according to instructions, isn't it?"

Whybrow smiled. "That's splendid, Sergeant," he said. "Couldn't be better. That means we have only the visitors who came down by car this morning left in the house."

The man considered.

"Yes, sir, that's right," he said at last. "There were two cars noticed this morning, and someone is thought to have arrived last night, although, of course, as we weren't on guard then we can't be sure."

Whybrow turned and, catching sight of Robin's white, agonized face, decided to push on. With a word of thanks to the sergeant he climbed back into the car, and they sped on down the road towards the sinister building which Robin had such good reason to loathe and fear.

As they came nearer, Robin got his first clear view of the nursing home by daylight. The long, low building looked very austere and prison-like with its huge surrounding wall. An immense iron fire escape led up to a gallery surrounding the glass roof of what was evidently a recent addition to the building.

Robin recognized the operating theatre with a shudder.

Madame Julie's quiet voice from behind him brought back the scene still more vividly to his mind.

"I climbed up there that night and peered through. There's an iron staircase leading up to the escape at the back of the house. We might use it again."

"We must be careful, Robin." It was Mowbray who spoke. "I know how you feel, but we're up against desperate men. He may put up a fight, and as he's under cover and we're not, the advantage will be with him. I want you to stop outside the gate at which Madame Julie here met you when you brought the girl out before. Then we can advance through the bushes."

Fuming at the delay, and with a secret feeling of dread at his heart, Robin did as he was told.

They pulled up outside the little postern gate and sat waiting for some moments. There was no sign from the gaunt house. It might have been empty, so lonely and silent it stood.

The occupants of the police car trooped slowly through the gate under cover of the protecting bushes.

A second car followed them, containing a sergeant and three plain-clothes detectives, and now each man in the little army took up his position with silent efficiency.

If the Dealer was hidden in this sinister fortress he would not escape with his life.

Madame Julie was forced to remain in the background. The police would not permit her to take any unnecessary risks, and it was Robin who led the way through the shrubbery.

He turned and spoke to Mowbray over his shoulder.

"I'm going out into the open. Once we can get into the porch we're safe from gunfire from the windows."

As he spoke he darted out onto the gravel and sprinted across the drive to the porch, but there was no splatter of bullets from the house. The place remained silent and gloomy as a tomb.

Mowbray and Whybrow with the sergeant came up into the porch just as Robin was putting his shoulder to the door.

"Steady, my boy, steady! We don't want to run into a trap."

Old Whybrow spoke warningly, but Robin was past caution.

The sergeant leant his weight to the door, and presently the great wooden panel burst open and with a clatter the men charged into the deserted, stone-flagged hall.

In the silence which followed as they stood listening, the damp unfriendliness of the great building seemed to rise up to meet them.

And then, just when a sense of frustration was descending slowly but surely upon the group, the unexpected happened.

A scream, shrill and terrifying, echoed from the floor above, and the next moment there was a patter of feet upon the wooden staircase as Jennifer herself, her golden hair dishevelled, her grey eyes wide and frightened, came flying down to meet them.

She caught a glimpse of Robin and threw herself sobbing into his arms.

"Oh, you've come! You've come! Oh, thank God you've come in time!"

As they crowded about her, eager for the information they most desired, she suddenly pulled herself together.

"You must hurry," she said. "You must hurry, or he'll get away. I suppose he heard you coming and that's why he left me. There!"

Her last word was occasioned by the second startling sound which had shattered the silence surrounding the gloomy building.

From somewhere outside had come the crack of a revolver shot, and the next moment there was the roar of a car engine and a scream of brakes as it swerved out of the drive.

They rushed to the door just in time to see one of the plain-clothes men reeling from a wound in his side, and to catch the tail of a car as it turned down the road.

It was Robin who spoke the general thought.

"They'll stop him, of course. He won't get by those traps. And yet—no—good heavens! He's taking the old coast road!"

He turned to Whybrow.

"He's staged a getaway. Come on, this is our chance!"

He flung himself through the shrubbery and leapt into the car. The inspector scrambled onto the footboard as the boy let in the clutch, and the car bounded forward in pursuit of the fugitive.

As they swung onto the uneven surface of the old coast road they caught a glimpse of their man. He was bending over the wheel of an open sporting car.

Robin strained his eyes, but it was impossible to recognize that crouching figure. True, there was something vaguely familiar about him, and as they gradually gained upon him Robin realized that the person who had leapt into mind at a first glimpse was none other than the inspector who sat even now at his side.

It was evident that Whybrow had noticed the resemblance also, for Robin caught the old man's muttered exclamation of mingled bewilderment and anger.

The police car was going all out. The surface was abominable, and Robin knew that any false move must send him and his companion into the muddy slime below which stretched out for the half-mile or so left by the tide.

The mists had thickened, it seemed, and the salt tang in the air keyed up the senses of the two men in the car, adding to the agonizing thrill and anxiety of the chase.

"There's the pier." The inspector's voice was low. "Does the road run past it, I wonder?"

Robin took his eyes off the track long enough to glance out to where the dark structure of an elementary pier loomed out of the mist. The thing was little more than a skeleton of rotten planks, but as they raced towards it they suddenly caught sight of something at its far end which forced an exclamation from old Whybrow's lips.

"My God," he said, "a yacht!"

A little boat, full steam up, lay in the deep water at the far end of the derelict pier.

Now the whole purpose of the man ahead became apparent. This, then, was his objective.

The inspector gripped his gun.

"I wanted to take him alive," he said. "He won't dare to run the car on that crazy spider's web. We'll get him when he pulls up."

But the inspector was wrong. The car ahead slowed down, it is true, but as the driver turned and caught sight of them bearing down upon him, he seemed to change his mind, for he turned his car onto the rotting structure of the pier and drove on.

In that instant they caught a glimpse of him. Although his face was not recognizable at that distance, his clothes and bearing were typical of Whybrow himself, and the old man caught his breath.

"It's like a nightmare," he said. "Like a nightmare."

Robin did not answer. He gained the end of the pier and pulled up. The rotten timbers were creaking and the supports rocking beneath the weight of the sports car, which was forced to go slowly to prevent the uneven planking from shooting it over the slippery edge.

Suddenly the car ahead stopped. Two revolver shots struck the bonnet of the police car, and then all was silent.

The inspector caught Robin's arm.

"Look," he said. "The planks have given way completely there. There's a gap. He'll have to come back, or climb on foot. Sit still. Don't expose yourself. I rather fancy we're in luck. Anyway, I'm going to take the risk."

And before Robin could stop him he sprang out of the car and stood exposed upon the rickety planking of the pier. But although he was an easy mark, no shot came from the man ahead.

"I thought so. His gun's empty. Come on, Robin."

It was a perilous journey over the rotting timbers. Some distance ahead of them the man in the sports car had also dismounted, and as they caught a clear view of him Robin's heart leapt. In his hand he carried an iron-bound box.

"Don't fire," the inspector panted. "I want this bird alive if I can get him."

They raced on. The figure was scaling the slippery joists which alone connected the two ends of the pier. Beneath him the tide was slowly creeping in over the grey, sinister mud.

And then it happened. In attempting to glance over his shoulder, the man ahead of them missed his footing, staggered, and clutched the side in an effort to save himself.

But the weight of the box he carried was the deciding factor. It slipped from his grasp, and in snatching at it he missed his hold and fell through the aperture into the shallow water below.

Robin and the inspector dashed forward.

"We've got him!"

The inspector was jubilant.

But as they came up with the gap in the planking and peered through, a sense of bewilderment passed over them.

Of the strange fugitive and his precious burden there was no sign whatsoever; only the water lapping gently some fourteen feet below.

The inspector looked about him wildly.

"But this is absurd," he said. "The water's only about eighteen inches deep there at the outside. Why, Robin, what's the matter?"

The boy, white and shaken, pointed to something showing just beneath the surface of the grey water, something dark, something terrible, a human head.

"Quickmud."

Robin spoke the words through frozen lips.

"This coast is full of it. For six feet down, in patches of about eight feet square, the mud's like a quicksand. I was nearly caught in it once when I was a child. That fellow dropped straight through into liquid mud up to his neck and the water's done the rest. He's been drowning slowly as surely as if he were held under, and we can't get near him."

The inspector stepped back. His stern old face was grey.

"He deserved a horrible death," he said. "But I hadn't reckoned on that for him."

It was more than half an hour later when the combined efforts of the local detectives and the Scotland Yard men, with the aid of ropes and a couple of cars for hauling purposes, dragged the terrible suffocated thing out of the ooze and laid it upon the planks.

The yacht had made off immediately after the tragedy, and already all ports had been furnished with a description of her.

Robin and the two inspectors stood on the pier, bending over the slime-covered figure which lay at their feet. The

Scotland Yard sergeant knelt beside the body and carefully wiped the face.

There, beneath the grey sky of a late afternoon, lay revealed the white, expressionless countenance of a man who might have been a recognized genius had he chosen to exploit his gift in any other way. The eyes were closed, but Robin thought of their colourless depths and shuddered.

The fairish hair was limp and matted, and the countenance was smooth and untroubled, as that of a child.

Mowbray turned to Whybrow.

"Nelson Ash," he said. "Well, I'm damned!"

Chapter Thirty
After the Storm

"Robin, Inspector Whybrow says we shall never recover the box. If it's true, I'm terribly glad. You're sure no one can ever get hold of it again?"

Jennifer stood in the room where she had experienced that fateful interview with her father only a few days before and looked up at Robin as she spoke, her young face earnest, her voice anxious.

"If the police can't get that box, no one can. It's buried heaven knows how many feet deep in slime. No, Jennifer, that's gone for ever."

Robin put his arm round the girl as he spoke and held her very close to him.

She leant back, her head against his shoulder, her face raised to his.

"I've seen Daddy. The whole thing's been a most terrible shock and strain for him, but he's going to be all right. He told me he simply had to get up last night and come down to find me. Apparently he broke in here and shouted for me until that dreadful little doctor had him locked up in one of the bedrooms, where the police found him this morning. Oh, Robin, if you hadn't got here in time, that man would still be alive to torment us. Even now I can't realize it's over."

Robin kissed her lips.

"Don't think about it, darling," he said. "Thank God I've got you safe."

They were interrupted by the arrival of Inspector Whybrow. The old man put his head round the door, a tremendous grin of satisfaction spreading across his face from ear to ear.

"Robin, I want a word with you," he said. "Here's your father, Miss Fern. I expect you've a great deal to say to one another."

He stepped aside as he spoke, and Sir Henry Fern came into the room. The old man was not very steady. His recent experiences had left their mark upon him, but there was a new expression in his eyes, and his face lit up as he caught sight of the girl.

"Jenny, my dear," he said and held out his arms to her.

Jennifer flung herself across the room towards him, and Robin left them together.

Outside in the corridor Whybrow took Robin's arm.

"Sir Ferdinand is downstairs," he said. "We've got a formal deposition out of him, but I thought you might like to hear the unofficial chat, as it were. He's taken it very well. Poor devil! He thought that if we couldn't get hold of the box there'd be no evidence against him. The discovery that we know about the Camden Gun Scandal came as a bit of a shock.

"He's a queer sort of bird," he went on thoughtfully. "He was in on all that terrorization affair down here, don't you see, but it doesn't seem to have struck him quite what an infamous business it was. It'll be the trial of the century. He deserves his stretch. And he'll get it!"

Robin accompanied the inspector downstairs to the little room which Dr. Crupiner had used as a private office.

Sir Ferdinand Shawle sat at a table, a plain-clothes man on either side of him. Inspector Mowbray, whose stern official expression could not quite hide the jubilation he felt, sat opposite him.

Whybrow and Robin took up their positions on the hearthrug, and the informal conversation, a procedure which Inspector Whybrow was reputed to have brought to a fine art, continued.

Sir Ferdinand was speaking, his lean, grey face expressionless as ever, and for the first time in his life Robin felt something akin to admiration for the man. At least he was a stoic.

"I realized from the beginning of this year that we were up against some question of disguise," he said. "You must remember," he added grimly, "that neither I nor my colleagues were in any way partners of the Dealer. He was a blackmailer—we, his victims."

For a moment the angry spirit of the man showed in his eyes, and two spots of colour appeared on his cheekbones. He recovered himself instantly, however.

"I never guessed, of course," he went on, "that we were up against such a master, and it amuses me when I remember that I went to the trouble of interviewing several make-up experts in the hope of getting a line upon him. It never occurred to me, you see, that the man was a facial mimic rather than an artist with greasepaint.

"I got these experts to visit me at night. I thought the Dealer had no idea what I was doing. If he had, of course, he probably laughed at the puniness of my imagination."

He stopped speaking, and the other men in the little room remained silent. It was a feature of Inspector Whybrow's "conversations" that the prisoner usually did most of the talking.

Sir Ferdinand appeared to be lost in his own thoughts, but suddenly he glanced up, a light of bewilderment in his eyes.

"Of course," he said, "you're wrong. You're wrong. He's eluded you. He's won, after all. It couldn't have been Nelson Ash. It comes back to me now. I knew there was something at the back of my mind which was warning me to take this story cautiously. How do you account for the letter?"

Whybrow bent forward, and his voice had a soothing effect upon the excited man.

"Suppose you tell us about it," he suggested gently.

"Of course I will. It happened in my own office only two or three days ago."

He plunged into the story of the telephone call from the Dealer which Ash had received in the banker's office, and of the mysterious letter thrust under the door.

The inspector listened patiently to the end. Then he sighed.

"Sir Ferdinand," he said, "if that had happened to me or to Inspector Mowbray here, our search would have been at an end from that moment. That's an old trick, and very easily worked. If you remember, all the voice on the telephone—which you took to be the Dealer's—actually said to you was to inquire if Ash was present. All the rest of the story Ash told you himself."

"But the letter?" the banker demanded.

The inspector's voice was very kindly.

"My dear sir," he said, "when Ash's confederate phoned— a confederate, mind you, who knew nothing save that he was required to call up his employer at your address—you answered the phone. While your back was turned, how easy for our friend to drop the specially prepared letter just inside the door and to slide it halfway through the crack with his foot. Not very difficult, was it?"

Sir Ferdinand sank back.

"I see," he said dully, "I see. My God! If I had him here I'd force the life out of him with my own hands!"

The flare of this sudden outburst died swiftly out of his eyes.

Mowbray shrugged his shoulders.

"You couldn't have made his death any more unpleasant than it was, Sir Ferdinand," he said dryly.

When the banker was led away, Robin and the two inspectors stood for a moment looking down into the fire. Mowbray was frankly jubilant.

"Well, that's that," he said. "If I hadn't seen it with my own eyes I wouldn't have believed it. An astounding case, a fascinating case, and one, I think," he added with justifiable pride, "that reflects well upon us all."

Robin sighed. "Thank God it's over. I think I'll go and join Jennifer now if you don't mind. Somehow," he added with a tired smile, "I'm not happy if she's out of my sight for a moment."

As the door closed behind him Mowbray frowned.

"I don't see now why Ash took such an infernal risk in kidnapping the girl again if he didn't mean to kill her," he said.

Whybrow looked at him curiously.

"It may not have occurred to you, Bill," he said, "that Miss Fern is a peculiarly attractive young lady. It may well have been that our friend the Dealer was not altogether unsusceptible."

Mowbray raised his eyebrows. "Very likely," he said. "I never thought of that."

Voices on the lawn without attracted their attention and, crossing over to the window, they stood looking down upon the scene outside.

Jennifer paced the lawn between her father and Robin. She was radiant; excitement and happiness had brought back the colour to her cheeks, and her eyes were glowing.

She glanced up and, catching sight of the inspector, hailed him.

"Congratulate us," she shouted. "We're going to be married."

Robin slipped his arm round the girl's waist and waved to the two men in the window. He looked like a schoolboy in his elation, and Mowbray grunted as he and Whybrow went back into the room.

"Can you beat that?" he said. "He's escaped death by a miracle, had one of the most gruelling experiences in his life, been instrumental in catching one of the most remarkable criminals of the age, all in the space of the last twenty-four hours, and now bless me if he doesn't want to go and get married to top it all off."

Whybrow regarded him slyly.

"I seem to remember a brilliant young sergeant some years ago who went even more dippy over a girl, whom he afterwards married, and made much more of an exhibition of himself than even our young friend out there," he observed. "A nice fellow he was, but he got a bit cynical in his old age."

Inspector Mowbray had the grace to blush.

Love Maxwell March?

Discover Margery Allingham's other creations and get your next stories,

FREE

If you sign up today, you'll get:

1. Two Margery Allingham stories only available to subscribers; Caesar's Wife's Elephant and The Beauty King
2. Exclusive insights into her classic novels and the chance to get copies in advance of publication
3. The chance to win exclusive prizes.

Interested? It takes less than a minute to sign up. You can get the novels and your first exclusive newsletter by visiting www.margeryallinghamcrime.com.

11407384R00176

Printed in Great Britain
by Amazon